Molecules and Women

Paola Giorgio

iUniverse, Inc.
Bloomington

Molecules and Women

Copyright © 2012 by Paola Giorgio

All rights reserved. No part of this book may be used or reproduced by any means, graphic, electronic, or mechanical, including photocopying, recording, taping or by any information storage retrieval system without the written permission of the publisher except in the case of brief quotations embodied in critical articles and reviews.

iUniverse books may be ordered through booksellers or by contacting:

iUniverse
1663 Liberty Drive
Bloomington, IN 47403
www.iuniverse.com
1-800-Authors (1-800-288-4677)

Because of the dynamic nature of the Internet, any web addresses or links contained in this book may have changed since publication and may no longer be valid. The views expressed in this work are solely those of the author and do not necessarily reflect the views of the publisher, and the publisher hereby disclaims any responsibility for them.

Any people depicted in stock imagery provided by Thinkstock are models, and such images are being used for illustrative purposes only.

Certain stock imagery © Thinkstock.

ISBN: 978-1-4759-4994-0 (sc)
ISBN: 978-1-4759-4995-7 (hc)
ISBN: 978-1-4759-4996-4 (e)

Library of Congress Control Number: 2012916757

Printed in the United States of America

iUniverse rev. date: 9/19/2012

In loving memory of Tamara Malia

Contents

Preface ix
The Night the Wave Broke 1
Girls' House 15
Molecules and Women 33
Still I Dance 41
Li'l Sister's Love 45
Kindergarten 59
Where Is the Camino? 83
The Laundry 93
Into the Puddle 113
The Painting 121
Enora's Purse 143
Cape House 153
Return Home 167
The Promise 185
Louisa's Cardboard Box of Life 205
Acknowledgments 219

Preface

These fifteen vignettes in *Molecules and Women* are enactions of some of the voices that have spoken to me over the years. They represent a beginning but also an end to one chapter of a life journey that has yet to cease to surprise me. The seeding for this web of interconnected stories can be traced back thirty years to a dream I awoke from, in which I was thumbing through a book whose chapters bore the names of women, some of whom were my closest friends and others who were still unknown to me. At the time, I was a single mother living in a beach cottage with my three small children, struggling to make ends meet each day. But I thought, *Yes, I must write that book—when I am wise enough.*

The quickening occurred four years ago. The first shoot that rose up was a short story that pushed through the earth's crust during a week's stay in a hermit's hut near Amherst, Massachusetts. I was in the woods, recording the experiences of my pilgrimage to Santiago de Compostela. I awoke in the middle of the night and sat up to record the movie that was playing in my head—of a child and her mother, sharing chores on a Sunday afternoon. I could barely keep up with the rolling tape of Philomena and Leona's story that was playing in my mind's eye, and I started typing as fast as I could. Even though all of their history was unveiled, I knew that the entirety of it was germane only to me and that my job was to stay focused on the moments unfolding during that one afternoon together.

The next night, the tape began to roll again, fast-forwarded to years later, when a life fully lived was reaching again into nature, on its journey home.

That was the beginning. Upon returning to California, I intended to return to my original manuscript, but at every juncture I got detoured. It seemed that every meeting with a friend or acquaintance included their relaying to me, in an often-obscure manner, some event that caused the movie projector to whir in the night.

As in the day I sat in silence, writing with Elena, a dear friend, and she blurted out, "I loved Aunt Amelia and her blue tennis shoes, with the sides cut out so her bunion wouldn't rub. Now why would I think of that?" she said with a chuckle. As she began sharing with me the intimate details, I became intrigued with her recapturing of a tender part of her childhood.

By the time of the unfolding of the fourth story, I realized that the process had become an invitation for me to listen and record, a responsibility even. "Paola, you must write about Girls' House." And the rest, as they say, is "herstory," or *our* stories. These voices of real women's lives speak of learning and teaching, loving and losing, and they belong to all of us.

Certain details were filled in by the storyteller in me. I do not claim that all of the information is accurate in its specificity, but when I started writing, it was less of a creative process than a documentation of how what I was hearing intersected with what I just seemed to know intuitively. I honor and respect the women who offered me the width and breadth to fill in blanks from my own muse—details lost, forgotten, or simply never known: trusting the mysterious energy that thrives on waking me up at 3:00 a.m. to start the projector rolling. All the locations, however, are authentic and true to their geography.

The process of weaving perceived facts with plausible fictions took on a life of its own. One of the great joys I experienced was when Lei Ling read a draft of "Girls' House" and was redlining the story, for accuracy about China. "No, she did not wear a brown skirt.

It was brown trousers. You have not put in the barter for the bride. It was important, the nines." We were sitting at Ristobar on Chestnut Street in San Francisco, and she placed the last page down in front of her cup of coffee. As tears formed in her eyes, I panicked, thinking I'd screwed it all up. Girls' House was important to me, because she had wanted me to record its existence. I had even been given the opportunity to meet with her ninety-year-old mother, Jung, and she shared the wedding practices and girl's good-bye song. Lei Ling said, "No, no, Paola. I just never thought my story was important enough to tell."

The immense value of these gifts in my life cannot be quantified, and my great hope is that in sharing this work, the gifting will flow forward to others.

Let me end with the words of one of my teachers, John O. Donohue:

> Gather yourself and then your traveling does become a pilgrimage, a pilgrimage to the inner regions of your heart, even though your body journeys on the outside. Alone in a different way, more attentive now to the self you bring along, a journey can become a sacred thing. Travel in an awakened way gathered wisely into your inner ground, so you might not waste the invitation that waits for you on your way to transform you.

The Night the Wave Broke

The dark Spanish stairs, wood worn to a paper-thin sheet on top of the carved stone, welcomed me home. I noticed for the first time, as I bent to touch their heads, the iron nails had worn down too. Stopping to rest on these steps I had climbed many times each day, I now wondered where the wood had come from. The only trees that graced these stone hills were ancient olives, mostly abandoned during the Spanish Civil War. A few seemingly dancing groves survived and lined the road into Chert as welcoming sentries to the village; their short, gnarled limbs spoke volumes of the harshness that was this land. Was olive wood hard enough to construct stairs?

A handful of farmers still harvested their bitter olives, but the war had wrought such devastation to life and palate that the locals failed to notice the stale quality of their olive oil. Amaranta, our eighty-year-old landlady, proudly sold me last year's bottling, but it was too rancid for my taste. *Had there been forests here at one time, centuries ago?* Noticing how the moonlight entered the second-story window, our only window, lighting the stairwell for me, I was grateful for a second time this long night for her helping me see clear passage. She had lit the broken cobbled street too, giving me a path to follow between the narrow, crumbling walls. *How foolish I am, to stand here on my stairs, to ruminate the source of this ancient wood.*

Earlier this evening I had pondered the very future of my life as I walked around and around the abandoned church plaza, remembering the portent that Beatrix's husband Mario had read in the tarot cards.

"Your husband has a deep fear that he must confront before his twenty-eighth birthday, or he will be lost. If he does not absolve his anger and surrender his sorrow, they will become his soul mates," he'd said, intently focused on the display. He glanced up from the cards and fell silent. I pressed him for what he meant. A cool breeze blew through the room, upsetting the cards' formations. The words "Pandora's box" came to me as I watched Mario sweep them up hurriedly, as if they burned his fingers, and throw them in his small satchel.

"I hear Beatrix calling," he said. "Silly tarot. Promise me now not to mention the cards. She hates when I bring them out. Carla, pay no heed to my foolish talk. Let's go and eat our dinner."

We were new friends then, and just arrived in Chert, I had done as he had said and let the tarot reading go. That was six months ago. Now, I could not stop hearing his words—*What had they meant? Chango just completed his twenty-fourth year. Does that mean there is time for his wound to heal?*

I would be there still, at the old church plaza, pacing, shivering, frightened, if Mario had not appeared. He took me into his workshop, below his and Beatrix's home, and comforted me. I sat on a stool, the coal heater below my skirt warming me, and watched him oil and knead the hides, preparing them for carving. In the silence of his heavy hands rubbing the leather, he listened to my fears. Mario's technique coaxed the skin into revealing its grain. He conversed with the leather, very different from Chango, who dominated, molded, and shaped it to his will.

Soothed by his gentle manner, needing to tell someone, I revealed to Mario what Chango had done, finishing with, "Mario, Chango didn't know who I was."

Mario remained calm, but I saw his carving blade slip and gouge the belt he was working on. Stopping his work, he put his thick hands on my shoulders, his voice steady. "It's a terrible thing you tell me, and Chango sometimes goes deep inside, but he would never hurt you."

"Mario, how can you be sure of that? He almost did! He didn't know who I was," I repeated.

"Because, Carla, I didn't see it in the cards. I'll talk with him, help him." He put in arms around me to comfort me. I began to yawn uncontrollably, in the safety of his embrace.

"Now, I must go before I fall asleep on the workbench," I said, and yawned again.

"Carla, please let me walk you home."

"No," I whispered back to him. "It's not far, all downhill to our house. Go to sleep now. Hurry to your bed; Beatrix is waiting. I have my sister the moon to guide me home."

"Careful for the ruts," Mario cautioned as I left his workshop.

I waved good-bye and noticed the worried brow crease his forehead.

Climbing the stairs now, the weight of my swollen belly, along with my sadness, drained the last strength out of me. At the first landing of the stairs, I paused to observe the night, so quiet and still before the *Madruagada*, the hour before the dawn. I listened for my husband, not sure if I would wish him awake to greet me. Perhaps he worried? Maybe my leaving had cooled our bed, and he had roused and found me gone; possibly he was out looking for me, his disappearing Rose. I leaned against the wall for support and heard above, through the silence, his labored breathing that escaped from our bedchamber and drifted down the stairwell. I remembered he had run out of the nasal spray that controlled his asthma, and we had not been to Castellon de la Plana for weeks. I debated calling out to awaken him.

How was it that Mario and not Chango found me walking the abandoned plaza at the top of old town? My husband had not stirred, nor noticed his wife and unborn child absent? So many questions there were no answers to.

The baby kicked hard, as if to say, "Get to bed, Mama. I'm tired of your wanderings. I'll be here soon." With that I found the strength to climb the last stairs, slide out of my sandals, and kneel into our manger. The shadow that was my Chango turned over when I slipped the bedcover over me; the straw crunched beneath the brown burlap-sack cloth and white sheets that covered it.

"Where have you been, my Rose, on this night so late?" he spoke into the dark.

"Oh, so you did notice I was gone?"

"I notice the rustle of your skirt as it sweeps the floor, every tear you let slip down your cheek, your sigh when our baby kicks, and the moans that escape you when lifting the heavy logs up the stairs. There is nothing about you I do not notice, woman of mine."

"And still you let me go out alone?" I blurted.

"What would you have me do? After the harm I have caused you, I could not fault you for walking away and never returning. My own guilt stayed my chasing after you."

I sat back up and turned to him. "I would think your guilt would have tried to stop me, or run after me and prayed for me not to leave?" Anger again filled my throat.

"Well, I lied. I did follow you out into the street. I tracked you up the path to the end of town. I held back in the shadows, to not disturb you. I watched you circle the plaza in front of the old church; every time you reached the outer wall, I ached to reveal myself, but I was afraid what words you might lash out with. I stayed hidden, guarding you. Then I heard Mario come up the steps from his workshop. Your face smiled as he crossed the plaza to you, and covered you with his poncho. I was grateful he was late working and knew he would take care of you."

"And I was wishing that it would be you to comfort me; yet you left that to Mario?" Furiously, I grabbed his shoulders and shook him. "You told me, when a man loves a woman, he nourishes her. Is this what you meant?" I wanted to hurt him, and for the first time I saw into Chango's tear-stained, dark-circled, terror-stricken face. He was trembling. His long hair was wet; his shirt was damp and cold. I realized he must have stayed out all night in the harsh winter air waiting for me to return, probably arriving only minutes before me. His face appeared shifted from the fear; his aquiline nose appeared blunt somehow, and his thin lips full. My anger drained out my tired arms. I wrapped myself into him and him into me, wondering whether *I could trust this man ever again.*

I gasped as the first strong cramp reached out and grabbed my womb, clenching the breath out of me. I fell over onto the bedding, and a cry escaped from my diaphragm. "Ooh, he was right," I muttered.

"Carlita, where do you hurt? What have I done? Forgive me," he begged, kissing my brow, my hands. Then he added, "Who was right?"

"Mario. He saw me flinch while he wrapped his poncho over me. He took me into his workshop and prepared chamomile tea. He told me my eyes shone the same radiance he saw in Beatrix right before she went into labor with both Dunia and Aisha. He sent me home saying the baby was coming and to find a way to forgive you, that fatherhood terrifies men and makes some crazy. Then he told me to get some rest and that he would send Beatrix over this morning. Is that it, Chango? Are you crazy?"

I shivered uncontrollably. Dawn's red glow was lighting up the white plaster wall across the bedchamber.

"Yes, my Rose, Mario is right; I'm crazy, and, no, that is not what I meant by nourish. I'll pray you will find the way to forgive me, but now you must rest." He took our one blanket and his poncho and covered me up. "Gather your strength and please sleep. I'll watch over you, and prepare the fire."

I closed my eyes, felt his lips touch my fingers as a second wave of contractions bore down on me. My hands clenched. I opened my eyes and saw the hurt in his. Taking his hand in mine after the contraction eased, I whispered, "No, no, it's not your touch, but the womb that makes me grit. In time, my little prince, I must forgive you. I do not understand any of this, but I do know I won't live in fear, nor will our child. It can never happen again. Can you promise me that now?"

"Si, Carla, I can do that. Let me start the fire and bring you warm soup; you didn't eat last night. Trust me; it won't happen again, I promise. Never."

"I'm too weary to talk. But I promise you this. I do not forgive twice; I'll go and not look back. Know it in your bones. Now, you need to take care of me. Leave me in peace, and go make a large fire so that I can feel the heat."

I pulled the poncho up over my chest and began to rub my belly in deep circles as I had seen a pregnant woman do at the clinic in Barcelona, to soothe the baby. *Patience, little one; let mama rest a bit. Let me clear my thoughts.*

I drifted off, listening to the crackle of the fire, the kettle rattling as the water boiled. I heard Chango sing a *Chamame* folk song from Argentina as he ran up and down, gathering wood from under the stairs.

Set the white dove free,
Set the white dove free
From the talons of the hawk

I realized the beautiful lyrics were tragic, haunting—like all the songs he taught me. My body relaxed as I floated in and out of a light sleep. The contraction came and went.

The tumult began to slip away. Then, abruptly, the events of the day before woke me in a startle, just as a stronger contraction arrived. "No, child, not now. You do not want to come today."

Was it only yesterday that Chango's five minutes of madness threatened the serenity of my life? The memory replayed itself like the terrible surreal movie it had been. I had arrived home with my basket full from the farmers market, calling to my husband as I climbed, "Chango, put on the kettle for mate. My feet are aching."

A stranger in my husband's form stood waiting upstairs. His eyes, smoldering and foreign, his three words spat at me, "Who are you?"

My basket fell to the floor as the knife blade rose against my warm throat. Engulfed in terror, I backed up against the window;

the pressure of my shoulder pushed against the cold glass, my head pressed hard on the wood jam above the window. I could see Beatrix outside, waiting as she always did for me to reach the window. She smiled up at me from the cobbled street—she'd heard my body rap the glass—thinking it was our signal, she waved and walked away, blind to my peril. I was unable to call out or raise my arm for fear of the blade against my neck. I pleaded with my eyes but could not stop her leaving.

I'd closed my eyes—for seconds, minutes, I didn't know—powerless to breathe, until I'd heard the sharp thud of the knife as it fell to the wood floor, bouncing once, and then lay at my feet.

Still afraid to move, listening to Chango's footsteps tramp down the stairs, I opened my eyes and gazed out the glass and saw him come out of our doorway below, cross the street, jump the stone wall, and flee up the hill out of view.

I bolted straight up in the bed, and gasped out, "No, stop!" I knelt on the straw mattress, rocking, praying in English, "Santa Clara, please let me forget, help me forgive; I can't dwell here. Grandmother Alessia, assist me—thirteen babies you birthed from your womb—help me to do this right. I must bury yesterday and be ready for this child who knocks on my heart."

I lay back down. Hearing my prayer in English reassured me and allowed me to release the memory. Rubbing my heavy breasts and arms, I surrendered in exhaustion from the last twenty-four hours. My body relaxed, a quiet surge of deep calm ran up my legs; the warmth of the fire reached under the blanket to my feet, and I slept.

A soothing voice woke me, "Carla, can you hear me? It's Beatrix."

I opened my eyes to the love that was Beatrix; her black curls fell over her eyes as she knelt beside me. She took my hand in her delicate one. Her fingers were blackened from the wood fire she used for making herbal infusions for women whose ailments the doctors didn't understand.

"Oh, Carla, how exciting. Are you ready to pop this *bebe* into our world?"

I had postponed thinking about this day since we'd left Barcelona. One day blended into the next—meeting Beatrix, Mario, their girls. *I've been in love with all of them, Chango, and my life. What had I been thinking? I am the crazy one. In my country, women go to hospitals and doctors to give birth, and here I am on the floor of a five-hundred-year-old crumbling building, in an abandoned village on a mountain in Spain, and for the first time since I got pregnant I ask myself if I am ready? I look around the small room of bare stone and the cracked, peeled plaster, anxious, aware of the remoteness of our village.*

Looking up to Beatriz, I finally answer, "I don't know. I can't believe these six months have passed, and here we are. Am I ready?"

Beatrix laughed. "We are never ready, woman, but we continue to bear our children, love our men, wash our hair, and live our lives. Of course you're ready, and I'm here. I won't leave you." Reading my thoughts she continued, "Mario is in charge of the girls, who will make a surprise for you and the baby. I have sent Chango to fetch vegetables and Dr. Sanchez."

"But the doctor told me last week that he would not attend my birth. He advised me to go to De la Plana, to the clinic. Could he have been right? I'm so confused." I sat up and pulled up my dress, exposing my taut, stuffed belly. I noticed that it no longer rode high; the baby had dropped into place, preparing for the birth.

"Look, Beatrix, it's happening. And the doctor didn't believe I was nine months along, that fool. Look at me now. Let him come tomorrow and see my baby. I do not need him."

"Carla, I know, I know. But he may be needed, and Chango will bring him. Men won't say no to each other, at times like these. Now, let me see, has you water broke yet? Are you wet?"

"No, the bed is dry. Is it late in breaking?"

"Hah, silly woman, it happens when it happens. All in good time; I want you to sit in a chair. I have some soup here. You will drink it; then I'll get the chamber pot, and you can do your business.

Important before the baby comes that you do it, because it can be messy."

I did as she instructed. I should have been embarrassed to use the porcelain pot instead of going below to the stable or up the hill to the boulders to relieve myself, but there was no time. Another spasm gripped my womb; the pains were closer and much stronger. In between, Beatrix helped me up to put on her favorite nightgown. She told me she had birthed both her girls wearing it, and all had gone well. I pulled it over my head and shoulders. I was so much taller than her. The gown barely covered my thighs. But the yellow cotton was so soft from years being pounded on the washing-house stones. The cloth felt like Beatrix's arms were holding me; then she really grabbed me and held me close. Her coarse red wool skirt brushed against my legs. She stood on her toes so she could look into my eyes.

"Beatrix, I'm frightened," I said in English.

Beatrix smiled softly, "I know, Carla; Mario told me everything. It makes no sense. I have never known a man as deeply in love as Chango is. Maybe he is *too* much in love. There will be time enough for him to make it right again, just not today. Do you hear me?"

"Chango promised me when a man loves a women he nourishes her." My voice trembling, "Mario would never have done that to you?"

"Ah, my woman, what men do? Or us women to them! Yes, a man must provide always, and when a woman loves a man, she sets him free. All that has gone before is over; all words, actions, and decisions disappear. With this baby, your life begins anew. Never again will you be alone, and never again will you be completely free. You have made a bargain with the divine to release you and all of your worries. Now, it's time to be present, Mama Carla."

She handed me another cup of her garlic soup and pushed me into the fire room so she could work. I noticed the sun low in the sky. Soon it would be twilight—the short winter day was almost gone. I threw some pine wood on the fire, and a flame shot up, brightening the room. Such a humble palace for my child to be born, these two small rooms where we lived: three straw chairs, a table, a few plates and cups on a shelf. The twenty-pound sack of brown rice stood in the corner next to the crate of bottled milk. Above the table, a basket hung with fresh herbs, garlic, onions, eggs, and a piece of cheese. These were our prized possessions. I started to laugh. "Oh my child, I hope you come with the loaf of bread that Amaranta promised all babies bring." Beatrix called, and I returned the ten paces to our bedchamber.

The room had been transformed; Beatrix had prepared my birthing space. She'd brought everything. We had never discussed the birth, but she had once told, "Carla, do not worry. I will bring everything; it will be my gift."

And she had. She'd placed clean sackcloth over our straw mattress and covered it with the beautiful embroidered white sheets she had purchased from Amaranta. Next, she covered the bedding with a piece of tarp to protect it all. Then she remade the bed with my worn muslin sheets, for easy removal afterward, and placed a big white enamel basin in a corner for the afterbirth. Her favorite blue enamel vase, filled with fresh rosemary, lavender, and bay leaves, sat in the other corner, and she'd lit two kerosene lanterns, bathing the room in an amber glow. As I scanned the area, my heart ached in sweet gladness until I saw her take out a small sharp knife, and I cried out.

"Why did you bring that?" I asked accusingly.

"Carla, it's only a knife, for under the bed. Here, take it."

"No. I don't want to touch it."

"Woman, you must. Stop this now." Her voice kind but firm, she took my hand and placed the knife in my palm. "It helps cut the labor, and later we'll use it to sever the cord. Who knows where these customs stem from? Maybe so the midwife knew where to find the knife when she needed it. I don't know, but it's the custom, and we shall use it. For it to work, you must be the one to take it and place it under the bed."

I took the knife and did as she said, holding it for an extra moment; somehow it calmed me. I placed it under the straw mattress, in the middle, just below where my waist would rest. She helped me back into bed and began rubbing my lower back strenuously, where my pain was worse.

"Yes, for some women, this is where they suffer. It's called 'back labor,' maybe from always carrying the weight of others on their backs," she said, and laughed.

The contractions were now coming hard and lasting longer. When the pain got too intense, Beatrix made me alternate between kneeling on all fours panting, and then lying on my side to rest. She hummed me a soft melody to help me sleep for the few minutes that separated the contractions, and that prepared me for the next one.

"Women's work," she said.

The last daylight hours passed in peace, stillness, then labor, until Beatrix's spell was broken by Chango's footsteps running up the stairs, calling, out of breath, "Clarita, Beatrix, I found the doctor. He was all the way in San Miguel. I found two—even better, yes?" He looked to Beatrix for approval.

"I hope you remembered the beets and yams? We'll need them to strengthen her blood afterwards."

I asked, "Did you run the ten kilometers to San Miguel?"

Behind Chango, two men appeared at the top of the narrow stairs, panting as they entered the bedchamber.

"Well, you made it just at the right time. Come in doctors. Come in and help this woman," Beatrix greeted them. My eyes barely made sense of the two tall men hunching over my bed wearing tuxedos, gasping from the steep climb up the hill. Chango stood holding up the kerosene lantern by my feet, so they could see into our room.

Sitting up, I mustered, *"Buenas tardes, Señores."*

After the hours of quietude, these three men were invading my sanctuary. They seemed incongruous, contradictory to everything Beatrix had created. A shift had occurred, and I looked to her for help.

"Do not worry, Carla. All will be well. They may be needed."

A huge contraction swallowed me for what seemed an eternity, and I fell back into darkness. But I could hear their voices, and tried to make out their conversation.

"No, no, impossible; you must take her to De la Plana! I already told you that, Señor, and I told your wife that last week too."

"But, Doctor, she's too far along. She *is* about to deliver," Beatrix interrupted.

"This is her first baby, yes? There is time. Señor, drive your wife to the hospital. That is an order."

"But I don't drive," replied Chango.

"Well then, Señora," he turned to Beatrix. "You drive her to the hospital."

"But I do not drive," Beatrix stated, "and my husband Mario," who had just appeared in the cramped hallway, "doesn't either. Tell me, doctors, why are you all dressed up?"

"Because, we were on our way to attend a wedding, when this crazy man," pointing to Chango, "accosted us. He stood in front of my car and refused to move. Then he dragged us up here on a matter of life and death!" the agitated doctor yelled at Beatrix and Mario.

"Who then drives the painted van out front that everyone talks about?" Dr. Sanchez demanded.

Three sets of fingers pointed to me. "She does!" they said in unison.

"OOOOHHHHHWWWW," I exclaimed, bearing down on another contraction. "I'm not driving anywhere!"

Dr. Sanchez pulled back the sheet and examined my womb. "Has her water broken yet?" he asked Beatrix, while he motioned to Chango to bring the lantern down closer so he could see. "I have not delivered a baby since medical school." He looked at his companion, who shook his head and mumbled something to Chango, wagging his finger.

Beatrix sat down next to me and whispered in my ear. "They will call a taxi, Carla. They will put you in the back and drive you the sixty kilometers over the mountain to Castellon, and your baby will be born in a dirty taxi, woman, if you don't hurry now. On the next one, bear down hard and push …"

But before she could continue, the wave rose inside me, and the pressure overwhelmed my whole being. I closed my eyes and fell back, and saw two large celestial orbs staring back at me. I cried out, and the waters broke all over the doctor, soaking him in amniotic fluid, with my baby cresting on it, landing in his and Beatrix's hands. She pulled my daughter up and laid her on my chest.

"It's a girl. It's a girl," she sang out to the room.

Sitting up, I saw my child's eyes wide open, the same eyes I had seen moments before, laughing at me, her mouth open, calling to me, not a cry, but an exclamation, as if to say, *I'm here.*

"No taxi for you, Cielo, my water baby," I said with a laugh, her wet body dripping on mine, christening me, too. After only a few minutes of rest, and much to my surprise, another large spasm came, just as strong; I fell back again, holding my baby on top of me, instead of in me.

"What's that?" I cried out.

"That is good, Carla." said Beatrix with a smile. "You must sit up again, Carla. It means your body knows what to do. Now, Doctor, it's your turn to work. Let's get the afterbirth out and clean this brave woman up."

Their movements seemed separated from me, holding the soft flesh of my child against mine during the second wave. My vision was blurry, until I heard Dr. Sanchez ask Chango for a knife. I focused on my husband and saw the elation of the moment drain from his face, replaced with shame. He didn't move.

Beatrix called to him, "It's under the straw, Chango. Reach in and get it." His hesitations were clear, not wanting to touch a knife so near to me.

Beatrix had taken my daughter and, holding her in front of the doctor, barked to Mario, "Get us the knife, husband."

"No, Mario." I interrupted her, seeing an opportunity. "Chango, please reach underneath me and pull out the knife. It has cut the pain, and now it will cut the cord, so our child can join us." I'm sure my words confused him. But my smile was genuine; my pain had dispersed, and the grace to move forward here in this moment was real.

"My Rose, all that you ask, I'll do." He reached under me and pulled out the blade, handing it to the doctor to sever our daughter from the divine womb into our world. Beatrix swaddled my daughter and handed her to her father, smiling, "Here, Papa."

He took her hesitantly. A moment of fear crossed his brow, and then, as he looked deep into those blue eyes staring back at him, he kissed each eyelid and exhaled. Lovingly, he handed her to me. "I won't fail."

"Nor I," echoing his love back to him, sensing a new door had opened for the three of us. As I took my daughter in my arms, a clear understanding of Beatrix's words, "You have made a bargain with the divine," enveloped me.

Yes, we had.

Girls' House

"Ama, I want to go to Girls' House!"
"No, Ling, you're too young. I've told you, one must wait until the right time. Now, go play with your rocks and jewels, and let your poor mother work."

Jung bent down in the potato patch, digging around each plant in the rocky soil so the vegetables could flourish in the windswept earth.

"I don't want to wait. I go now."

"Yes, child, go play now," muttered her ama.

Lei Ling picked up her small basket and stomped down the furrow, determined to walk to Girls' House. Before she reached the end of the row, she came across a butterfly perched on a young potato vine. She sat down in the earth and laid her treasured red cloth on the soil. Next, she removed the largest of her stones and placed it in the middle of the cloth.

"Wise butterfly, I'll make sacred altar to you. Please show me how you change from caterpillar to butterfly. I must change from too young to girl!"

Lei Ling spread out her glass beads and seeds, imitating the patterns she had watched her grandmother make, eyes closed, chanting quietly.

Jung stood up to rest and looked down the channel of vines at her precious daughter bent over the earth, the red cloth placed in front of her. *So like my mother,* she thought. *Sooner than I would wish, she will be going. It will be my greatest gift to her.*

Head bowed on the prayer stone, Lei Ling imagined herself a butterfly, flitting around the valley, up the river bank, wings fluttering in the breeze, blown here and there, joyful in her lightness. She visited the flowering crops, sipped sweet water from the rice paddies, and then allowed the wind to push her wings high in the sky. She saw her mother stooped over the earth. Her brown trousers and blouse blended into the soil, as if she was growing from the soil. Lei Ling flew next to the mist-shrouded mountain, where large forests of bamboo flourished. The same breeze blowing under her wings stirred the giant bamboo stalks to hum a melancholy tune. In the strong wind, their green hardness bent deep as if they were kowtowing to the mountain, their tops curved over gracefully, just as her Popo had taught her to do.

She heard her popo's voice coming from the forest. "Watch, Ling, the bamboo is strongest when it bends in the wind and does not snap like the pine limbs. So it is when we meditate. We bend our wills in prayer so that we can flow in this harsh life and not break."

The child-butterfly slowly fluttered back to Lei Ling's bent-over body sitting in the dirt. The child opened her eyes, sat up straight, stood, and then ran back to her mother, positive she had been transformed into a girl.

"Ama, Ama, look! Have I not grown? Look at me now!"

"Sweet breath of mine!" Jung knelt down; her gaze melted into the black moon eyes of her only child. "Soon, Ling. Ask Quan Yin for patience. Before long your time will come. An important part of your popo's teaching is to accept what appears on your path each day."

Jung sighed and pointed to the bamboo baskets strung on either side of the pole. "Now, help me lift the burden of the world on my shoulders. Daughter, when you're strong enough to carry this weight of the earth on your shoulders, then you will be old enough to go to Girls' House."

"Yes, Ama, I understand. I'll practice every day."

That night, when Lei Ling's father arrived home from his work, she stopped him at the door. "Baba, please, will you make pole baskets that fit on my shoulders?"

"Why would you need them, Ling? What do you need to carry but your trinkets and your doll?"

"Oh, I'll fill them with the sharp rocks that scatter in our potato field and carry them to the pit. That will help Ama, and I'll grow stronger."

"Little one, so soon you wish to carry the weight of the world? Why not take these few years and play? They will soon be gone. The rest of your long life will fill with work enough!"

"But, Baba, I want to go to Girls' House," the child pleaded, holding her father's hand.

"Already you want to leave your mother and me? I cannot understand, when you are all we have until your mother's belly grows fat again." Lifting his cherished one up into his arms so their eyes could meet, he hugged his daughter and whispered, "I'll see when I can get to it, but in the meantime, play, my child."

—

Girls' House stood on the south end of the village square. In this harsh era of the Cultural Revolution, only a few of its original features remained. The sturdy gray tiles and large timbers had been removed by the soldiers to roof their outpost. The stone lion totem that guarded the entryway was destroyed, for it represented foolish superstitious ideas that were no longer tolerated. Only the carved door still remained intact, a tribute to the craftsmanship of the village carpenters. The people were encouraged to abandon their old customs and were expected to dedicate themselves to the New Order. All the children received uniforms to wear and were taught Chairman Mao's revolutionary songs.

Although unique to Lei Ling's province, the house didn't offend the sensibilities of the communists. They tolerated the tradition as long as the villagers didn't waste any of the collective's resources on repairs. Twice a year, the village would gather and donate whatever materials they could to secure the tin roof or patch the walls with fresh mortar, to protect their daughters before the high winds and rains came.

When a girl reached the age of six or seven, Girls' House became her home. No matter what her family's standing in the village, all girls were welcomed. Each would learn from the elder girls how to sew, cook, and care for her female needs. During the day, a girl would return to her family home to eat her daily meals and work alongside her mother, but at night she would run to Girls' House to play and sleep. Once a member of the house, a child became the charge of the community and, as such, was protected by all the men of the village, so no harm could touch their daughters.

On days that Lei Ling was free to roam the village, she took her doll to play on the steps of the house. In the warm months, the wooden shutters were left open to allow for the cool breeze to enter. The openings were covered in cloth brightly decorated by the girls as a way of keeping their privacy. She would place stones and scraps of wood under the window and climb up to peer inside. The house was usually empty during the day, but Lei Ling hoped to catch a glimpse of the older girls' secret rooms. Several times she heard laughter and singing drifting from inside, which only increased her longing.

In Lei Ling's seventh year, her waiting ended.

On the last day of the harvest, she had run into the fields where her mother toiled. "Here, Ama, let me help you. Don't worry; I'll carry it to the barrel."

Lei Ling squatted below the bamboo pole and raised herself up. With all the strength her small frame could muster, Lei Ling wobbled down the field, carrying the load until she reached the barrel. Without dropping a single potato, she emptied the baskets and dashed back to her mother. She beamed as she reached the place where her mother stood smiling at this determined child.

Jung nodded to her child and lifted the pole and baskets from her shoulders.

"Ling, my how you've grown before my very eyes; you're no longer a child. You're a girl, and tonight I walk with you to Girls' House. We shall make sweet bean soup to celebrate, and you may take a pot to share with your sisters."

Proud daughter clamped her arms around her mother's legs, hugging her tightly. Jung filled with gratitude that, in these troubled times, at least Ling would know Girls' House.

At home that evening, her father said, "Come here, Ling. Can you not at least pretend to miss your Baba or your little brother tonight?"

Reaching up to her father, Lei Ling wrapped her arms around his neck. "Silly Baba, I'll be home in the morning to give you your good morning kiss and cup of tea as always. I'm not leaving you for many, many years to come. Do you not wish me to grow and learn to be a good wife for some lucky man you shall pick for me?"

"So wise you are to turn it back to me. At only seven years old you can outmaneuver your father. Pity the lucky man who tries to argue with you. Now off with you, so the night will pass and once again I'll see you."

Mother and daughter walked hand in hand to the square. The other mothers stood in their doorways, smiling as the two passed from their hut at the end of the village through the stone streets. Some gave Lei Ling small tokens—a ribbon, a handful of peanuts, a glass bead.

Sixteen-year-old Yin Lian, the oldest girl, stood in the carved doorway, bowing deeply to Jung. "Not to worry, Jung; we'll take good care of your precious flower."

"My tears are not of worry, but of joy. Listen to your big sister, daughter; she'll have much to teach you. Come right home in the morning so you may eat your rice."

For Lei Ling's first night they dressed her as a bride, arranging her hair with flowers and small berries, draping red cloth around her. A small throne stood at the end of the sleeping room, and there they sat her in the honored seat.

Yin Lian stepped forward. "We welcome you, Lei Ling. Tonight we celebrate your joining us and look forward to learning who you are. We have prepared the materials for you to have your own bedroll, mat, and washing bowl."

As she spoke, the girls approached with the items left behind by another girl gone and married.

"Come, let us sing and dance for our new sister. In time you'll learn our songs and dance with us. Enjoy this moment of celebration and the throne you occupy. There will be much to learn on your path to a woman. The next time you sit here will be the night before your wedding, but that is many years away."

—

The only joy that competed with Girls' House was birthdays, hers and her grandmother's. Twice a year, mother and daughter climbed the steep mountain to visit Jung's home community, and both times all the presents were for Lei Ling.

Upon reaching the outer edge of the village, Lei Ling released her mother's hand and ran all the way to her grandmother's door. Sung Lei stood waiting, but before they spoke, she would bend down and take Lei Ling's small hand in hers to caress and rub her fingers over the palms, infusing them with her love. Then she would lean into her granddaughter's face, staring directly into the child's eyes, holding the gaze until the two touched foreheads. Clutching Lei Ling's hand, she escorted her granddaughter to her altar, lit the incense from the oil lamp and bowed, offering prayers of gratitude to Quan Yin for the safe arrival of her granddaughter.

"Now, precious flower, you must be so hungry from the arduous hike up the mountain. Let's fill your rice bowl and after …," her voice trailed off. Looking around to make sure no one was near, "and after, we shall see." Winking to Lei Ling, her eyes motioned to the ceiling above. "Oh, lucky child, I remembered to save a cup of sweet bean soup; we shall let your mother eat the rice."

Jung stepped into the kitchen. "Oh, Ama, I wish to visit my sister. You two will be happy together?"

Sung Lei pointed to Jung, and said to Lei Ling, "Your mother was my first child, and you my first grandchild, so no matter whom follows, you two will always remain my first. Go, daughter; Ling and I have much to do."

Jung patted her mother's shoulder, smiling at the sweet words, and left the two generations, heads bent together, laughing and whispering. When Sung Lei was assured they were alone, she went to the ladder she kept outside and placed it under the trap door that led to the storage area. Granddaughter and grandmother snuck up into the attic. All was prepared for their clandestine ritual; a small pillow awaited Lei Ling. She watched her grandmother take the wooden cover off one of her grain baskets. On top of the rice lay the stash of specialties that she'd prepared and hoarded until Lei Ling's visit. In the dimness of the attic, Sung Lei spread out toasted peanuts, dried sweet yams, and the child's favorite, sundried mangoes—while captivating the child with descriptions of her family's years as members of the royal court.

"Eat, Ling. Eat slowly and savor each bite as it fills your belly. Ask your body to remember the fullness you feel right now. It will serve to replenish you in times of hunger. Like my mother, your Zeng Zumu, you have had the misfortune of being born in the Year of the Dragon."

"I don't understand, Popo. Was not my Zeng Zuma counsel to the emperor himself? How can that be misfortune?"

"Ah, little one, a person born in the Year of the Dragon is gifted with deep power. It's easy for a man to carry that power; he is respected and honored. But a woman is not intended to wield authority. Girls born in the Dragon years are destined to a very hard life."

"How can counsel to the emperor be a hard life? The dazzling jewels and servants! How I wish I could have seen the palace. Look at the silk tapestries here in this painting of Zeng Zuma; the fish appear to be swimming on her robes. How magical she is."

Lei Ling fingered the portrait that her grandmother hid in the attic. It must never be seen by the Red Guard; if found, it would spell disaster for her family.

Sung Lei continued, "Prosperity reigned for many generations during her life. The harvests flourished, and fresh fruit overflowed on the altar every day. The young emperor favored your Zeng Zuma and kept her as one of his trusted advisors. Lavish cloths spun of silk with golden threads were the daily dress at court, but the emperor was tainted by his fortune and allowed the peasants to starve when the famines came. He didn't heed his ancestors' wisdom or your Zeng Zuma's advice. He allowed the Japanese interests to gain foothold in his decisions and, for all his wealth, he could not save himself or your Zeng Zuma from the prison camps. Yes, she was regal, but study carefully the hardness of her eyes. Is there happiness there? I keep the portrait not to envy what once was, but to remind me of how quickly riches can be lost."

"But, Popo, such wealth! Is it not easier to be happy when the eyes are full of such beauty, rather than the pain of the bent back, sore on hoeing our hard soil?"

"Abundance in one's heart is what is to be measured! This is where happiness lives, not in the greed of the material world. For that reason the emperor lost favor, and his palace was overrun. The world of your great-grandmother is gone forever. We remain to carry the essence of her teaching, and practice stillness to hear it."

On Lei Ling's fifth birthday she was gifted a scrap of red silk left from that era, her first altar cloth. Though it no longer glimmered with brilliant colors, when Lei Ling closed her eyes and sat in meditation, she felt the threads glow. She silently added a prayer every day that she might know the outside world of which she'd heard merchants chatter. And when she napped in her grandmother's bedroll, dreams swept her across the mountains atop a metal bird that flew faster than the wind, viewing the brightly lit cities, the ancient wall to keep out the hordes of Mongolians, and the Forbidden Palace. She imagined herself one of the glamorous movie stars. Women with painted faces, beautiful dresses, and high-heeled shoes were pictured in the prohibited magazines that were passed from household to household, kept secret from the Red Guard.

"How can one be still if the stomach growls all night and refuses to lay quiet on the bed roll? At home, there are few bowlfuls to go around, and even fewer sweets."

"Easy, child; open your heart and feed love to the stomach to fill its hunger."

"Someone should tell my Baba; his stomach growls loudest of all. It doesn't wait for sleep even. At times, when our rice bowls are shallow, I can hear it across the room."

"Better still, little one, send your love to him, so his belly shall calm in fullness. That is why it's so important every day, during your chanting, to fill your heart with all that is left over from your love of Quan Yin."

"I shall try, Popo, but first I'll practice filling my own belly, so it will be easier to smile."

"Wise thought, Ling. You're learning."

On her thirteenth birthday, Sung Lei presented Lei Ling an unusual gift. After their feast she handed her granddaughter a carved water gourd. She had engraved the characters of Lei Ling's name into the side and prepared a beaded cover and latch to securely close the top, so water could not spill. Handing the filled gourd to her precious one, she spoke her warning.

"Ling, it won't be long before your life as a mother and wife will begin. Many hard years await you. Remember to always keep this gourd filled, and you won't starve. Never allow it to be empty, not one day, and you will be protected."

"I've never seen a decorated gourd, Popo. Does it come from the Emperor's Palace?"

"Don't be silly, child. I carved it!"

"I didn't know you could carve."

Taking Lei Ling's hand in hers, as she so often did, massaging the small fingers, Sung Lei answered, "There are many things you don't know about me, as it should be. Just remember the things I tell you."

Now at sixteen in Girls' House, two days before her wedding, a teak chest arrived for Lei Ling. The girls had encircled the mysterious bundle from Lei Ling's grandmother, which required two men to carry. Squeals filled the room as Lei Ling carefully untied the burlap-swathed trunk to reveal jade and ivory carvings inlaid on the ornate lid. Each had run their fingers over the figures, marveling at the intricacies that represented Chinese astrological symbols.

"Oh, my sisters, I've secretly loved this chest my whole life. I never dared touch it. How generous of my Popo; it's the last heirloom from her mother's family. I do not see a latch. Help me figure out how to open it."

They tried their hands at finding a way to open the endowment, until Jin, the carpenter's daughter, pushed her fingers gently on the handle, and it slid, exposing a small hidden key.

"I've seen my father make seamless wood slide. This has been made by a master."

"Now we have the key. But where is the lock?" complained Lei Ling.

As Lei Ling continued to inspect the lid, another girl asked, "What sign is your Popo?"

"She was born in the Year of the Tiger. Ah!" But when she played with the tiger, nothing moved.

"Try the dragon, Ling," the girls squealed. "You're a dragon!"

When Lei Ling pushed on the dragon, the lock became exposed. "Of course!" she sighed.

"But how is this so, Ling? If your grandmother has had this forever, it couldn't have been made for you."

"No, little sister, the emperor in the Forbidden City ordered it made for my Zeng Zuma. She was named for Lao Tsu, the supreme dragon, and I, in turn, was named for her." Lei Ling took the key, unlocked the latch and opened the chest to find it empty except for a small purse. Recognizing it immediately, she picked up the bag and put it to her chest, whispering, "Thank you, Popo, for all that you have taught me. I hope I'm worthy of this life that beckons."

Lei Ling placed the purse in her pocket, and laughed at her sisters' quizzical faces. "Do not worry, little sisters. I'll reveal it before I leave. Now, our last night, is it not a time to celebrate our games and secrets?"

That night they amused themselves with their favorite diversions and sang lighthearted songs to Lei Ling's weaknesses.

"Oh no, please, Ling, let someone else make the rice for you. Maybe it will be better for you to hire someone to bring it to your house, or your new husband will surely starve to death."

"Oh, big sister, your needlepoint is so unusual. Are you practicing a new technique with your feet?

"Laugh if you must. These feet have many talents."

The girls had occupied the evenings the past twelve months for sewing the four seasons' wardrobe for Lei Ling's new life. They wove baskets for her kitchen and filled them with grains and food stores from each harvest to ensure she would not starve in her husband's family home. They turned clay pots for her cooking and made straw mats for her floors. When each young woman left Girls' House to marry, all her childish ways would be left behind. As was custom, each girl left with the skills and materials required for running a home.

Lei Ling loved performing musical dramas. That night, she danced for her sisters. Mixing old Chinese rhythms with melodies she had heard over the radio, she caused the other girls to blush with her movements and songs, but then they begged her for more.

The next morning, Lei Ling awoke to the voices of her sisters singing the good-bye lament. They were packing her trousseau into the teak chest. Listening to her sisters' song, she opened her eyes and sat up, thinking about how wonderful the evening had been. A light rain tapped on the tin roof. She surveyed the sleeping room and found she was all alone. "How auspicious, the rain brings good fortune. Thank you, spirits of the clouds, for your blessings, and thank you, little sisters, for allowing me this moment of solitude," she whispered.

Her feet tired from hours of dancing, Lei Ling lay back under her bedroll, reveling in her fortune to linger on her last day in the house. Her thoughts drifted to memories over the nine years in Girls' House, and to how quickly time had passed. The years of preparation for this journey, the promise of answers to a new life unfolding, could not have predicted the threshold she was about to cross. Her betrothed, Shaozu, and her father were planning an escape over the mountains to Hong Kong before the winter's snows made the route impassable—a secret she could not share with anyone, even her sisters in Girls' House. Reliance on the villagers' trust was compromised, even in her remote province. The Red Guard planted spies; ears and eyes were everywhere. She looked at the teak chest and realized many of the gifts would be left behind, and a quiet sadness tapped in her heart. Then too, all the provisions meant for her in her new home would be used for everyone; they might spell her family's survival for the crossing. Lei Ling smiled, the sadness replaced by gratitude that all her sisters' work would have more far-reaching benefits than they imagined. It was to be a fierce beginning for Lei Ling, thrust into that outside world she had once envied.

Recent visits from the Red Guard bode ill for her Buddhist beliefs. The earlier tolerance by the Communist regime had been replaced by strict enforcement of their guidelines. Nothing was safe, even here in this remote village. Her fears of what her future portal would open to rose up into her mouth and left her with a sour taste. Not wishing to give in to her anxieties, Lei Ling sat up and shouted into the room, "Enough. Today is my last day. Let me enjoy my sisters!"

Running feet could be heard on the slat floors as the other girls responded to her shouts. "Lei Ling, are you all right? Are you sick?"

"No, little sisters, I'm wiping my uncertainties from the crevices of my mind so I can welcome my new life tomorrow."

"Must you wipe them so loudly?"

"So sorry to disturb you; forgive me. I know it's a day of quietude. I'll miss you all so much." She rose and stretched her arms to her sisters. "Before we wash our faces with salty waters, there's much to be done."

Her last day in Girls' House would be spent in silence. The girls made final preparations for her departure. None would go home to their families, or to their work in the fields. As Lei Ling dressed, they brought her fried mango and an overflowing rice bowl. Only she could partake. Fasting had already begun for the other girls. Until the sun set, all would sit in silence and meditation around Quan Yin's altar. Sniffles would be the only sound to break the stillness, tears to rinse away the childhood deeds and prepare Lei Ling as a new vessel.

Everyone wore the plain sackcloth dress and white scarf of mourning as a symbol of the "death" of childhood and entry into the "life" of womanhood. No longer would Lei Ling play or sleep among them, or chant with them. For Lei Ling, the anxiety of moving into her husband's household was replaced with the knowledge that not only her childhood would be lost, but soon the fabric of her daily life would be cleansed of all that was safe for her. Excitement and fear competed for her attention.

At dusk the oil lamps were not lit. The last ceremony was performed in the shadows of flickering candles. Lei Ling was bathed and anointed with special oil extracted from aromatic herbs and flowers. Lastly, she was swaddled in red silk and laid in her bedroll to sleep the last dream of childhood. The cloth would later be used to sew her married bedsheets. The other girls sat awake and held vigil around her so no demons could come and interrupt her repose.

The first shaft of light broke through the cracks in the wooden shutters and illumined the girls dressing Lei Lin in red robes and all her finery. The Ha Mu "Exemplary Woman" was summoned to the house. The girls selected the matron they deemed to be the most successful woman of their village. She may have the most children, or the kindest husband, or a mother-in-law who didn't beat her. This woman always bore a smile for them and dispensed wisdom with giggles. The Ha Mu arrived to comb out any snarls left in Lei Ling's hair that may hold unfinished business; she was accompanied by Lei Ling's Popo, mother, and aunties. All came to sing the "Goodbye Girl" song to ensure her future days be blessed in good fortune. With each sweep of the bone comb through Lei Ling's blue-black tresses, Ha Mu's voice carried loudly through the room, each verse repeated by the girls.

> *"Best endings to your childhood left behind.*
> *Guide gentle man with courage to face all obstacles."*

The next two verses always brought giggles to the younger girls.

*"Plant abundant seeds in their hearts and soil,
Grow healthy babies that giggle in the light."*

And then, all grew more solemn with the final verses, especially with the times so full of uncertainty. The comb pulled through deeper to the scalp so no hair was left untouched.

*"No lonely nights for any under their roof,
Sleep soundly and rest beneath the heavens."*

And lastly, combing through to the very tips of her long tresses, the final verse was repeated twice.

"Awaken, lucky woman, to new beginnings of this awaiting life."

When the singing ended, the Ha Mu wove the hair strands with ribbons, pearls, and silk. Surrounded by her sisters, Lei Ling struggled to hold back her tears, not wanting to ruin their hard work transforming her into a noble bride. They finished the final touches on her veil, and then all voices fell silent. Lei Ling chanted the sacred sutras that her grandmother intoned in the temple, prayers repeated for generations.

Eight men from both families waited outside the door with a palanquin to carry Lei Ling to her new life. From the doorstep of Girls' House to the doorstep of her new home, her feet would not be allowed to touch the ground. In this way, there would be no bridge for her to walk back; there would be no returning to her childhood.

"Please, blessed sisters, before you prepare to give me away, allow me one more prayer."

She knelt before their small altar, overflowing with their humble offerings of the last twenty-four hours. Lei Ling lit her white candle for the last time and bowed her head to the mat.

"How different I am, Quan Yin, from the child running up to Popo's house always yearning for stories of the palace of my mother's ancestors, to this new wife, who would be content now to rest in our village and live the peaceful ways of my father. I have made a circle from here to there and back again to here. Give me strength to walk this path you have offered, and not forget where I have come from. The lightness of being a girl is now leaving me, and I am being called to places I do not know."

She rose and took from her pocket the threadbare silk purse that had been in the teak chest. The last gift from her Zeng Zuma had hung above the bed-mat where her Popo slept. Once, when she had fingered the silk, her grandmother had stopped her, saying, "No, Ling, that is not yours, yet. One day it will be the bridge from the past, for you not to forget." Lei Ling removed the simple gold tiger bracelet contained within and held out her hand to Sung Lei. Dragon's gift to tiger daughter now returned to dragon's great-granddaughter.

Taking the bracelet from Lei Ling, her grandmother placed it on her wrist. "This bracelet was gifted to me on my wedding. Your Zeng Zuma knew that its simplicity would ensure its longevity. It does not call attention to itself or to the wearer. Even so, in these times of poverty every bride must have a piece of gold to start."

A loud knock at the door, as the main groomsman pounded and called to the girls.

"We have come for Lei Ling."

"Who calls for her?"

"Shaozu is here," answered a loud voice, "and he does not like to be kept waiting. Hurry, foolish girls."

"There are no foolish girls here. What lucky money have you brought for our most treasured sister?"

"I hold a generous offer of one hundred yuan."

"Oh cheap man, go away. How you insult us to offer such a pittance. Do not waste our time."

"You think your sister is so valuable? Then we will offer one hundred and ten yuan. Now open the door."

"Now you're the foolish one. We will keep her with us."

"Well, then, what is her price?"

"Nine thousand, nine hundred, and ninety nine would be fair for such a flower."

"Crazy girls, have you been sucking on rancid meats?"

The bargaining ritual continued, with insults thrown generously and laughter on both sides for the best taunts. Finally the Ha Mu intervened, opened the door slightly, and reasoned with the groomsmen.

"A precious flower such as Lei Ling has no price high enough. Her lineage alone calls for an emperor's treasure, but we understand these are difficult times. Not a penny less than nine hundred and ninety nine could be considered. After all, more nines spell good fortune for the marriage, yes?"

Pretending foul play, the main groomsman handed over the prearranged purse to the Ha Mu. "Count it, old woman. You will find every yuan there."

"No need, sir; such a noble man as your lucky brother is beyond suspicion. He is so fortunate to have won our finest flower. Come, she is well worth your family."

The door was finally opened, and Lei Ling was lifted onto the ceremonial chair. Shaozu, holding the golden chord that wrapped around the dragon's head of Lei Ling's palanquin, led the procession. Listening to the sobs of the sisters left behind, Lei Ling positioned herself on the wooden bench to best tolerate the stiff ride. With head bowed and trembling hands, she quietly spoke the mantra.

"In gratitude I acknowledge all ancestors gone before me, after me, and with me now. I request their help to protect this marriage, offering my heart to them and Quan Yin."

Peering through the red veil, Lei Ling could only see the feet of her husband, dust rising onto his black trousers, transporting her to an unknown future. For the first time since being told of his and her father's plan to flee to the West, the prospect of her future became clear in its uncertainty.

Did my Zeng Zuma know how far-reaching the emperor's folly would extend? she wondered. *Not only the palace, but even our homeland lost! Can our prayers sustain us?* Fingering the tiger bracelet, Lei Ling smiled. *You knew Popo, what was coming. I wonder, all the sessions in the attic to prepare me for this, was I the good student?*

Just then the front men stumbled for a moment, the chair jostled, and the water gourd from Popo fell out from under the pillow in front of her. Lei Ling reached out and caught it. Bringing the gourd to her chest, a small giggle escaped from her heart, fear and joy intermingled.

She turned and saw her Popo leading the procession of women, behind her. Their eyes met, and she spoke softly to her, knowing the old woman could hear her heart.

"I am a dragon, and have the ability. Your gifts will fill my belly. And, yes, it won't be easy, but I shall not starve."

Lei Ling turned to face forward, sitting tall in her seat, smiling to embrace what awaited her, realizing this might be the last time she would be afforded such luxury.

"And I am not afraid."

Molecules and Women

A tall woman stood leaning over the upstairs porch of the ramshackle farmhouse, shaking out her newly shampooed hair. Droplets of water flung against the railing like mosquitoes dancing on a river's edge; she was unconcerned with the splatter around her. She raised her head and allowed the cool water to trickle down her neck into small rivulets along her spine. Tilting her head as she gently combed through her golden curls, drowsy sighs released with her snarls. Her body swayed to the comfortable ritual that she welcomed once a week as her time to herself.

A clatter and clank disturbed her reveling, and reluctantly she moved out to the balcony to seek the source of disturbance. Her sharp blue eyes spotted the large tin tub that usually sat on a stump under a leaking water spigot to catch the drops. It had tipped over and rolled across the yard.

Dang that girl, always running off, leaving something half done, she thought. She called to the empty yard, "Willow, Willow." Hearing no response, she leaned over the railing and raised her voice again toward the woods, "Philomena Jackson North, you answer me. I know you can hear me out yonder. No way you can run that fast; our washtub is still rolling!"

The tin basin finally came to rest at the base of the tall cherry tree that provided shade in the otherwise barren, dusty back garden.

The woodshed door below the porch swung partly open, and Willow popped out, waving up to her mother.

"Yes, Mama, here I is. I'm checking on Miss Purrfect to see if she's had her babies yet. She seems to have settled in behind the woodpile. I was just bringing her an old towel to lie on. She sure has a bellyful. Its sooooo big, it's rubbing on the ground when she walks. I wonder how many babies we're gonna get."

"Never you mind her; you get over there and put that tub under the spigot where it belongs. We can't squander one drop of our precious water. Then get in here and help me get the laundry hung out on the line. No use in it sitting in the basket; no way it's going to dry there. Who knows how long this warm wind will last. There are clouds moving fast out there, and my fingers are aching, a sure sign a change is coming."

Willow turned back inside the shed, patted the slumbering cat on the back, and gave her ears one last rub. "No way I'll be gone long, Miss Purrfect. You wait now, and I can help you get all those little ones out of you."

Standing up to leave, she caught her dress on a sharp splinter of a log and the soft faded cotton tore. "Oh no," she cried.

It was Willow's favorite. She'd worn it most every day that summer, taking it off only to launder it. The gift had come from Josie, her best friend. When Willow had unwrapped the pink box, all the girls squealed. It was the most special dress ever.

Josie boasted, "I picked out the pattern at the general store, and my momma already had the green plaid material. She told me it would look so special against your warm caramel skin, Willow. Then she added the velvet collar."

"Oh, Willow, it's the same color as the sea green flecks that swim in your chocolate eyes. But it's too fancy for play," her mother declared. Looking at the stitching, she said, "Your mama sewed this up right nice, Josie. This is better than any store-bought dress. You make sure and tell her how grateful Willow and I are. Let's save it, child, for special occasions." But once Willow had put it on, no amount of coaxing could get her to remove the delightful dress.

"But Mama, you're always telling me I'm growing like a weed. If I wait for the holidays, surely it won't fit. Then where will I be? I won't have worn it at all." With her daughter's pleading, determined face, Leona knew there was no point in asking Willow to put the dress aside.

"Remember to be careful then, child. It's not often such a special dress will come your way."

She lifted the skirt and sighed. "Now I have gone and torn the hem. But no bother, I'll fix it right quick before it frays, soon as the clothes are hung," she said to Miss Purrfect, who meowed in agreement.

Willow shut the door easy and ran to the house before her name could be called again. "No good can come if my name is called again. No good at all!" she said to no one. Philomena Jackson North was always chattering, conversing with the trees, with the rain that fell on her face, with the crows that flew overhead, with any living creature, and even with some that weren't. She collected the errant tub and placed it under the spigot. "Now we won't waste a drop." A gust of wind captured dry leaves and sent them swirling around the yard.

Willow exclaimed, "My, oh my, the wind is blowing keen right now. It will be no time at all to get the wash dry on a day like today, no time at all."

She tried to lift the large basket filled with their laundry, just as Leona stepped out from the kitchen to help. "Now wait up, child. You can't carry that all by yourself. Let me take one end. Oh, Willow, you haven't even combed through that nappy nest you call hair! What have you been doing all morning?" Leona exclaimed. "I bet you haven't brushed your pearly whites, neither."

"Oh yes I have, right after breakfast. I never forget them. I don't ever want them to hurt like they did last winter, and Dr. Fox got that drill and started digging like he was searching for gold or something, no siree. I promise, Mama."

"All right, I believe you. But that still doesn't answer about your hair, now does it?

"Well, you see, it's like this. Josie promised to come over after chores and plait my hair. I was gonna wait till she got here. She's gonna have to brush it right hard then, and, well, no use in frittering time away and doing it twice, now is there, Mama?"

"Oh, Philomena Jackson North, you do like shortcuts. And you always have an answer too. Your hair needs brushing every morning no matter what. You hear me? No matter what. You know how easy it turns to a tangled mess. One hundred strokes, just like me. See how luxurious my hair is, so silky? It doesn't grow that way. You have to care for it."

"But, Mama, my hair's never going to be pretty like yours, never. The light dances off yours like fireflies in twilight. No, I'm just happy when it's out of my face, so I can see where I'm going when I run like the wind."

"No more about it, you hear me? As soon as the wash is on the line, you march in there and do two hundred strokes," her mother scolded gently.

Every Sunday, Willow and her mother hung the laundry together, a weekly chore to share, and a favorite for both. Willow would drag the oversized basket and hand her mother each piece of clothing and a clothespin. Leona loved all things wet and clean, not easy in this dusty town. Willow just loved all things.

There were only the two of them left in this rambling old house. On weekdays, Leona headed out early to the post office to collect and deliver the mail. In the afternoons, she walked the three miles to cook at the local boarding house and served the evening meal to the workers there. At night, she hurried home with a delicious meal for Willow and herself. Leona didn't talk much, but she did have the listening ear that a child like Willow required. They did all right for themselves, each carving out her place next to the other as best they could.

"Mama, tell me again how you met my father."

"Oh, child, so long ago, and you have had me tell you that story so many times. You can probably tell it better than me."

"I know, I know, but your voice gets all soft and furry when you mention him. Your voice is all I have of my daddy. I can't even feel sad because I never knowed him. I can't decide; should I call him my father or my daddy?"

"Knew him, not 'knowed,' Willow," Leona corrected. "Child, it's important you learn to speak right, not like most folks do around here."

"Okay, Mama. But what happens when someone dies? I mean, what is heaven anyway? I heard Josie's mama say …"

"Sweet pea, your mind never stops moving, now does it? You can jump from one idea to another faster than a cricket over a leaf. Let's stop our cackling and get these clothes up before the rest of the morning is lost. You will learn soon enough about death. And as far as heaven, well, there will be the time to think on that. But for now, there is a big, wide world that will open to you, as soon as I can save enough to move us away. Now, give me another clothespin." Leona held out her hand for another clothespin at the same time that she captured the large sheet that a sudden gust of wind had whipped from her grasp, wondering whether she had a good enough mind to answer all the questions that her daughter would most certainly raise. Willow helped her mother quiet the ballooning sail and handed her a pin to secure it. "Willow, honey, is your mind ever at rest?"

"That's just it, Mama; there are so many things I want to learn about. But I do rest. When I get tired, I lay on the rocks by the pond and make like a snake. I slow my breathing so I can't see my stomach move. Then, I let my feet slip into the water and close my eyes, not tight but softly, so I can listen to the rocks. Sometimes I think I can hear them breathing underneath me as they warm my back and hands. I make myself so still I wonder if that's what death is. You become so quiet that you're not moving, but everything else around you keeps on. The longer I stay there, the more I can hear the fish under the water talking to each other. It's so precious. I think then that I never want to move again, just stay there soaking up all the molecules in the trees and sky."

"Why child, what a peculiar word? Whatever do you know about molecules?"

Leona took the final pillowcase and firmly attached it to the last sheet. As she walked back up the line of clothes, she pulled each piece of cloth tightly between her graceful hands so they might dry wrinkle-free. Willow followed right behind, duplicating as best as her small frame would allow, and ran her hands on the bottoms of the clothes she could reach, so her mother would not have to bend down.

"I saw it in a book in the basement with my daddy's things. It was called *Molecules and Men*, by a man with a funny name, Francis Crick. I read a whole chapter. I didn't understand it much, so I looked it up in Grandma's big old dictionary and learned all about them. Well, not everything, but I do understand they are so small you can't see them, but they are filled with life. Did my daddy understand about molecules?"

Leona gazed into her daughter's bright face and tousled the unruly hair. "Oh yes, your father knew all about them and many more things. He would have known how to explain these things to you. Is it any wonder you're always going on and on about such oddities? My darling child, you're your father's daughter for sure."

"And yours, too, Mama. We might not have the same skin or hair or color of eyes, but just look—we have the same hands and feet. And our toes are funny. The middle one is longer than the rest, see?"

Willow fell down on the ground, and held her feet high up in the air so her mother could see. A smile crept into Leona's sky blue eyes. She carefully inspected the child's toes and nodded her head in agreement.

"No question, I would know those feet anywhere. They are a replica of mine. Nothing gets by you, Willow."

Lying beneath the billowing laundry, the child added, "Look, Mama, we're all done. We surely do make a good team!"

"Yes, you're my baby too, and we do make a good team. Now you get up there off the ground before the dripping clothes turn the dust to mud all over you. Willow, honey, I worry that you spend too much time alone. When you're making like a snake, do you ever wish not to be alive?" Leona held out a hand to help lift her child, trying to hide the concern in her voice.

"Oh, I'm never alone. I have all the molecules and the trees and animals around me. Don't you worry, Mama, I like being a snake. But when I'm quiet for a long time, I get to thinking, what if I was to stay there? Then I get a big ache, because I wouldn't see you or Josie or Miss Purrfect or the new kitties that are coming, and learn all the things there are to learn. So, then I jump in the pond and rinse all that ache away. That's okay, isn't it, Mama?"

Leona laughed loudly, a scarcity these days. Taking her daughter's hands in hers, she began to circle around the cherry tree, dancing. "Philomena Jackson North, yes, it's all right. I don't understand all that you say, but I know you will teach me before we are done." Together they sang:

Ring around the rosy, pocketful of posies,
Upstairs, downstairs, we all fall down.
Ring around the rosy, pocket full of posies,
Ashes, ashes, we all fall down.

Stopping, out of breath, they both fell down onto the hard soil, not minding the dust that scattered all over them.

"Now, my little snake, how about we take care of your hair? Go and get my brush from my dresser, and I'll brush it for you gently, two hundred strokes until it shines like silk."

"Okay, Mama, but can I go check on Mrs. Purrfect first? I promised her I would be back to look in on her, in case she needed my help and all. I wouldn't want her to think I'd forgotten. Once those babies start coming, they might just be all too much for her to handle, her first time and all. And it just wouldn't be right, leaving her alone to do all the work, now would it? Please, Mama, you will wait for me, won't you, right here? I promise to run like wildfire and come right back!"

Before Leona could answer, Willow flurried off like the warm wind that had been blowing all day. Yes, she would wait and lie down against the tree and remain very, very still. Maybe make like a snake, too, and see if she could feel the molecules of the cherries ripening above her head.

Still I Dance

I have been dancing long into the night not listening to music but of the beat, beat … beat
Of my heart
I have not been sleeping while I listen to this beat … beat
Of my Heart
It takes all that I am to give up these satin shoes, to walk away
From this Dream
So many say, "Willow, you can't possibly continue," and I know
They are Right
But all I ask for is a few more nights, a few more moonlit nights
In the Garden
One more Cycle
So I may feel the crush of the grass under the souls of my feet.
One more pirouette, one more cartwheel, backbend, fireflies in my face,
The jasmine singing her fragrance, the nightingale's engaging answer.

Then I'll gracefully untie the laces and put away my childish no sense and
Pay close attention to the molecules,
To this heart that goes beat, beat … beat … … … beat.
Each night I notice the gap growing larger in between and still,
I dance.

Everyday my daughter comes to bring me my lunch and spend the afternoon with me, until she must pick up her own children. Today, she spies the nightgown on the back of the chair, damp from the evening's frolic.

"Please, Mama! Please tell me last night was the last time. Look at you. Your skin is paler still and your breath is shallow."

I slurp my coffee and nod. "Almost, my dear. I promise soon, at the darkening of the new moon, I'll stop."

She takes our plates away, sighing.

"And what if you don't last till then? It's not right, Mama. It's not fair to the rest of us. The doctors said …"

I raise my hand to silence her. "I know. I know what they said. Trust me, my sweet. I know what I'm doing."

"No, Mama, I need you to promise me right now that you will stop."

"Shhh, my darling girl. You really shouldn't worry so; it's not good for you. Your eyes have deep dark circles under them. Are you sleeping well?"

Finishing the dishes, Susanna wipes her hands and lays the towel on the strainer. As she turns, I see tears pooled in her frightened blue eyes.

"No you don't! You don't get to do that. It's not right," she stammers as she slams the front door.

I call out to her, "You will be back tomorrow?"

I hear her footsteps crunching the gravel beneath them. She opens her car door and yells back, "I love you, Mama."

Looking up at the clock, I put my hand to my drum.

Beat, beat, beat … beat, beat, beat, beat.
Ah, still good. Rising slowly, I watch her car disappear,
Then turn and step into the potting porch,
Past the wicker rocker that beckons,
Reach for the satin shoes hung by the door,
Push gently on the screen; the rusty hinge squeaks.
The flowers look up, trees sway, and leaves drop at my feet
Anticipating my arrival
My garden has prepared a welcome carpet for my ballet
To this heart that continues to beat, beat, beat.
And still I dance.

Li'l Sister's Love

The two hikers reached an outlook above the canyon, a temporary reprieve from the dense forest heat. A slight breeze whispered over their faces. The woman, seizing the opportunity, pulled her water bottle off the harness and poured it on her head. The soft air cooled her as an air conditioner would. She smiled to her companion, passing the bottle to him. "A little trick I learned in the Pyrenees," she said.

Across the canyon, hawks were circling, riding thermals. Joanna dumped the rest of her water over her head and stood, arms outreached, turning ever so slowly. Water ran down her chest, soaking her thin shirt and shorts, allowing her breasts and muscles to be clearly defined.

"Wow, woman, I can see why I had a hard time keeping up with you. You always had a superb body, but now it's a machine. Are you going to jump and soar with those hawks?

"Funny, when you spend a lot time in high altitudes and the hawks, vultures, and falcons are your neighbors, it seems feasible. I've stood on outcroppings and closed my eyes in the Andes and half expected to lift off." Looking at her companion, she turned, seeing the laughter in his eyes. "Okay, no, I'm not thinking I can fly. It's just a feeling one has. Surely you have felt it too, sometime?"

"Maybe when I'm charging down a black diamond at Whistler, snowboarding, I've a sense of launching, but not from a quiet standstill like here. It's okay; I already knew you were all hocus-pocus. I bet if there is a way, you might be the one to find it."

Taking out one of the smooth pebbles she always carried in her pockets, she threw it at him. He started laughing, so she threw a handful at him. "Okay, make fun of me, but let's get a move on. We have at least five miles to go. Your pansy-ass will have to pick up the pace if we want to get a warm pool at Sykes before they're all taken. How much younger than me are you? Twenty years? Too much time at the negotiating table methinks, sucking down beer, and not enough working those legs, my friend. Hope you can keep up."

Joanna strapped her backpack on and was climbing over the boulders like a billy goat. In seconds she reached the forest trail, grabbed her walking stick, and began marching before Dan had climbed off the rocks.

"Don't wait up or anything," he yelled after her. "That's okay. As long as I've that tight booty to follow, I can keep up."

She turned and shot him a scowl and then wondered why. Joanna kept the pace up, more so she could have the free time to organize her thoughts. She stopped only to pick up a few smooth river stones to roll in her hands as she marched, remembering the old man in the Pyrenees who had mentioned, "Important to keep a walking stone in your pocket." It was great being in the wilderness again, but she was wondering if having agreed to take Dan with her had been such a good idea. Clearly, he assumed there was an invitation for more than just a strenuous twenty-mile hike up the backcountry of Big Sur. Now she was faced with the reality. *Was there an invitation?*

At first it was innocent, she thought.

Over the years, she had taken to calling him Big Brother, referring to his size, as he was twenty years her junior, at least in age. They had planned weekend trips sailing or hiking, when he was her sister Susan's partner. Salt air and dusty trails didn't compare to rock concerts and all-night dancing in clubs, as was Susan's passion. Her sister was glad Dan had found someone else to burn off those desires. He partied with her as the best of them but found the outdoors just as nurturing, and established a sweet kinship with Joanna. Their points of view at times ran parallel, and at other times were fodder for intense banter. One time, they had been in a heated discussion for hours, the three of them at first, but Susan had tired of the conversation and gone to run some errands and to bring home wine for dinner. When she returned, Joanna and Dan hadn't even moved. They were still deep in turning over the "golf ball" to see what other sides to the political issue they could argue. Usually on the same side, the two had a different angle on how to resolve this current hot topic.

"What? Are you two still at it? Shit, maybe you're with the wrong sister," she'd tossed out jokingly.

Dan immediately jumped up and, hearing the undercurrent and potential danger, began attending to Susan. After that weekend, Joanna's visits always included some time when she and Dan would find a moment for an interesting exchange, when Susan would be busy elsewhere. She abhorred politics. *Always innocent, right*, Joanna mused. Three years had passed since those days, and life had moved on for the three of them separately, the façade of friendship between Susan and Dan a dim candle.

Dan caught up with her and tapped her on the shoulder. "Slow down, Joanna. What world are you in? You passed a trail marker back there and didn't stop."

Gazing up at those baby blues encircled with black curls, the rest of his hair loosely pulled back in a ponytail, Joanna felt the heat rush into her. Surprised by his effect, she quickly recovered her composure.

"I'm sorry. I get lost in the beauty. It happens to me a lot when I'm in the mountains. That's why I brought you along, Big Brother, right? Do you need me to slow down?"

"No. But I shouted out three times, and you didn't stop. Every hiker for a thousand yards heard me. I definitely don't want to get lost and have more miles to do today than necessary. When you said a ten-mile hike, I thought you meant round-trip, not one way."

"Sorry, you're right of course. I'll pay closer attention. Time for a break, huh? I'm hungry. What did you bring for snacks?"

The two went back to the trail split. "Well, lucky you, Joanna, you accidently kept on the right trail."

"It was no accident; it's what happens when you commune with the journey, City Boy. Here's a good place to rest." She followed the path back to the stream that followed the secondary smaller trail, dropped her pack on a log, and stepped near the water, placing her scarf in the shallow water.

"City Boy here has the food and drink, and has been carrying all the weight, my friend, so be respectful. Now, do you want a sandwich or an apple?"

"Poor boy, it must be a drag, picking up the slack for an old lady," Joanna said, and bowed. "Better I keep it light; just an apple and a slice of cheese. I'll save the sandwich for dinner."

"I think I'll settle on a liquid lunch; less weight to carry," Dan said with a sigh. He cracked open a beer and began to guzzle.

"Better mix that up with some water, my friend; you don't want to dehydrate. Look at you; you're sopping with sweat." She slapped his back hard.

"The better to cool off your hot body." He grabbed her, pressed his arms around her from the back, and scrunched himself into her, leaving her sopping.

She laughed, feigning anger, and slapped him with her wet neckerchief. "So this was the fun I missed not having a big brother growing up."

"I wasn't thinking brotherly thoughts, Joanna," he replied. Moving close to her, he brushed her hair out of her face. "I hope you're not going to keep going there. That ship has sailed. Last night wasn't exactly sisterly."

Pushing him back, she said, "What are you babbling about? You were sleeping before you even hit the bed. You must have been dreaming, my friend. Now, let's get moving and stop our jabbering. I heard that the last three miles are a brutal ascent."

"No, I don't think I was dreaming. And what do you mean you 'heard'? Haven't you done this hike before? I thought you knew where you were taking me."

"What's the fun in that?" she called back to him, quickly trekking up the trail.

Damn, she thought, *I was sure he was sleeping.* The memory of slipping from the accepted family protocol the night before smarted like a bee sting. Dan had arrived late to the motel, and she had already fallen asleep. When she had checked in, they only had one room left, with a king bed. Dan had showed up after midnight, wiped out from a marathon drive down from Oregon. After showering, he fell into bed and, after apologizing for waking her up, was snoring within minutes.

His long muscular body next to hers, naked, had awakened her more than she wished. The nudity wasn't new, but had always been in situations that could be explained—the hot tubs in the Napa Valley, and once jumping into the ocean, anchored off the coast, to cool off from sailing. Not in a bed, alone, away from family ties or eyes, together. Hearing his breathing deep and heavy, his clean showered skin inviting, she had stroked his back, running her fingers up and down his spine gently, and had slipped into a trance until her lips touched his skin. She froze. Listening to his heavy breathing continue in deep slumber, she rolled over, grateful for escaping detection. She slipped out of bed and changed from her skimpy nightshirt to sweats and a tee, and went outside for a walk; the cool air was a welcome shift from what she'd left. *Silly bodily functions*, she thought. *No, it wasn't him, just a pleasing warm body*, she convinced herself. *They creep up at inopportune moments.*

Returning, careful not to disturb Dan, sleep was quick in coming, but her dreams, not surprisingly, were of Susan. The baby sister whose long blonde hair Joanna would spend hours untangling and combing through and braiding. The one who followed Joanna everywhere in the summers, happy to be a part of Joanna's world, glad for a little exemption from camp. Once Joanna received her driver's license, their mother allowed her the freedom of the family car three times a week, as long as baby sister tagged along. Susan was as much a chaperone as Joanna was a babysitter, and Joanna always suspected their mother's motive was to keep both daughters safe. Susan had been a cool kid, smart and sassy.

Joanna's dreams bounced about from summertime beachcombing on the rocky shores of the Oregon's wild coast holding her sister's hand, to lying in the Columbia River on a raft, spying for water snakes. Susan so cute she almost never got in the way. Her dream settled upon a memory of a small child sitting in a high chair. Joanna was usually in charge, during the week, of cooking the family dinner. But on Thursday nights their mother always left work and went to get her hair done, and then had dinner with her best friend. Those nights Joanna would take out a box of cereal, fill up a bowl, pour some milk and place a spoon in front of li'l Susan, until the night that Susan slammed down her spoon and cursed.

"Every goddamn night Mom goes out, I get cereal."

Joanna knew then that this baby sister would be a force to be reckoned with. Bribery became her favorite tool to avoid detection when their excursions took them to unauthorized events.

In her senior year of high school, Joanna left home for California and any other place that called to her. It was Susan that she would make the trip back home for, at holidays. It was Susan she would buy presents for in whatever wayward town she found herself. Silly souvenirs—playing cards from Winnemucca, Nevada; engraved teaspoons from Sparks, Utah; a Chinese fan from San Francisco's Chinatown; a Sears Tower replica from Chicago. Stupid mementos that Susan cherished and placed on a shelf set aside for Joanna treasures.

And then Joanna traveled across continents and oceans, too far for visits—five years in Europe and South America. By the time she made her way back to Portland, Susan had grown up. No longer hanging onto Big Sister's every word, all the sweetness had been replaced with aloofness. Of course, Joanna reasoned, Susan was a teenager, playing her music and getting stoned with friends; her life no longer depended on Joanna.

The next ten years, the two sisters followed divergent paths. Their ideals, lifestyles, and interests separated them. Susan was a city girl; Joanna, her husband, and children settled in the country. Neither sister wasted any time with pretenses. Kisses and hugs abounded

Molecules and Women

at holidays, and a shared wit made their encounters fun, but it had become mostly superficial—Party Girl meets Earth Mother.

Susan, though she excelled in school, chose to ignore her "God-given brain," as their mother liked to remind her, and took odd modeling jobs here and there to support her way into the life of the theater. The hope of a New York discovery to Broadway kept her churning for ten years. Minor local community and summer stock successes sustained her enthusiasm.

At first, when Susan met up with Dan, it appeared to be a mutual fling. Then the all-encompassing biological clock started to tick away, pushing Susan to think ahead to a home and family. They settled down and bought a house, his support unwavering for her to follow her passion into the theater.

At the same time that they were beginning, Joanna's marriage was ending. Ironic that Susan settled down on the heels of Joanna's new freedom. She elected to return south to more sunshine in California, where she had always thrived. The wet, mossy Oregon coast had now become more of a prison than a garden. She packed up her two children and moved back to the Bay Area to study holistic health and open her own practice. When she returned north at Christmas for a family holiday and met Susan's partner, it was an unexpected welcome. Dan's outrageous style and humor reconnected the sisters. Her friendship with him grew easily, and when his work took him south, it was easy to visit her and her kids and stay with family instead of hotels.

That morning when dawn had finally come, Joanna had arisen exhausted, realizing the line between dreaming and reliving her past with her sister had been crossed. She was not even sure how much she had slept, but with one glance over to her bed partner, she jumped up and yelled, "Five minutes to the car, Laggard. We don't have time to linger. It's imperative to be at the trailhead by 7:00 a.m."

Now, as she walked in this dense forest, she wondered what her feelings for Dan were exactly. Susan had started a new career after her breakup with Dan, opening a fitness studio, while continuing her interest in theater. It was a major success, but what little they had in common before diminished further, and Joanna and Susan returned to their separate lives.

She stopped to look behind her and saw that Dan was a ways behind. She motioned to him, inquiring if he wanted her to stop, but fortunately he waved her on. *Good, he was on point. Funny how the two of them could usually communicate without too much effort.*

So many times, it was Dan she would call from different airports when she had layovers. They could pick up a thread of conversation wherever they left off, and it was seamless. It was Dan she had spent the last night in Seattle with before flying off to Mount Kilimanjaro, listening to him rant and rave and cry at his and Susan's breakup. Joanna had remained quiet, not wanting to share with him the loneliness of her own recent breakup with a man she'd had high hopes for. She felt lucky in life, just not so in love. She kept silent her thoughts of how foolish her sister was for leaving him. He was everything Joanna looked for in a partner, and Susan cast him aside, not knowing what she was giving up. It was Dan who somehow was able to pick her up in San Francisco one year later when she returned, and drive her up to Mount Shasta to pick up her car. They had gotten pretty drunk, the one night he stayed over before driving home to Oregon. They were at a cousin's home, and after all the lights were out, she heard him rouse and come to her sleeping bag. Resisting all his pleas, she had kept repeating Susan's name.

"No, Susan would never understand."

"But she left me! She's moved on; she would never know," he countered.

"But I would know," Joanna said, and held firm.

Another year had passed, and here they were climbing to secret warm pools, deep in the forest where no one knew them. Of course he was hoping for more.

Joanna admitted to herself that perhaps she hoped for more too. *But could she betray her little sister? Would it be a betrayal? Susan was living with someone else. Still not married, but clearly not thinking of Dan anymore.* "No," she said out loud. "Susan would be wrecked. She would never believe that we had not faltered during their relationship."

There had been suspicions, even accusations the time Dan and Joanna had stayed up all night by the fire, while Susan had gone to bed. The fact that nothing had happened was no less incriminating, as desire, though silent, was present.

Yes, Joanna said, and smiled. *There had always been a silent desire. He always found an excuse to rub my neck, saying it was to help with my headaches. Then there were those late night visits back from corporate meetings in Northern California, when he always managed to fly into the San Francisco airport instead of Sacramento.* "The schedule to SFO is much better," he claimed, leaving the conferences and showing up at her door at midnight, with a bottle of wine. In the morning, with no sleep, he would catch a 6:00 a.m. flight home after keeping her up all night laughing and talking, maybe with a back rub thrown in, but always stopping just shy of any cause to appear guilty. *It had been more a tease that a serious idea*, she thought.

The last year that Dan and Susan were still a couple, Dan stopped mentioning seeing Joanna. Susan was so involved in her career that she never questioned Dan's trips. Still they remained true to Susan, never allowing for even a hint.

Joanna stopped on the trail and spoke out loud, "When has enough time gone by that makes it okay to be with a sister's partner?"

Just then a couple of ravens scattered from a tree, squawking, her voice having disturbed them from their sanctuary. Joanna looked up as they flew away. "Right. Never!" she said.

"Never what?" Dan surprised her, coming up from behind.

"Can't a person have a private thought?" She laughed.

"Sure they can, but then they usually don't consult with birds. But maybe you do. So tell me what significance are ravens in your medicine cards. I'm sure they're something important." Then he added, "Can we take a five-minute break?"

"Yes, a break would be good. See that rise over there?" She pointed to the trail's switchback going up a steep grade. "If I'm correct, Sykes should be a downward descent into a small canyon after the crest, where we'll find our hot pools."

Dan climbed onto a low boulder, breaking out a beer from his small cooler. "You're one tight woman, lady; my hat's off to you!"

He removed his cap and placed a few ice chips from the cooler on his neck. "I need to go to the gym when I get home. I'm keeping up with you out of sheer ego. It just dawned on me we have to turn around in the morning and do this all over again. Look at you; you seem almost as fresh as when we started. Damn, girl."

"I thought you were crazy rigging up that cooler with two wheels. But I have to confess, you may be on to something."

"My years of fishing on the back rivers, keeping the beer cold became an imperative," he said with a laugh.

"Pass me a water bottle, please. Okay, which is it?"

"You will have to get it yourself; I can't move for at least five minutes. Which is what?"

Joanna got up and went to reach into the cooler that lay at Dan's feet. "Lady, woman, girl, you just called me all three." Joanna laughed and took out a water bottle. "Here, let me help refresh you." She removed the cap and doused him with it.

Like a flash, Dan reached up and grabbed her arm and pulled her on top of him. "All three, and right now you're being a naughty girl. I might have to spank you."

Trying to escape his grasp, she said, "Hey, respect your elders, young man, I'm old enough …"

"To kiss me," he interrupted, and then, holding her with one hand, he reached up and pulled her pack strap to him, and kissed her long and hard. "Resistance is futile," he breathed.

Surrendering to the moment, Joanna kissed him back, and it was all she had fantasized. His taste, salty mixed with beer, something she normally would hate, was appealing. His tender full lips begged to be gobbled. His taut muscles against her flesh were responsive, tempting her. He loosened his grip, and she bolted.

"Hey there, you can't tell me you didn't like the flavor," he quipped.

She picked up her hat, which had fallen off in the tussle, and brushed it off against her legs and walked over to a log on the other side of the trail. Wiping her brow with the hem of her T-shirt, she caught his look of approval.

"Give it a rest, Dan." Joanna sat and stared at her desire, her nemesis. "Harbinger from Spirit," she mumbled.

Dan looked up, confused. "What?"

"Raven medicine is a direct message from Spirit. Ravens show us human beings how to break through old paradigms and belief systems, and help open the door into a more expanded reality." Joanna spoke quietly, as if hearing the words she was saying for the first time.

"Well, then, what's the problem?" Dan sat up and gave Joanna all his attention; the tone had gone to a place he had waited for patiently. His desires long ago out of the closet, he now welcomed the opportunity to make headway, even if it came from a bird. "Why then do we hold back from what we feel and know to be true, just because of what others might think happened in the past? We know we played by the rules. Hell, if anyone broke the rules, it was Susa …"

"Slow down, cowboy. Yes, breaking old, outmoded belief systems, sure, but Raven also teaches the right way to live, and the way not to be. It's a spiritual message; we are healers, granted in different mediums, but healers nonetheless. You go around the country teaching conflict resolution to, of all venues, union collective bargaining disputes. Who's the one always touting that the single woman's needs are never considered? We must act with integrity, not harming any by our actions. Look at me now, and tell me that Susan wouldn't be devastated if we acted on our desires? She would never forgive me, ever. And my children, they're your friends. How would they view us as anything but platonic? Don't even answer. I'll tell you. They would be confused, hurt, and rightfully so."

"I won't argue with you any of that, but does that mean we can't experience the fullness of what we feel towards each other? Can't our actions be ours alone? Does Raven control the physical too?"

"No, we control the physical. I can't believe you're going to try that old line on me." Looking up to face his piercing eyes, she was met with fire. "I don't know, Dan, what to do. Right now, I won't fight your fire off. Let's get to the pools, eat, and see what other messages might lay in our path. Truce?"

His face broke into a broad grin, and he laughed his trademark dynamic howl.

"Truce it is, me lady. Your reason always wins in the end. Now unfurrow your brow or you'll get the dreaded frown lines. Can you believe she taped her face every night?" shaking his head at the memory of Susan going to bed with scotch tape on her forehead. "Well, actually, I think the Botox ended all that," he said a bit snidely. "But this conversation is not about her; nor is it over. I'd never cause you harm. On the contrary, it's pleasure I wish to cause you, and me too!"

Dan came over and, reaching out his hand, crossed his heart. "Scout's honor, I won't bite. Take it." He helped lift her up from the ground, embraced her, and gently whispered, "I would never do anything to risk losing you."

"Now that's what I'm saying," she hugged him back. Letting go, she began to march. "Last one to the top has to give the foot rub." His last bitter remark about Susan sank into her heart. *He is still attached to her, even if he doesn't know it.*

Watching her walk ahead, he heard the ravens squawk. He looked up and saw two birds playfully chase each other above the trees, pecking, then diving, then rising on the thermals side by side.

Joanna had stopped to watch them also, admiring their playfulness, plunging at each other and then swooping together in unison, circling and rising higher and higher. Raven medicine is said to instill the ability to hear and know others' thoughts and feelings. Very useful for healers, to know which path to take in helping others, what they're really ready to engage in, and how far it is safe to go. Raven's medicine helps show you the true and correct path, when one happens upon a crossroad. Then she thought, *Okay Raven, have I learned the right way, the true way? I cannot risk losing her, my little sister; there are more roads for us to take together. She is so much more fragile than she pretends. Some boundaries are just not meant to be crossed.*

Looking back at Dan, she knew he was solid, no risk in losing him. He was her friend, yes, and the one that she kept no secrets from. She called, "What are you waiting for, an engraved invitation?"

"Don't taunt me, woman; I can still catch you," he shouted. "Yes, I can wait for that invitation, and I'll be ready when it comes," he said quietly.

Kindergarten

A blonde, petite woman paced back and forth from the yellow kitchen to the small dining room, gripping a phone whose base was anchored on the kitchen wall, listening intently. She paused at the table, reached for her tea mug, and stopped to respond, her voice loud and strained.

"This is ridiculous. I've *been* patient, and in fact I've been on this phone for thirty minutes as you pass me from one person to another. How many people work in your admissions office?"

She listened to the voice, lifting the mug to her lips, the liquid now cold; she gulped a mouthful, and then placed the mug with the brightly painted words "Best Mummy" down hard on the table.

"Yes, I understand that it's not your decision, but it's not rocket science either, just kindergarten; yes, I'll remain calm, and, no, it's nobody's fault, I just …

"Yes, I'll hold."

She placed the phone to her chest. "Mother Prudy, you have to help me understand what is wrong with these people," she blurted to her mother-law, who was quietly holding Nicole in her lap, feeding her cookies and milk. "What is so hard to comprehend? Nicole already spent four months in kindergarten; look at what she made me in class." Holding up the mug, she continued, "And for a small technicality of her birth date being a few days off, they want me to hold her back a year until September."

"Karen, calm down. You will wake the baby from his nap. There is no use getting excited about this; it won't do any good. Rules are rules, and if Nicole needs to wait another year here, then she must wait."

"Mother Prudy, that's absurd. How can she wait when she has already started?" Before Prudy could respond, Karen's attention returned to the voice in the phone. "Really? Another school district? Where? Farmers' what? Well, how far outside of town? Okay, give me the number."

Karen picked up the dishes and brought them to the kitchen sink. She pulled the curtain aside to look through the ice crystals formed on the glass, into the white expanse that purported to be her garden.

"Really, Prudy? Something will grow out of all this?"

"Yes, Karen, not to worry. You will love it come summer when everything is in bloom. Now what did they say about Farmers'?"

"I'll take your word on that." She closed the curtain with a little shiver. "Oh, yes. It appears the next school district from Streator is Farm Ridge, appropriately named as it's comprised of dairies and corn farms, and it has a more relaxed standard. Because of the demands on families during harvest, the school works more with the parents' schedules. What a concept! They told me to take Nicole in on Monday to register. I'm not sure about the commute though. I'll have to drive her, and with this weather, how will that work?"

"Oh, Karen, these storms will be over soon; you'll see. And it's not like you've never driven in the snow—all those holidays up in the California Sierra, skiing."

A chubby toddler wandered out of the bedroom holding his tattered Brownie, a bear that had seen more life in three years than ever intended for a stuffed animal—from bathtub scrubs to dunks in Lake Merritt, to tin cover slides down snow drifts at their new house in Streator. David imbued Brownie with superhero properties, so that no matter where the bear was thrown, dropped, or doused, it felt no pain and suffered no misfortune. No amount of coaxing or pleading to take gentle care of the companion could convince the child that the bear might be capable of feeling harm.

When he saw his grandmother he ran to her and tugged on her sweater, reaching into her pockets for the treats she usually hid there.

"Mother Prudy, can you watch David on Monday?" asked Karen.

"I'm sorry, Karen. Monday is my bridge luncheon, and it wouldn't do to have him underfoot while we play. You understand, right?" She kissed the child's head, letting him dig into her pocket.

Trying to hide her disappointment, Karen picked up her boy, taking the candy from his fist, and carried him into the kitchen. "No sweets for you, little one, until after lunch," she said, plopping David into his chair and quickly strapping the moving target to his seat.

"Of course. I understand. "We'll just bundle up this little monster and have a Mr. Toad's wild ride on Monday. Right, David?"

"Love you, mummy, soooo much," came the answer as she placed a plate of cut-up hot dog and creamed corn in front of David.

Nicole hugged her mother's legs and asked, "Mummy, when I go back to school, will my friends be there?"

"No, sweetie, remember, there will be new friends in your school. I'm sure they will be just as nice as your old ones, and I bet during recess you will go outside and make snowmen and snow angels. Won't that be fun?"

"I make snowballs and throw them like this!" David flung a piece of hot dog up at the ceiling.

Prudy made her way onto the storm porch to bundle up in all the trappings one needed to venture out into the icy Illinois winter. "Don't worry, Karen, the good news is this storm is breaking up, and by Monday, they say clear skies. It should be all right. You'll see."

"I'll take your word on that too, Prudy. That would be great news, if it's true. Run and give your grandmother a kiss, Nicole, and thank her for the new scarf she brought." Karen waved good-bye to Prudy before standing on a chair to wipe the smudge from the ceiling where the hot dog had hit.

"Now, my baseball pitcher, let's put that food in your belly instead of on the ceiling."

Monday morning, the children ate breakfast while Karen pressed her forehead against the cold glass, soothed by the icy window. The last flurry of snowflakes swirled and became transparent. She rubbed her temples for a minute, trying to remove the headache she'd awoken with that morning. Bernie had not wanted her to enroll Nicole in the Farm School. Just like his mother, he thought rules were to be followed. He was a policeman in California, and it fit him. He'd tried to convince Karen to not go to Farm Ridge. "Nicole will adjust," he barked. "Streator was a decent, safe place to grow up in. It was good enough for me."

"Oh, Bernie, please not that argument again. It was so good you left the minute you turned eighteen and graduated high school. So good, you headed straight for California to pay to attend college, instead of stay here where it was free. So good, that you paid for your parents to come to California every year for vacation, so we wouldn't have to go to Illinois." Karen's voice, rose at each "so good," until she was yelling. "So good, that for seven years, you never said one nice thing about it."

"All right, I hear you. Lower your voice, or you will scare the children."

"Bernie, I've said yes to all of this. I'm still unclear as to exactly why you gave up your career to come here and help out in your father's store. I said yes to uprooting my home and moving here, and now I need something from you. Please don't fight me on this."

"You know why I came."

Nicole ran into the room crying and grabbed Karen's legs. "Mummy, I can't find the pink scarf and hat that Granny Prudy gave me. You said I could wear it to school."

"No problem, honey, let me come and help you look for it. We want everything to be perfect for your first day at your new school, don't we, Daddy?" Karen looked over to her husband.

"Yes, Karen, you help Nicole get ready for school. I'll catch breakfast down at the café in town." Bernie tugged gently on his daughter's pigtails, bent down, and kissed her forehead. He brushed past Karen brusquely, leaving without saying good-bye. Nothing had been resolved, but at least she won on kindergarten. Looking out the window, she could see the outline of the sun pushing though.

"We better get a move on, little ones. The snow is abating, and if I'm not delirious, I do believe I see sunshine coming through the clouds. Maybe Prudy was right after all. Nicole, as soon as David finishes slurping, will you help him out of the chair and put his rubbers on over his shoes? Mum's going to warm up the car and get it all toasty for us."

Karen walked outside onto the porch, happy to see blue sky above her until she slipped down the icy wooden stairs and landed on her bum in the fresh snow.

"Damn, these leather boots are no good in this godforsaken weather." Carefully, she climbed back up the stairs to the storm porch, and slipped galoshes over her boots. Successful in her second attempt, she saw that the windshield had vanished beneath the fresh powder the night had dropped. *Sure*, she thought, *it'll be all right; piece of cake, right.*

She dug into her parka to remove the scraper, deftly cleaned off the windows, then got into Bernie's green Ford Torino. "This is a preposterous car to have here," she murmured to herself.

Karen turned the key; the engine stuttered, whirred, hiccuped, and shut off. She released the key and listened to the silence. "Please, just start, one more time." Karen pressed the gas and turned the key. The engine turned over, sputtered again, and finally engaged, spewing some white vapor out the back, eventually settling into the low rumbling that her husband found exhilarating. Ever since they'd left California for the freezing weather of Illinois, the muscle Torino found it hard to cooperate, almost as if it too didn't want to pull its head out from beneath the covers to face the expansive flat white nothingness.

"Why did I let that husband of mine talk me into leaving the station wagon and taking this prize to Illinois?" Karen groused to the rumbling Detroit metal, slamming the car door so hard that snow fell to the ground, covering her feet. She gingerly climbed up the steps. "Better clear these off now before all of us end up on our bums."

She picked up the smaller snow shovel and scraped each step until she reached raw wood. Her nurse's training nights in the ER had taught her all the ways humans harm themselves in the simplest of places. Normally more cavalier than cautious, she felt grateful she had learned to pay heed to details. Her career provided a balance to her otherwise hasty methodology to get things done. She stomped to the doorway to shake off the powder still on her galoshes.

Thank God Mother Prudy is as small as I, she thought. *At least she supplied me with a few practical boots, gloves, and a parka. Hardly makes up for her number one son, though.*

"Oh, settle down, Karen, it was just one fight. Things will get better," she scolded herself. She opened the front door and called, "Nicole, sweetie, Mummy's all wet and doesn't want to track snow in the house. Are you and David ready?"

Nicole appeared with David in hand. Both children were topped with hats, muffs, and scarves; only their noses poked out.

"Great job, sweetie. Are you sure you two can breathe? Let me get David into his seat, and I'll come back for you, Nicole. I don't want you to try it alone." Scooping him up, she headed for the stairs.

"I can do it by myself." Nicole followed her mother to the stairs. "I'm a big girl; I'll be careful."

"Yes, you are. Okay, sweetie, hold the railing, and take one step at a time. Isn't this exciting, your first day in your new school?"

"Uh huh. Daddy said he will bring me home a surprise from work today."

"Let's hope it's a new car to drive around in this mess," Karen muttered under her breath.

She piled the children into the back and then jumped into the front. "We better get a move on, before this one decides to stop." The grumbling green Torino pulled onto the road. The salt crackling beneath the tires reminded Karen of driving out into the gravel roads of Mount Diablo. But that was where the similarity ended. In California, from the top of the neighboring mountain she could see west to the spires of the San Francisco bridges, and to the east, views of the high Sierras shimmered in the summer heat. Here the road looked onto the clear expanse of white for miles and miles and miles. And come summer it would be exchanged for miles and miles of corn rows. The only mountain one could glimpse from a bird's perspective here would be the new Sears Tower in Chicago. The flatness of this middle land left Karen disoriented. Where was west? North? The sun would be coming from where? Walking out on the few clear nights after they arrived, she couldn't figure out what direction to look for the moon.

The Torino hit a patch of black ice and abruptly began to swerve. It took all of Karen's focus to keep her hands on the wheel and turn into the swerve, back and forth across the road until she finally came to rest a few inches into a snowbank. Her hands trembled clutching the steering wheel. Looking at them, she understood for the first time what white-knuckled referred to, and resisted the urge to scream for her children's sake.

"Mummy, Mummy, I scared!" cried little David from his car seat.

"Oh don't be such a baby. That was fun. Can we do it again?" squealed Nicole.

"It's all right, David, darling. It's over, and no, we'll not be doing that again. First thing when we get home today is putting snow tires on this green brute." Karen squeezed through the bucket seats so she could reach her children, one with glazed eyes of joy and the other with fear. She exhaled, relieved and grateful no harm was done. "Are we having fun yet? Worthy of Disneyland, don't you think, sweeties? Now let's check. You're both still strapped in safely?" Reassured, Karen put the shifter in reverse and slowly backed away from the snowbank and maneuvered the car, pointing back onto the roadway. This time, she put the Torino in low gear and drove down the road slowly.

"No good in hurrying and not arriving. We might be a little late, but we'll be in one piece. Now how about we put on some music? Neil Diamond? We can sing along like we did when we drove cross-country."

"Yes, let's sing 'Cherry,'" shouted Nicole.

"I want 'Song Blue,'" David whined.

"Well, let's just see what song comes first, and we'll play both of them twice."

The music started playing loudly as the car crawled through the white tunnel the plows had carved though the weekend's blizzard. The snow-covered cornfields only became visible when they came to a crossroads to turn off the main highway onto a smaller country road.

She had tried to make light of their mishap, but she had read in the Sunday paper of a mother driving off the road into a lake with her children in the car. *Had Bernie been right about not letting Nicole go to school so far from home?*

While the children sang, Karen wondered what else waited for her in this heartland. Since they had suddenly been uprooted by her husband's family, nothing felt comfortable or familiar. Not since leaving England as a teenager and arriving in California, after the death of her mother, had Karen felt so lost. But, then, that had been an exciting place to land—with warm weather, beaches, mountains, and friendly people, happy people. So far, here in Streator, the townspeople were polite but cold and distant. *Their glances speak volumes of disapproval,* she thought to herself. *Maybe I'm imagining it. After all, it's winter, and my clothes probably seem funny and out of place. Perhaps here in the Farm Ridge School, the women might be nice. Let's hope so.*

"Come on, Mummy, sing with us," Nicole begged. Their three voices filled the car the rest of the way to school.

Song sung blue, everybody knows one; song sung blue, weeping like a willow.

Suddenly the snowbank was interrupted by a four-way intersection, with the two-story red brick schoolhouse on the corner. Pulling behind a row of parked cars, she shut off the engine, letting the last of the song finish before turning off the music. Looking up at the schoolhouse, Karen gasped. "Look, kids, the snow is so deep that one could climb up the snowpack to the roof."

"We can climb to the roof, Mummy?" Nicole asked.

"No, of course not. I'm just being silly, honey. That would be dangerous." Catching herself, she thought, *Be careful, Karen, Nicole is capable of trying it at recess. That child is so confident.* "Come on; let's go see what your new school has on the inside."

The red brick stairs and the front of the school had all been cleared off. Someone had even taken the time to clean off the bell in the front that hung from the roof, making the building inviting in spite of being buried. They tumbled out of the car. Karen's eyes took in the corner crossroads that represented the community of Farm Ridge. Town would be too strong a word, for other than the stop sign, the Purina Grain Store, post office, hardware store, and the two-story school in front of her, Farm Ridge had nothing to offer. The gravel parking lot was filled with old pickup trucks and even a few John Deere tractors. On one end a basketball hoop emerged out of the snow bank as a lonely sentry; across the lot a tetherball pole and few metal tables, wiped clean, sat forlorn. Behind the building a chain-link fence kept out the open acres of cornfields that would crop up in the spring. As they approached the steps, a dark-haired matron in rubber boots came out to meet them and escort them into the school.

"You must be Karen Madison, and you must be Nicole," she said, patting Nicole on the head. "I've been keeping an eye out for you, hoping that the weekend storm wouldn't keep you away. My name is Mrs. Wozniak, and I'm the principal, secretary, and school nurse. Oh, I see you have brought Nicole's records." She took the manila folder from Karen's hand and shook it vigorously. "And who is this little jewel?" she asked, pumping David's hand quickly.

Not waiting for a reply, she opened the folder as they walked up the school steps.

"This is wonderful; it will make my job registering her so much easier. Why don't you take Nicole into our kindergarten room, the first door on your right, and get acquainted with her teacher, Miss Penguin. Class is starting. There are mothers in the room helping get the children settled. Just introduce yourself; they are a helpful bunch." She pointed to a door with a colorful cartoon penguin. Mrs. Wozniak rushed across the hallway to another door decorated with a cartoon nurse sitting at a typewriter and disappeared as quickly as she had appeared. Karen looked down the hall and noticed all the doorways had similar artistic expressions with different images.

"Well, children, no lack of creative expression here. I guess we are in the right place. Come on! Let's go meet Miss Penguin."

A warm, animated room greeted them. The teacher quickly noticed the newcomers and called another child over. "Shannon, please take Nicole to the cloakroom and let her pick out her very own cubby. Then the two of you go sit in the circle, please."

The teacher, a young, lanky woman wearing a colorful smock with hand-sewn pockets, black curls falling from her loose bun, hurried over to Karen and David.

"Class is starting," she said, extending a hand. "We can meet after class." Pointing to an adjoining room whose accordion doors were half open, she said, "You're welcome to stay in our art and music room and observe for a few minutes." Her smile, although quick, appeared genuine, and complemented her alluring green eyes. She turned back to the waiting class, clapped her hands, and began singing a welcome song to each child. All of the children's attention immediately centered on their beautiful teacher, and they eagerly waited for their name to be called—to stand up and bow or curtsy.

As the class settled into its routine, three mothers drifted over to sit by Karen. They were excited to meet the newcomers. "Hi. I'm Anna Kowalski. This here is Sofia and Agata Pawlak. Rumor has it you drove over from Streator. We don't see too many townies in our rural community, and you're the first to venture into our schoolhouse!"

"Nice to meet you; I'm Karen Madison, and this charmer is David, and that blondie in pink is my Nikki. I must confess it wasn't my first choice. Now that I'm here, I'm guessing this is the best thing that could have happened. Miss Penguin has magic. Look at her captive audience."

Pulling on Karen's arm, David squealed, "Want to go with Nikki."

"Oh, darling. I'm sorry; you're too young. We better go, before we interrupt the class."

Karen turned to the mother closest to her, Sophia. "Is there somewhere we could go sit and wait until noon? It was a slow drive from Streator; it might be easier to wait in Farm Ridge. David will never settle quietly in the midst of so much activity." Thinking about their drive over, Karen wasn't too eager to jump back into the car. "We've had quite an exhilarating morning. He'll be ready for a nap soon. A library or coffee shop?"

"We don't have either of those things here in Farm Ridge. You would have to go all the way to Ottawa, which isn't much closer than Streator. But you're certainly welcome to come to my farm."

"Oh my, how generous of you. I feel more welcomed here in twenty minutes than three weeks in Streator. Are you two sisters?" Karen asked Sofia and Agata.

"Yes and no. We married two hardheaded Polish brothers," Sofia laughed.

"Yes, I hear that the Polish are a force to be reckoned with around here." The three women's blank stares alerted Karen that her attempt at humor had failed.

"Sorry, silly city humor. Wozniak, Kowalski, Pawlak; it's a mouthful. I'm still trying to figure out Miss Penguin. How did she make it to the clan?

Anna scooted her chair closer and, not wanting to distract the class, lowered her voice. "Well, actually, that's a funny story. Her grandfather's name was Jakob Pencheizwoska. When he landed at Ellis Island, the clerk took one look at the name and then looked up at the man with black clothes, black hat, black shoes, and white scarf, and said, 'You might as well be Jack Penguin, because I'm not going to attempt to pronounce that name.' And so the family became the Penguins."

"They never went back to using their Polish name?" Karen whispered.

"No, Jakob was an actor and minstrel in Warsaw. When he arrived in New York, Vaudeville was in its heyday. His talent gained him a position in a traveling repertoire company, and Jack Penguin made for a good stage name. He traveled with the troupe around the country for five years. When they arrived in Chicago, he met his Emiliana. Their love story is what movies are made of. And we are blessed to have their granddaughter Emma as our teacher. She inherited Jakob's talent and his beautiful voice. She teaches our children the Polish folk songs."

"How lucky for Nicole to land here, and, if you really don't mind, I would love to visit your farm. I haven't been in the country since my family left the Cotswolds in England." Karen looked over to Nicole, who was engrossed in the activities. "I don't think she'll even notice I've gone; so much for a hard transition."

"Well, then, let's get a move on." Sophia stood up. "Agata, do you still have your quilting bag in the car? We can circle this morning at my house." When they reached the parking lot, seeing Karen approach the Torino, Sophia offered, "Your car wouldn't make it on our gravel roads until the snow melts. Besides, you wouldn't want to hurt such a pretty green car. Why don't you come with us?"

"Pretty? I can't stand that car. All it does is make a lot of noise and rumble. It's not suitable for a family, but my husband just loves it, and we could only afford to take one car with us from California. He won the coin toss."

They drove down the road, and Karen noticed how many houses were freshly painted in various shades of green. *No wonder they liked the car*, she thought.

That first morning, the four wives stayed together at Sofia's farm. After a collective effort to help straighten the house and prepare the meat and vegetables for the family's dinner, the women sat down and engaged in what was to become the first of many morning cackle-fests.

In Sofia's sewing room, a checkered partial-quilt hung over a large frame. Generally, the women met every Saturday afternoon and worked on different quilts for each other's homes. Deciding that breaking with tradition never harmed a soul, they put Karen to work on Sofia's quilt, instructing her on the different stitches possible to apply.

She found the delicate needle stitch not unlike the sutures she had learned in the emergency rotation of her training. At first, head down with rapt concentration, she sped through a whole square, trying to keep pace with her new friends, until she looked up and saw the women watching her, smiling. She compared her work to theirs and shook her head, crestfallen. "Wow, yours are so skillful compared to mine, and lovely to look at."

"Don't be disheartened, Karen. We have been doing this since we were children. It takes practice. Relax and have fun. We're in no hurry." Agata took the needle from Karen's fingers, where she had been holding it so tightly it had left an imprint. "You're not sewing skin together to hold back blood. It's important to hold the needle gently with love and joy as you stitch, imagining the pleasant dreams that those who will lie beneath the quilt might have. This is our playtime. Listen, we might be simple country folk, but we have a few tricks in our baskets."

Agata's words hit home. She realized that she had stopped hearing their conversation, so single-focused to complete her task. She had missed the last fifteen minutes.

Amazing. I've become such a taskmaster that I've forgotten how to just be me and smell the roses. School, career, and marriage and babies, she thought. *The last years have sped by, and I'm wondering why, or when was the last time I just listened.*

"Oh, Agata, you're so right. I seem to have forgotten how to have fun. There were other mothers—my neighbors, my friends—and we'd take walks together in the mornings, strapping the babies on our backs. And sometimes for no reason, we would gather at one of our kitchens and bake batches of cookies. But since I went back to working the morning shifts nursing, there's never been any free time, until now. I loved my work and miss it, but sitting here with you, I sense that there are other things for me to learn."

The morning passed with Karen answering their endless questions about all the myths and truths about California. Yes, the weather is wonderful. No, they don't have oranges on every tree; that is more southern California. No, no movie stars, especially not in Alameda. Yes, San Francisco cable cars are fun to ride. Yes, the earth does quake regularly, but most of the time you don't even notice. And, no, the ground doesn't open and swallow people. It was so unusual for people to move from there to Illinois.

While she answered their questions, she wondered about their families, and husbands. These women spoke of their menfolk in kindly voices. It reminded Karen of her father, so kind to her mother, so different from her husband and his father. She had wondered which one was more typical. Their Polish hospitality, such a welcome respite from the icy reception in Streator, relaxed Karen, and allowed her to confide more than was customary among such new connections.

"Now I want to know why you moved here in the first place." Agata asked what they all were wondering. Everyone stopped their work and looked up.

"It for sure wasn't my idea. Bernie's father suffered a minor stroke, and he needed help in his office supply store. Actually, I'm not really sure why we are here. He could have hired on a helper for much less than moving us out here. But for richer or poorer, sickness or health, Illinois or California, I vowed, and so I followed. The last year has not been a happy one for us, and, well, I think I was hoping that the change might do us good," Karen blurted. Then, looking around at these friendly faces, she added, "But, I'm here, and knowing all of you will make this an adventure I know will be well worth it."

A momentary silence filled the room. Sophia jumped up. "Here let me fill our cups. We sure are glad you came to visit our small community."

Agata joined in. "Absolutely, Karen, you have certainly perked up our morning. How about tomorrow you come to my house? Tuesdays are egg days for me. You and David can help me sort and box them for shipping to the mercantile."

Before she could answer, Sophia suggested that Wednesday, Karen and David could come and help her put up some cheese.

"Hey, there, let me have a turn," Anna interrupted. "They have to come to my farm too. I make the patterns all us mothers use to sew our children's clothes. I could teach you how to make much better and prettier clothes than you can buy at department stores."

"Whoa, ladies, I'm so flattered, and I want to come visit all your homes. Nikki is not the only one starting a new school today. I accept, I accept. Did I mention my mother was a farm girl too? After her death, we migrated to America with Pan Am …"

"Mummy, I can't find Brownie," David called out from the couch, where he had fallen asleep for his morning nap.

Glancing at her watch, Karen went to pick up David. "Look at the time. The morning is gone. No worries, sweetie, he must be in the car. We are going to get him and Nikki, and, look, the sun is still shining."

Agata perked up. "I can't wait to hear about England. Karen, you're so exotic."

"Not really. No, tomorrow I want to hear about your family. And you must all promise me that you will all come to Streator one day. Promise me."

"Yes, of course. Do you have pictures of California?" Sophie asked.

"Yes, albums full," Karen said, laughing and thinking now she had a reason to unpack her box of photo albums. "Hey, as a matter of fact, I always carry my camera. No one move." Karen went to the diaper bag and pulled out her Kodak Brownie camera.

"I never go anywhere without it. It has become my passion. Agata, you scoot closer to Anna. David, stop slouching. Sit up so Mummy can see you. I want to make sure I get the whole quilt in the picture. That's perfect. Now smile everyone; say kielbasa!"

― ―

Driving home, Karen was rejuvenated by her prospects in Illinois. For the first time in a month, she felt inspired to cook a big family dinner, *or supper*, she thought to herself. *That's what they call it here.* She stopped at the local meat market in town and splurged, purchasing a leg of lamb, usually a Sunday dinner meal. She felt like celebrating. When she pulled into their street, she saw that the warm day had made a dent in the snowbank lining the sidewalk. Even their driveway had melted clean. "Maybe I just need to make a better effort," she said out loud.

"What, Mummy?" Nicole asked from the backseat.

"Oh, nothing, Nikki, Mummy was just talking to herself again. Now, after we get the groceries into the house, we'll sit and have a snack, and I can hear more about school today. Then you and David can go play with your toys, and I'm going to make the family a special dinner. We can even bake an upside-down apple cake. You can help, if you want."

Karen caught a glimpse of herself and saw she was smiling. *Yes,* she thought, *things will get better.*

The table was set, and the children sat in the living room watching the Mickey Mouse Club. Karen was in the kitchen pulling out the roast from the oven when the phone rang. "Damn," she muttered. "Please, not again tonight."

She picked up the receiver. As usual, Bernie was already talking. "Sorry, Kar, I know it's not what you want to hear, but I've got to stay late—inventory. Don't hold dinner. I'll eat when I get home."

"Bernie, I made a leg of lamb, your favorite."

"Why would you go and do that on a Monday? That's a foolish waste. What were you thinking?"

Karen placed the phone to her chest, counting to ten quietly before answering, something her mother had taught her when she was a young teen. Before she reached ten, she heard Bernie say good-bye and hang up, not waiting for her to explain, to argue. She stared at the receiver and listened to the drone of the dial tone. A tear escaped. "No, no, no, no, I won't let you do this again," she said, putting the phone in its cradle. "No more tears."

"I hungry," chirped David from the living room.

"Let's eat then, shall we? Go wash your hands, you two."

"Aren't we going to wait for Daddy, Mummy?" Nicole asked, coming into the kitchen.

"No, darling, the dinner is ready, and we are hungry. I can't wait to try our cake, can you?"

After dinner, bath, and story time—she had to read three stories before they would finally fall off to sleep—Karen was able to turn off the light and go downstairs. The table still had the dirty dishes and cold food sitting, waiting for her husband. She picked up the roast and carried it into the kitchen, resisting the urge to put it into the garbage can. "No, I'll heat it up on Sunday dinner, and he can eat it then." All of her earlier hopes and goodwill ran out her toes. *So this is what it's going to be*, she thought. *Just like California. Inventory! That was last week's excuse. Typical Bernie, a phone call, and he's off the hook! Well, we are here, and there is Farm Ridge. I won't let him take my joy from today.*

Four months passed, with Karen spending her weekdays engaged in her new community. After a few attempts to interest Bernie in visiting her new friends on weekends were met with a raised eyebrow and the "look," she kept the treasure they represented inside. She bought the materials to start her own quilt, and some canning jars and a pot from the general store. She loved the idea of putting up summer fruit like she'd seen in Agata's cellar. She had to settle for a rabbit hutch in the toolshed for her farm animals. Sophia's husband made it for her, small enough so it would fit in the trunk of her Torino. Streator would not have approved of chickens running around in the backyard.

Bernie barely took notice of her projects, indifferent, as long as it didn't require any effort from him. Their relationship returned to what it had been in Alameda—a separate, passive coexistence. His work was his passion, or so he claimed, but it did her no use to prod. Bernie was a master of aloof. He did try to be present with the children, at least on the weekends at the family Sunday supper. More of a show for his parents, she suspected. They slipped into complacency until he dropped the bomb one Friday night.

"We are going home," he said as they watched the Johnny Carson show.

"What?"

"We are going home," he repeated. "I hate it here. I've called the precinct, and they assured me my job was waiting for me. I contacted the Browns and told them they had thirty days' notice to find another place. I figure we could stay in a hotel for a couple of weeks until then. Why are you looking at me like that? It's what you want, isn't it? You never wanted to move here in the first place."

"Well, of course it is, I guess. But how do you get to make all these decisions and not talk to me about it? What about your father?

What about this house? Didn't we sign a lease? How long have you been thinking about this?"

"Come on, Kar, why are you concerned with petty details? I'll take care of it, like I always do. You just get the packing done and have the family ready in two weeks when school is out. I figured we could leave the next day. I knew you wouldn't want to leave before that. See, I was thinking about your needs too."

Bernie rose up from the couch, turned off the TV, and announced he was done for the night, adding, "Coming to bed?" *And that was that? In his mind, everything is settled?* The confusion bubbling in her mind left her speechless.

Karen nodded, waiting until he left the room before she grabbed a couch pillow and covered her face. A mixture of rage, elation, thrill, and distress swept over her. Her family was English, the masters of control; yet, so many thoughts were racing through her mind that it was anything but controlled. She had pretended for months that this was her home. She'd practiced the words until she could believe them. And in only four words from his mouth, "We are going home," it was all erased. *Of course, the children will be happy, Bernie will be happy, but what about me? Will this be what makes me happy?*

—⁂—

"Is this where I went to kindergarten?" An athletic young woman came into the bright, sunny kitchen where her mother sat drinking tea, sewing an appliqué on a square for a quilt.

"I've been going through the family photo books for a school project, and found this small album tucked behind the yearly ones. The cover reads, 'Kindergarten in Farm Ridge.'"

Looking up from her needle, Karen smiled. "Yes it is. I'm glad you remember."

"Actually, I don't remember. I just read the cover. Who are all these women, and these farms? I don't recognize anyone."

"Here, hand me that, Nicole." Putting down the cloth on her lap, she took the book from her daughter. Karen's heart skipped. "Of course you don't. How could you? You were in school all morning. That winter, David and I spent the mornings in the homes of the local farm women, mothers of the children in your school. Do you remember your friends Shannon and Cherril?"

"No, not really."

"Let's see if we can't find their pictures."

Flipping through the pages, Karen stopped at a small black and white snapshot of three women sitting at a large pine table, an intricate quilt laid out in front of them. Below that, a color picture of three little girls and a boy in front of a red brick schoolhouse.

"Here you all are," Karen said, pointing to the photo of the children. "This was one of my first rolls of color film. And here are their mothers," touching the top one. "Look at that little towhead brother of yours sitting with a cookie in his hand. They were always slipping him one when my back was turned."

Nicole glanced down at her mother. "Wow, Mom. Look at you. You're smiling ear to ear. I do remember going to school in the snow, back at Grandma and Grandpa's in Illinois. That was when you taught me to make a snow angel. I remember Daddy was so unhappy, we hardly ever saw him. At night, after we went to bed, we could hear you two arguing. David would crawl into my bunk, and I would sing him funny songs I learned at school, under the covers. Now, that's odd. I haven't thought of that in forever. My teacher, she was pretty. What was her name?"

"Oh, yes, Miss Penguin. Everyone's favorite. You're right, it wasn't a fun time for the family, but I had a secret life. Your father and I weren't talking much, and when we did it usually didn't end well. He didn't want to get involved with the farmers, probably beneath him, so I kept it to myself. I'm sorry that is all you took from that time in Streator. It was such a crazy time, and then it was over, and we came back."

"I remember; we were so happy coming home to California in the summer. You said everything would be all better. It was at first. I remember the fighting stopped for a while. I guess I forgot about Illinois. And even though Daddy still worked a lot and was gone all the time, you were great. You always had something for us to do together after school. By the time you told us about the divorce, I had stopped thinking about you two together. You did everything separate anyway. Now thinking back, it must have been hard on you. When you're a kid, you only think of how it affects you. And things didn't get worse for us like my friends said it would."

Stunned by the kindness of her daughter's matter-of-fact words, Karen felt a shift in her breathing. She exhaled the long-buried guilt. These powerful words lessened the pain of the failed marriage. By the time Karen realized her husband had been having affairs, she was no longer in love with him. The shock of betrayal had been tempered with the resilience to create her life anew, and fill it with beautiful things and people that mattered to her. Now Nicole had opened the door for her to share some of that wisdom.

"I learned a lot in Streator. Why not grab a cup of tea and sit with me? Let me share with you my wonderful time there. In fact, that is where I learned to quilt and can fruit and so much more."

"That would be great, Mum, but I have soccer practice at four, and I need to get my books back to the library before then. Can we do it another time?" Nicole stood up and walked to the door.

"Sure, another time, sweetie; we can do it later." *So much like her father*, Karen thought.

Nicole turned and saw the smile leave her mother's face. "No Mum, I mean it. I want to hear all about it—the farms and the women. Tonight, after practice, let's get pizza. It's David's night at Daddy's. It will be fun, just you and me. You can tell me everything. Done?" She blew her mother a kiss, and left.

"Done!" Karen replied to the empty doorway. It was an expression she learned from Sophia, back in Farm Ridge. When an agreement was made, you said, "Done." *A commitment not to be broken;* her smiled returned. There were many things she had learned from her Polish friends that had translated into Karen-speak. Friends in California always thought they were English idioms, and Karen, never knowing how to explain her Polish side, allowed the misnomer. She had grown into herself in those few months in Farm Ridge. She had become a woman, not someone's daughter or wife or even mother. And it had taken other women to show her the way. Not enough to resuscitate a flawed marriage, but enough to rescue herself.

When she opened the first page, there was Nicole holding up the mug she had painted for Karen in her first kindergarten class in California. *Now where is that?* she thought to herself, closing the book. Pulling over the step stool, she climbed up and reached to the back of the cupboard. *I see it. Won't Nicole be surprised I saved it all these years*, she thought. Karen reached in and pulled out a chipped painted mug from the back of the closet, the handle gone and a hairline fissure running through it. *No worry; I bet it's still good.*

She poured a cup of tea, placed the mug on a saucer just in case it leaked, and sat down at the table. She turned the mug, looking at the letters. Only the letters ST MUM had survived from BEST MUMMY. "Saint Mum, sounds right to me!" She found herself laughing out loud in the empty kitchen. She remembered Agata declared one day at the quilt circle, "Some of the best giggles I've had are when I'm in the kitchen doing a chore, and I remember something funny, and I sit there all alone laughing silly, sometimes to tears."

Anna had questioned, "All by yourself, you sit alone cackling? I always thought you might be a bit touched in the noggin'; now you confirmed it."

"Hey, why, I'm some of the best company I know, and seeing as I'm always with myself, I think it's right smart of me to find pleasure in it. What you say, Karen? Am I crazy?"

"No, Agata, I think that is one of the smartest things I ever have heard."

She opened the book again, the California afternoon light filtering onto the pages. She found the section of Agata's farm. Karen remembered the series of photos she took on one of their egg days. There stood Agata, with her plaid green apron, in her cellar holding up an egg to the candle, to make sure it wasn't spoiled. In the next one, David was placing the egg on the tin plate, bending over to read the fading numbers on the rusted scale. In the third one, the two of them packed eggs into a sixty-four-holed cardboard crate, and in the final one, the two of them were holding eggs pressed to their eye sockets, big silly grins on both their faces.

Yes, she taught me to laugh, Karen mused. Turning the pages, a small snapshot of David waving from atop a tractor fell out from behind another one of Sophia standing next to her quilt stand. That morning, her husband Albin had ridden David on the green John Deere. She remembered that she had hidden the picture behind the other one so Bernie might not see it. Not that he ever looked at her photos. She wondered if David had any recollection of the farms. *Bernie would have been furious with me*, Karen thought, claiming it was an unnecessary risk. David managed to keep that secret. Even at his young age, he'd figured out how to keep a low profile with his dad. Fingering the small faded black and white, the smile from the little towhead clearly visible, Karen's smile faded thinking of how she'd felt she had to hide happy things from her husband, while he was hiding the real sins.

The last one was of the group of friends dancing on Anna's porch on a late spring morning, next to an old-fashioned turntable, propped up on a chair, playing a 45 rpm record. Karen remembered listening to the song, called the "Great American Farmer." John Deere Company, in honor of the bicentennial, had recorded a country song. Remembering back to dancing with her friends, Karen's laughter returned.

No one would ever believe me if I told them. She'd even come home from Illinois and had taken a square-dancing class at the Parks and Recreation Center in Alameda. She forgot how much fun that was. Bernie rolled his eyes at the suggestion he join her.

"Oh, well," she sighed to herself. "His loss."

"Never mind," she spoke into the kitchen. "It will be fun sharing all this with Nicole tonight." For a moment, Karen's heart welled in sadness. She never had the time with her mother to ask questions about growing up in England. She had died when Karen was so young. These women had filled in some of that gap. *It's time I shared their gifts with Nikki, and many of my own. Stop and smell the roses; yes, before they are wilted and gone.*

Karen got up and went over to the wall phone, next to the sliding glass door. She thumbed through the phone book on the counter.

"K, K, here it is: Kowalski," she said out loud.

Just then her cuckoo clock chimed. Four tweets and then the dancing milkmaid came out of the house and danced to the other door. That last week in Farm Ridge before school was over, Sophia and Agata had dragged her out to a German farmer's barn sale one morning and insisted that Karen should buy the clock. "It will be something to remember us back here in Illinois."

"But it's German, not Polish," Karen had protested.

"Oh, phooey, we have been conquering each other for centuries. Our fathers and brothers keep finding ways to war, but they're all related," Sophia had said, laughing.

"That's right," Agata exclaimed. "We're all one family, if you go back far enough." Karen started laughing again as she took down the receiver from the wall and began dialing Agata's number. *They should be just finishing supper. Maybe I can catch her before she goes out to call the chickens to their pens*, she thought.

"Hello, Agata, it's Karen from California. I know it's been a long time, too long. Is now a good moment to chat?"

Karen listened to Agata's welcome laughter. "You're right, Aggie, it's always the right time to cackle."

Where Is the Camino?

I received the pilgrims' call when all else was being taken away, until all that was left was the empty road. At a moment in my life when everything appeared grounded and well organized, I entered the hurricane force of fate: my boat sunk, my car was stolen, my office burned, I received an eviction notice, and I lost someone I loved. All of this came together in a matter of weeks, uprooting me from the soil that I regarded as deeply seeded. I was being called to what, I did not know. But from a new silence of the inner regions of my heart, my awakened inner voice answered loudly:

Well, you have my attention. Now what?

I did not have to wait long. In the middle of the night a few weeks after the forces had begun, my oldest son, having heard of my trials, called to ask, "Mama, are you all right?"

"Yes, I have no other choice but to be all right—at least until the dust settles."

"Well, I was wondering, do you have any debts that concern you?"

"What an odd question, Santo! But no, dear—no debts, and no tethers it seems either. Why?"

"If I bought you a ticket to Italy or wherever else you would wish, would you go back and write your story?" He was referring to an interrupted manuscript.

"Be careful, Santo, I just might say yes. Anywhere?"

"Yes, anywhere! It would be a long overdue Mother's Day gift."

What an offer from a son whose only financial asset was the American Express card he carried, and used for emergencies!

"I can't think now; I am on my way to the airport. They need my help in Missouri, to attend to a friend. I will call you back in a couple of days after I get settled. You may have just made me an offer I cannot refuse. Love you."

Immediately upon arriving in Missouri, as a guest in a small South American community, I began to see signs in the most unlikely of places. As a healer, I was no stranger to the possibilities of the unexplainable, but my naturally pragmatic self kept me rooted in the practical realm for everyday life. On the second day, the family I was staying with brought me to a graduation ceremony of a friend; I went along to care for Barbara, who was suffering from a severe brain injury. A woman had been watching me feed and care for Barbara, and she approached us, saying, "My name is Isadora; I am a healer from Guatemala. I have been watching you take care of your friend there. I see the light emanating from your heart, the gift that you carry. You have a long journey ahead."

When I asked the stranger what she meant, she responded with a whisper into my ear, followed by a kiss on my forehead. "You already know, Paola. Just remember you are not alone, and will be guided all the way."

That night I had much difficulty in sleeping. The following evening I attended a Brazilian dance ceremony, not a normal event in Missouri. One of the cigar-smoking dancers pulled me aside and whispered to me, "You will find the strength to complete the journey you are embarking, and it will be very physically difficult, but you will persevere."

Too tired to question, I smiled and nodded, thinking that the water in Missouri must be spiked. After another sleepless night, I rose at dawn to call an elder mentor to ask for help.

She answered the phone brightly at 6:00 a.m. her time. "Paola, how wonderful you called. I have something to share, but first, why did you call me so early?"

I recounted the strange occurrences that had been happening since my landing in Missouri, and asked, "Elena, am I losing my mind?"

"Well, I should say not my dear. You have been on my mind a lot in the last few days. I have been reading this book, and came across this passage about St Francis's journey, a pilgrimage in Spain."

Elena knew of my connection to St. Francis's life. As a child I was drawn to his simplicity. His gentle temperament and connection to nature always brought harmony to my heart. And as a teenager in the '60s, I thought of him as the original hippie. The book Elena had been reading spoke of Francis's quest for clarification about the resistance to his mission from the hierarchy in Assisi and Rome. He elected to follow in the steps of pilgrims to Compostela, in Spain, where the bones of Santiago (St. James) are believed to repose.

"Elena, perhaps you have delivered the calm to my storm. I need to do some research." The next day, a trip to the Columbia Library opened the world of the *Camino de Santiago* to me. I was surprised to find so much written on such an ancient route. The Way of Saint James had existed for over twelve hundred years. It was one of the most important Christian pilgrimages during medieval times, and, together with Rome and Jerusalem, a pilgrimage route on which a plenary indulgence could be earned. After centuries of being all but forgotten, the ancient route attracted a resurgence of interest in the 1990s, largely due to two popular books, *The Pilgrimage*, by Paulo Coelho from Brazil, and Shirley MacLaine's *The Camino*. I had read neither book. Suddenly, I remembered my son's offer. I wondered, "Is this what I am supposed to do? Walk in St. Francis's footsteps? What possible value could there be in this foolish idea?" But as I pondered, my doubts were replaced by intrigue. Nothing was holding me back. I called my son, and he readily offered the magic AMEX number, and the journey began.

What I had discovered about the *Camino* sent me following the Aragon route St. Francis had traveled. A six-thousand-mile flight led me to a frantic Madrid taxi ride in a downpour, during a national strike, to the train station. An old, languorous train took me to the most northern tip of Spain. Finally, twenty-four hours later,

I found myself in the French border village of Somport, hidden in the Pyrenees, along with others walking with guidebooks and tourist maps. All along the route, the scallop-shell symbol of the pilgrim is posted as a guide. Carved stone, ceramic, or wooden shells are embedded in walls or in the cobblestones. Signage was posted along the highways, along with more minimally painted yellow arrows, and, of course, there were the stars. So many pilgrims walked unaware that they were trekking the ancient Celtic trade route that followed the Milky Way, predating Christianity, *Compostela*.

In the following six weeks, many jewels fell from the sunny skies, starry nights, and rainy afternoons. I chose to walk alone during the day; in that silence I became keenly attuned to the timbre in some voice or in the stillness of nature. Such an attunement that walking with an ant did not seem out of place. When I got lost, it allowed for the deeper mystery to emerge as part of the walking. In every instance, thresholds were unveiled, and they opened into feasts: an apple grove appeared, branches heavy with ripened fruit yearning to be plucked; a pan full of frying crepes was offered by a charitable woman who cooked for the passing pilgrims every morning in O'Cebriero, at the highest peak in the Leon Mountains. At other times I found nourishment for the heart by discovering hidden ruins and chapels or abandoned routes. In each case there was a deepening of trust in the pilgrims' path, knowing that I was never lost, just detoured in order to cross another important portal. Somewhere, deep in the wet green forest of Galicia, after an intense eight hours descending the Leon Mountains through difficult terrain, I came upon Antonio in the middle of the road. Turning in circles, mumbling epithets, and waving his staff in the air, he was a vision, a cross between Moses shaking his rod at a burning bush and a beachcomber waving a metal wand looking for treasure. I had been walking for hours in silence and solitude, and seeing him tickled me.

Antonio was a Spanish pilgrim whom I had met in some of the *refugios* over the last month. Our occasional shared evening meal usually ended after a bottle of wine in heated discussions of the value of spirituality versus the constraints of a cruel, unjust world. He had been a banker but was forced into early retirement with the expanding Spanish economy. This was a windfall to be sure, but its arrival left him untethered to his life. For the first time since he was seventeen, he was afforded time to ponder the path he had chosen. At age fifty he took the opportunity and freedom to explore his desires; he left his home in San Sebastian and began walking to find his way.

When I approached, he stopped flailing, and his eyes lit up. "Ah, Paolita, a vision to behold in these deep dark woods, maybe you can help me in my predicament. It seems I have been walking and not paying attention to the markers, and now at this crossroad there is no shell, no indicator to follow. I have taken both paths for some distance, to no avail. I returned here to the junction again and still do not see the way."

"Well, Antonio, now that you say the words, I too have been lost in this beauty." Looking around for a few moments, I continued, "You are correct. There is no visible indicator, but let us consult with the *Camino*."

By this juncture, the road (camino) had taken on its own persona for me. She was my companion, my teacher, my nemesis. Turning slowly I observed the split: a high, wider road on one side, with a stone wall bordering an apple orchard, and a lower one that dipped deeper down a gully past a dilapidated farmhouse in the distance. "I suppose we need to take the low road."

He looked at me, shaking his head, and said, "That's ridiculous; it makes no sense." He argued that the high road was wider and clearly more traveled.

Sitting down on the moist earth, I listened and said, "No, it is the low road."

He became agitated and asked, "What are you listening for? You have no map; you have never been here before or walked this road."

"I have been experiencing this *Camino* now for thirty-five days uninterrupted and so have you. Haven't you heard it by now? It sings to us, cries to us, and especially laughs at us."

He looked at me, shaking his head, certainly not convinced, but he followed behind me arguing that for sure I must be mistaken. As we dipped deeper into the valley, he moaned, "*Loca. Loca.*" (Crazy. Crazy).

Not believing me, but also not wanting to go it alone or leave me, he cajoled, "I am sure you think you are on the right path, but I think we are lost. You need to come with me. I must go back to where it makes more sense to me."

He turned to backtrack up the path.

"Wait," I called out. "There is the farmhouse," I pointed. "Let's knock and ask someone."

"Woman, you are crazy. Can't you see it is abandoned?"

"Well, then we won't be bothering anyone, will we?"

I approached the bottom door and rapped with my staff. When no one answered, I stepped back and called up, "*Buenas Tardes. Hola, hay alguien?*" (Good afternoon. Is anyone home?)

"You are wasting your …"

Before Antonio could finish the sentence, the upper wooden balcony door creaked open, and an old crone stepped out on the balcony.

"*Que quieres?*" (What do you want?) she called out.

"Afternoon, Senora. Sorry to have disturbed you. Can you please tell us which way is the *Camino?*"

"Foolish people, foolish question. You are standing on it, are you not? Continue and cross the stream!" And just as abruptly as she appeared, the door closed.

"*Muchas Gracias, Senora,*" I called to the empty balcony. "Now can we continue on in peace?"

We crossed the stream and, as promised, there on a crumbling stone wall, a peeling painted yellow arrow awaited us. Our conversation started up again, with Antonio questioning: how it was that he had walked this *Camino* the year before, and I, a stranger, guessed which way to go.

"But, Antonio, I did not guess; I listened. Sometimes answers come when we are the quietest, no?"

"Oh, you are talking women's intuition."

"No, it is not women's or men's. It's human intuition."

"No. A man must work hard to provide, listening to reason and what is demanded of him," he barked.

"I am not talking about that level. I know what you are saying. What I am expressing is the deeper questions of our purpose, our destiny. How is it we are walking here, for no other reason than to experience this path? Why, of all the pilgrims, did you and I stop to talk together? Do you think it is an accident that you found me today after days of not seeing me? Have you not learned anything from this earth, this sky—about messages to the heart?"

"Oh, easy to be spiritual when we are not working, but when it is survival, there is no place for intuition. You may have been lucky about which trail to take, but …"

Just then, for a second time in less than an hour, Antonio was interrupted. Out of nowhere that was clear, a woman appeared standing in the middle of the road and greeted us. She had heard his words and said in a firm voice, "There are no 'buts' between men and woman; there is only honor and partnership."

Antonio's presence softened. He walked up to the specter and asked, "What is your name, old woman?"

"Vasilisima," she replied.

Her long, wavy, silver tresses pulled back in a bow glistened in the forest light. Her red and gold blouse was tucked in, with a shawl to match cinched loosely on the long black skirt. Her eyes, an endless watery blue, were most unusual in their intensity and deep shade.

"Vasilisima," cried Antonio, touching her shoulder, "was the name of my favorite relative. I have not thought of her in years." He sighed.

"When I was a young boy, outside San Sebastian, I spent many weeks during the summers on her farm. She shared wonderful stories with me and cooked me amazing foods; there was no going to sleep on an empty belly. She taught me to mount a horse and trusted me to ride into the village to sell her vegetables at the market. We had very little to eat in the city, during Franco's reign; fried fish in rancid olive oil, potatoes, and onions were our staples. She had wanted me to stay on and take over the land for her. Her husband and sons had died in the civil war, and she favored me among my cousins. It was my choice, but I could see no future there. I chose the city and found an entry-level position at a bank. I have forgotten how special she was to me. I always wondered, 'Had I chosen the right direction?' She was perhaps the one truly happy person in my family. I only remember her smiling or laughing."

When he was finished talking, Vasilisima reached up and took Antonio's face in her hands and, bending him down to her, kissed his cheeks. "You are a good man; remember what I say. Slow down and listen to the path. Remember what is important."

She turned and beckoned me to come closer. I walked up and took her hand into mine and felt the softness that belied her apparent age. Sinking into her eyes, I felt comforted as I had not known in years. She put my hands to her lips and gently kissed them. It was a gift.

"And you, you come from far, far away, and a much longer journey ahead." Turning my hands over to look at my palms, she continued, "You are open-hearted, and that is good; it will serve you. Some will meet you with skepticism; do not doubt your feet." She waved us good-bye. "Safe journey to you both." She blessed us.

Continuing on down the path, all his previous agitation seeped into the ground, Antonio fell quiet for the first time. We moved as if in water, seamless with the earth. A spell had been cast, and we were alone in a different way. The forest stillness captured our tongues; the only sound, our footsteps on the ground. It could have been five minutes or an hour that we walked until a red fox darted across the path, stopping for a moment to startle us, and then jumped over the stone wall that bordered the path.

"Did you see that?" I asked, not sure if it was imagined or real.

"*Si. Si.* We must be close to a village."

Confused, I replied, "Why does the fox mean we are close to a village?"

"Because they eat the eggs. We should be coming on Sarria by now."

And just like that, we came out of the forest onto a well-worn dirt road, the spell broken, entering the edge of a village. As we passed a mechanic's workshop, I saw the shingle hanging from a post for a local bar. Noticing my body's call for attendance, I mentioned my need for the facility, and Antonio said, "Let me buy you a cappuccino?"

"I don't want one. Do you?"

"No, but if you want to go inside, we should buy something."

"No," I replied, "I just need to pee."

"Well, you cannot go in and not buy something if you intend to use the toilet."

My banker was back, "Oh, don't be silly, Antonio; I can do what I want. I am a pilgrim, remember? If you are embarrassed of me, keep walking; I will catch up."

I entered and waved to the barista, who was busy watching a soccer game. He looked up and smiled. I motioned to the WC, and he nodded. When I took off my backpack and sat down, a huge heaviness overcame me. When I was done I could barely stand. Splashing my face with cold water in the sink in an attempt to revive myself had no effect. Barely able to boost my pack on again, my feet felt a hundred pounds each. Only moments before I had felt so refreshed and revived. I struggled out the bar doors, and a glare from the late afternoon sun struck my face. Disorientated, I tried to walk back to the center of the road, my arm raised, my hand shielding my face from the glare. Just then Vasilisima was standing right in front of me. She took my hand from my face and gazed directly into my eyes. As if in a trance I returned the gaze, and it deepened; we stood there in silence.

Slowly, everything around me disappeared—the ground, the trees, and the wind. I heard the words, "You will be okay, Paolita, and you will make it all the way." She let go of my hand and walked off.

"Wait!" I called, and tried to follow. She was gone. I ran back up the road where we had come from, looking in the brush to try to see where she disappeared. But there was nothing except the empty path that led back into the forest. Turning around, I found my strength returned, and I began walking at a fast clip to catch my friend. Antonio was leaning against a tree, smoking a cigarette some twenty yards ahead.

"Did you see her?" I asked him.

"See who?"

"Vasilisima! She was waiting for me when I came out of the bar. You were standing right here. Are you sure you didn't see her?"

"Si, Paolita, I have been watching the door the whole time. I didn't see anyone but you come out. You are agitated?"

"Yes, well, no; I mean, it's, I just had the strangest experience, and then Vasilisima came and somehow made it better. I don't even know what happened to me."

I could see confusion rising in his eyes and realized that this was my mystery, and I would need to sort it out, as Antonio would be sorting his. Looking up next to the tree, I saw a stone pillar with a cobalt blue ceramic shell encased on its top. The *Camino* beckoned.

"Come on, Sarria is just another kilometer. I'll treat you to Tapas. Are you tired? Do you want me to carry your pack?"

"No," I answered. "But I would like you to hold my hand, until we get to the bridge up ahead, *mi hermano.*"

"*A sus órdenes, mi hermanita.*" By your orders, my little sister.

"Gracias, Antonio," I said. "But I think it is at the request of the *Camino*."

The Laundry

Angela decided today would be the day she would attempt to crack the hard shell that encased Signora Fellini. Noon bells were ringing, and school had been let out. The small street filled with uniformed children, laughing, ducking into doorways, on their way home for lunch and siesta.

Ah, maybe one of these children will end up in Fellini's store, and I'll learn something, she thought.

She pushed open the door, loving the jingling bells above her head that announced her arrival. Large fragrant cheeses and dried meats hung from hooks attached on the ceiling; their aromas smacked her senses immediately. Giant jars of pickles, olives, and peppers stood on top of the glass cases, and huge wooden bins lined the walls with every type of dried goods she could imagine. Multicolored beans, rice, and pastas reminded her of kindergarten play, only these were to be cooked in savory sauces instead of glued to Popsicle-sticks or made into beaded necklaces.

"*Buongiorno, Signora*," she called out as she closed the door gently. Signora Fellini sat atop her perch at the end of the marble counter with her head buried in her ledger. When standing, the tiny woman could not see over the counter. Ladders were placed along the wall so she could reach her merchandise. Although not very old, she dressed only in black, with matching black hair pulled severely in a bun. She rarely spoke, only the words necessary to complete any transaction. A smile had yet to cross her lips in Angela's presence.

Four months earlier, when Angela and Roberto had arrived in town, empty-pocketed, the signora had not blinked when Roberto asked for credit. Without any hesitation, she responded, "*Che cosa vuoi?*" (What do you want?) Thinking he was not understood, he asked a second time, and again she replied, "*Che cosa vuoi?*" then added, "*Quale cibo desideri?*" (What food do you want?) The most words Angela had heard her say to date. Although the townspeople were more reserved than the Italians in the city, none were as silent as Signora Fellini. But the notable peculiarity was that the signora alone attended the store, whereas elsewhere in Formia businesses were family enterprises, and different faces appeared at various times of the day. Yet, despite the dry silence, the way the *Merceria's* merchandise overflowed was comforting, an explicit invitation to enter.

Angela swept in, approaching the counter, repeating, "*Buongiorno Signora!*" The shopkeeper raised her eyes above the ledger book as if to say, *Who dares disturb my peace?*

"*Si, si*, I heard you."

"Did you know your shop is my favorite in all of Formia? Not because you were the first to extend credit to us when we had no money, and not even because you speak fantastic English, which helps my poor aching head from working overtime. No, what makes your store so special is that it's brimming with the best delicacies begging to be eaten. I think you must spend hours arranging and displaying everything. I walk into a beautiful canvas every time I enter. *Abbondanza!* I think that is the right word?"

"*Si*, it's the right word."

"Do you work all alone, or are there elves that come at night to help you?"

"What is this thing, elves?"

"Oh, they are creatures of magic. I'm not sure how to say it, *elfo?*"

"*Ah si, folletto, elfo, tu sei pazzo*! You're crazy. There is only me that does all this work."

The small woman stepped down from her perch and walked to the front of the store, straightening the row of canned tomatoes. Angela could hear the pride in her voice too, and saw a hint of a smile on her pursed lips.

"Well, how sad you have no one to share your cheerful work with." Without thinking, her mouth continued, "Would you like some help? I would be happy to come in one morning and give you a hand, or during siesta when the store is closed. I mean, if you're not napping or cooking for your family." Immediately Angela regretted the suggestion; she could see raw emotion right below the surface, Signora Fellini's shoulders trembling.

"Foolish woman, how could you help me? Why would you help me? Does it not look perfect the way it is?" she snapped. The Signora's pride had been quickly replaced with hurt.

"*Ma no, e' perfetto;* yes it's perfect. I just meant that you have been so generous to me and my husband that I would like to return the favor. It would be my pleasure."

"It would be your pleasure? I do not understand these words."

"*Sarebbe un piacere, Signora Fellini,* surely you know the word pleasure? Your shop is like stepping into a work of art. The fragrances, the colors, the shapes—a beauty you have created. Think about it, and if you change your mind, send word with Marcello, Signora Carlotta's son. His band practices in the villa where we live."

"*Si,* I know. Everyone knows what those disorderly boys do over there. I'll consider it. Now, did you come here just to pester me?"

"No, of course I came to buy." As Angela began rattling off her list, she thought, *I guess her secret will remain for now, but I'll find out how she comes to speak English so well and where her family might be.*

She left Fellini's store absorbed with her mystery and started to walk down the street out of town, feeling perhaps she'd made some progress. She'd had a conversation of sorts with Signora Fellini. And she didn't throw her out at least; maybe next week. Her thoughts were interrupted when she heard her name being called. Looking back, she saw Signora Carlotta waving to her from the bakery.

"Angela, you do not stop today?"

Turning back, Angela walked back up to the bakery cafe, to a smiling Carlotta. Angela remembered how at first the cold stare from the shopkeeper was unsettling, but as she had grown more confident with the language, to her surprise, Carlotta had responded with delightful encouragement, and she no longer looked at her dusty feet.

"*Che bella gonna, signora, dove l'hai comprato, Roma?*"

"*Scusa non capisco?*"

How beautiful your skirt is. We do not see such clothes here in Formia. Did you get it in *Roma*?" Carlotta replied.

Surprised by the woman's English, Angela stuttered back in broken Italian, "Roma, *ma no, ho comprato a Londra.*"

"You speak English please. I need *la pratica.*"

"*Si, si, grazie, Italiano ma un po difficile per me*; I mean, it's still so hard for me. I bought the skirt in London, but it's from India. My tastes are simple; besides, in *Roma* the clothes are far more beautiful and too expensive for me."

"Do you have many such imported clothes?"

"Ah, no. All I own is this one skirt, one pair of pants, a pair of shorts, and three blouses. We have been traveling for eight months out of our rucksack and baskets. *Signora*, I have not heard you speak English before. It's so good. Where did you learn?"

"You compliment me. I have my son Marcello to teach me every night when he studies his English lessons. The American sailors stop here when they walk from the train depot to the port, Gaeta. It's important we can talk to them, invite them in. It is how you say, good for the business?" Carlota reached into the glass case and brought out Angela's favorite pastry, a *mezzoluna*. "Look, you have not put your sweet in your basket." She handed over the pastry wrapped in a white tissue.

Angela, thinking maybe this was her clue to Signora Fellini, asked, "Does Marcello teach others in the town?"

"No, I am lucky if he spends a little time with me."

Angela reached in her coin purse, to pay for the pastry. The *Signora* waved her off. "*Metta via i soldi, gielo offro io oggi!*"

"I'm sorry. What did you say?"

"*Scusi*, put your money away. My treat today. Go now and finish your shopping."

Angela smiled as she took the pastry. "*Grazie, sei generosa.*"

Carlotta responded, "How you say in English?"

"Generous. Something many here in Formia practice." Angela waved as she closed the shop door.

As she walked across the piazza, she recalled her last week's enchantment, when a nun sweeping the steps in front of Chiesa Del San Luca invited her in for an impromptu tour of the ancient stone structure. The sister had led Angela down a steep passageway into the bowels of the church, to the remains of an ancient temple with underground catacombs linking Roman pools to other villas. Iron gates prohibited any further exploration below; crumbling handpainted signs warned '*pericolo—non entrare,*' dangerous—do not enter. Angela sighed, expressing disappointment not to be allowed any further. Her guide pointed to the signs and shook her head. Taking Angela's hand, the nun led them through an alcove to another set of stairs. At the top, a short wooden door opened behind the altar, yielding a closer view of the spectacular fresco of Madonna ascending into a celestial vision. The little-known artist was daughter to one of the noble families of Rome during the Renaissance, and painted beneath the tutorship of Antoniazzo Romano.

"*E il suo lavoro non mozzafiato?*" whispered the nun to Angela. Isn't her work breathtaking?

Ordinarily not a fan of churches, Angela's sensibilities were flooded by the immense inspiration of the fresco, stunned that such a masterpiece could be found in a humble village such as Formia, where a woman's passion was so openly displayed, unfettered by any restraints.

"Si, Sister, it's magnificent, a true work of genius! *Mille grazie peraverlo condiviso con me.*" (Thank you for sharing it with me.)

Angela's smile helped carry her up the steep climb home, straw baskets overflowing with the week's provisions heavy on her slender shoulders. Her Thursday ritual, to explore the village shops and the farmers' market packed with fresh-caught fish, vegetables, and specialties, cheered her to no end. Today, she walked out of town, treading the Roman cobblestones, pleased to have landed in this part of Italy. The road narrowed to one lane as Angela crossed over the viaduct. From the middle of the bridge, the view upriver separated the valley in two. On the one side, large, square, concrete farmhouses scattered over the landscape, their adjoining fields linking one another—some separated by wooden fences, others by the shift in crops. Each farm's livestock were either penned in neat corrals or tethered to pieces of heavy iron so they could not wander. On the other side, groves of willows ran up the mountain, broken up by tall cypresses that surrounded abandoned villas, most in ruins from falling bombs dropped first by the Americans then later by the Germans.

Angela always stopped here to rest before starting the arduous climb up to her crumbling minivilla, one of the few on the mountain that had escaped the ravages of World War II. She climbed and straddled the stone wall, reaching into her basket, removing her sliver of *boschetto al tartuffo*. Every week, she treated herself to one extravagant purchase from Fellini's—an expensive handmade cheese from rare white truffles and a blend of cow's and goat's milk. As she ripped a piece of the *paisano* bread from the loaf and unwrapped the small treasure from its white waxed paper, she promised herself that this week she would take just a bite and save the rest for her husband. But as the delicacy touched her tongue, the futility of her intention was clear; there was no way to resist.

No bother; he has his nasty Galloise, é Io, il mio Boschetto, Angela reasoned as she reached in the basket to pluck a small stem of Baresana grapes to top off her picnic. Savoring the plump juice drenching her mouth, Angela thought Signori Benito was correct; *these are perfect with the cheese and bread.* She lay on the warm stone wall, imagining herself a lounging Roman goddess floating on the puffy clouds above, until cackles of voices carried by the wind from the foothills broke her spell.

Oh, my, with this hot breeze, they are washing today, she thought with glee.

Angela plopped the final morsel of delicacy into her mouth with the last grape, gathered her belongings, and hurried across the bridge. Up at the top of the path, out of breath, she paused and surveyed the cerulean sea that stretched out below, until her eyes landed on the Pontine Isles, glistening in the sea, allegedly the Island of the Sirens as told by Homer. Between them and her new home on the mountain slumbered Formia, the fishing village she had just shopped in, quaint but nothing like its notable history: the summer home of the Roman orator Cicero, who utilized the guarded treasures of local women's medicinal powers to relieve his debilitating joint pains, perhaps explaining Cicero's desire to have built a villa in these remote foothills with stunning meadows and valleys trailing all the way to the Tyrrhenian Sea. Her eyes settled on the stone tower mausoleum on the waterfront, where he was entombed after being murdered at the command of Mark Anthony. *Not such a bad place for his final rest!* Angela's imagination bubbled with the possibilities of what treasures might lay buried in these hills.

Voices echoing from below reminded her of the laundry. Leaving her ruminating behind, she continued on, through the small forest, eager to reach home. Unceremoniously, she emptied the contents of her basket onto the larder in the kitchen and ran up the stairs to their makeshift bedroom on the veranda. Quickly she filled the baskets with sheets and the well-worn clothes she and her husband possessed, and headed for the river, leaping down two stairs two at a time. She paused to glance into the workshop. She saw Roberto lost in his work, rubbing out the rough edges of the hides they had brought back from Rome.

"I'm off to the creek to do the wash. There is food on the counter if you get hungry," she called into the room. Not stopping for a reply, she began the trek down the path of tall grasses to the swiftly flowing waters that sprung from an underground river bound by an outcropping of boulders—a natural washing house formed by eddies, where the countrywomen convened to clean clothes and exchange news, recipes, joys, or heartaches.

In the first days of wandering about the mountain, Angela had noticed women gathering by the stream. She had spied on them from behind the reeds, shyly. She returned a few days later and found them again engaged in their chores. The loneliness of months without friends, and the longing for her female companions in Ibiza, overcame her timidity; she decided to plunge in.

Carrying her dirty clothes, she approached the shoreline, confident that her camping experience in California and Mexico at local streams to clean dishes or rinse out a bathing suit would qualify her. The women at the creek politely returned her greeting and continued on in their task. Angela watched as they used the boulders to rub the soap onto the clothes and scrub.

The women motioned her to an open spot in the boulders where she might put in to the stream. "Pretty basic stuff," she mumbled to herself. But soon, it became apparent that her attempts were awash with comedy more than laundering. They pretended not to watch, but when Angela stepped into the running water and began the slapping technique for rinsing the soap out of the clothes, she soon found herself sitting waist-deep in water. The women's laughter could be heard over the rush of the water that surrounded her. At that moment, Luisa, Angela's landlady, was crossing downstream with her basket, filled with fresh medicinal herbs and wild mushrooms, gracefully perched on top of her head. She was an unusually tall woman in her middle years with a poise and refinement that belied her country surroundings. She had stopped to rest for a moment when she caught sight of the spectacle of Angela's performance.

Luisa yelled as she came over, "Vergona, shame on you. Why don't you help her? She honors us in trying our simple ways."

Laying her basket down, she kicked off her shoes, hitched up her skirt, stepped into the stream, and reached her hand out to Angela. Her dark eyes silent, she allowed herself to chuckle only when she saw Angela was laughing and not crying. She took the garment from the water and artfully demonstrated that a simple flick of the wrist, not brute force, produced the desired results. Luisa then escorted Angela over to a shallow, safer pool, where the young woman could practice without disaster. She spoke a few words to the onlookers, and they came over one at a time and offered their hand, some more heartily than others, and a few with large smiles.

Now months later, arriving at the stream Angela greeted them, *"Ciao donne, che bella giornata, no?"* (What a beautiful day!)

The Maria sisters stopped their scrubbing against the rocks and waved a cheerful welcome. Suspicious of Angela at first, they had soon become her favorite supporters, especially since Angela volunteered to help with the mountain of clothes the two women would bring with them. It seemed the Fulano family had its fair share of twins. With only two pregnancies each, both resulting in twins, each sister had four babies. At first Angela felt sorry for them, but their zest for life illustrated that no sympathy was required. Living on farms adjacent to each other, they took turns keeping all the children in one home or the other, thereby freeing each sister to attend to her chores. Visiting their homes revealed to Angela an appreciation for controlled chaos. They explained that neither of their husbands would risk having their wives get pregnant again, so at a very young age both women had completed their families.

They laughed and said, "We only had to get fat twice instead of four times."

After that first washing when Angela had helped, a small boy appeared at her kitchen window the next morning with a basketful of eggs. Each week another child would appear with an offering: fresh greens from the garden or a round of cheese.

Only a few women were by the stream today; the afternoon sun warmed the boulders comfortably. Angela lay on a flat ledge to rest after hanging her clean clothes on the surrounding branches with wooden pegs. Dozing for a few minutes, she awoke to the Maria sisters' voices approaching. Knowing her husband would be lost in work and not notice her absence, Angela elected to stay and help her neighbors. As she left the creek side in the midafternoon and began the trek back up the hill, her clothes already dried from blowing in the warm breeze, she paused to rest. She saw Luisa coming down from the upper terraces, a large bundle of wood sticks carried on her back.

"*Buongiorno, Signora*, I see your clothes are already dried. You remained again to help the sisters?" Luisa greeted her.

"Yes, working with them is joyful; they help me with my Italian and have such amusing stories to tell. What do you carry on your back?"

"Oh, it's the branches from the pruning of the willow trees; the bark and leaves are a good pain reliever, and the leftover stems are great for starting the fire. It's still a good deed that you offer your hands to help the Marias. *Non e´ vero?*" (Is it not true?)

"Yes, *Signora*, the good deed goes both ways. *Non e´ vero?* Will you show me how to take the bark from the plant to make the remedy?"

"Of course. You and Roberto come to our home for dinner tonight. It will be nothing fancy, just our simple fare."

"Oh, we would be honored. Can we bring something?"

"No, just your two skinny bodies. *Ciao*, Angela. See you later."

Turning to resume her climb, Angela realized she had no idea what time they would be expected. Running back she called out to Luisa, "What time should we arrive?"

"When the sun crosses the hills and sits above the sea," her voice carried up from the grasses.

Excited to share with Roberto her afternoon's adventure, and their first formal invitation, she sprinted all the way up the hill. *We will have clean clothes to wear. Hope there is time to heat some water and wash my hair too. I wonder what time it is when the sun sits above the sea?*

Losing the path in the dazzling glare of the setting sun, Angela and her husband Roberto ambled out of tall grasses onto the corral area where their landlord's livestock were penned.

"Careful, Roberto, where you step. We don't want to track muck into the house."

"Calm down. They are only farmers, not royalty. Such a fuss you're making. I still don't understand why I had to change my clothes. I know Signore Alessandro didn't have to change his."

"Perhaps, but humor me, please, and be the charmer that I love. They may be simple like us, but I adore Luisa, and she has promised to teach me some of her secrets."

"*Si*, Angela, I'll behave. Anything to see that smile you came home with."

Two young boys waved and ran to the house to announce their arrival. Typical of the area, the farmhouse stood out in the landscape—a large concrete-block structure coated in beige plaster, with no exterior adornments. Such a contrast to the ornate fading-pink villas that capped the hillsides, or the Renaissance structures with small balconies and columns that occupied the town. Farmhouses, austere and utilitarian from the outside, made Angela yearn to glimpse what lay inside.

Signor Armando opened the bottom door and greeted them as they approached. Roberto extended the bottle of wine Angela had purchased that morning from the wine merchant. They entered into a quaint old mud and stone kitchen where a tall hearth held a blackened clay pot simmering with aromatic fragrances. The walls were painted in brown plaster; their uneven texture suggested many more layers underneath.

"Roberto, accompany me to my cellar, and we can pick out the antipasti? I bet you have never tasted *sopresetta* like mine," Armando taunted.

"My good fortune. I'm sure yours will be the best."

As the two men descended into the cellar, Luisa appeared from a narrow stairwell behind the hearth.

"*Ciao*, Angela, welcome to my home." She reached for the giant wooden spoon that hung just inside the hearth and stirred the pot. Tasting the thick tomato sauce, she motioned to Angela to pass her the cup of fresh-cut basil that sat on the counter. The only light filtering into the room came from a small wooden window set into the thick wall above a stone sink with an iron pump spigot. Luisa added a handful of the herb to the pot.

"Hmm, smells delicious; reminds me of home," Angela said, surveying the small room.

"*Grazie mille.* The sauce must simmer all day to reach its full potential."

"Yes, my mother would cook hers all day on Saturday, and it would be prepared in various recipes during the week with different pastas or meats."

"You look surprised. Is my kitchen a disappointment to you?"

"No, of course not; it's warm and inviting. I'm just surprised that your kitchen is so old and small. I mean, your house is so large and new from the outside. I guess I imagined a larger kitchen."

"We built our farmhouse on the old storage room. Armando's parents' home was the villa you're living in. Before refrigeration, farmers built stone storehouses with cellars to preserve the cheeses and other products they prepared on the property, near the livestock. After the war, his brothers divided the family's lands, and each built a home on his share. As the oldest, he had first pick. This was the best parcel. After we were married, we decided this would be the cornerstone of our home." Laughing voices were followed by the men appearing from the cellar, arms full of homemade cheese and salami, and carrying more wine. "Mando, you prepare the antipasti. Save some for the table, eh? Come, Angela, would you like to see the rest of my home?"

Nothing could have prepared Angela for what awaited her up the narrow passageway upstairs that led from behind the fireplace. The staircase opened up into an entryway with a beautiful clock and a cloak area. Following Luisa down the hall past three large bedrooms, one for the boys, one for their daughter, and one for the parents, she came upon a complete modern kitchen: a gas stove and refrigerator on one wall, and in the back corner a washer and dryer. On a long wooden hardwood counter laid the willow branches and herbs that Luisa had carried down from the mountain. Angela gasped as they walked into the room. A yellow Formica table with chrome chairs stood in the middle. The kitchen separated the bedrooms from a formal dining room and a large living salon; another set of stairs led down to the marble entryway to the home.

"Luisa, how is it that you have all this and still cook on the fire and launder down at the stream, instead of using all your modern conveniences?"

"Oh, we use the stove and refrigerator here, but when I make the sauce that requires all day to simmer, while I get to be outdoors where I love to be, it just makes sense. Some traditions one cannot give up. These conveniences, as you call them, are not for me, but for my children. Armando and I have been blessed more than most, and

Molecules and Women

he insists our children won't be farmers. They will attend university. But for me, what do I need them for? My fire downstairs keeps me warm, and the washing creek is where my friends connect. I could not stay in my house all day, and what, be separated? Watch television or listen to radio and not know what is happening in my surroundings? What good would that be to me? Our ways won't be theirs; the world is changing fast. That is why I do not push them on my children, except for Silvano, our oldest, who is suited for this country life. Luigi and Stella will complete their studies in Roma. She will be a doctor, and he wants to be a judge. We shall see what life has in store for them. Now, how about you and I stuff the sausage for the sauce? Then I'll teach you how to scrape the bark and mill the medicines for the stiffness in my joints and the pain in Armando's aching back."

Back downstairs, next to the sink, Luisa set up the meat grinder and stuffer and showed Angela first how to mix the meat and spices and then take the handheld grinder, attach the pig casings, and fill them. The rhythmic grinding of the meat, the men's voices from outside cutting salami and cheeses, and the bubbling sauce pot on the burning coals filled the atmosphere of the small kitchen to the brim. That, coupled with the lively conversation between its occupants, steamed up its only window.

Smiling at her hostess, Angela whispered, "I can feel why you want to be down here."

⸺ ⸺

Angela, transported back to childhood memories of her grandmother's kitchen, imagined all the similar fragrances and conversations at an old wooden table. Her father being the youngest of thirteen placed Angela and her siblings at the end of the pecking order with her sixty cousins. Her *nonna*, already into her seventies by the time Angela was born, never spoke English. So many daughters and sons surrounded the old woman at family gatherings that Angela and her peers were usually marched out of the kitchen. Except for the hug and smack on the cheek when she arrived, and the holiday dollar bill pressed into her palm upon leaving, there had been little opportunity to know her. Sometimes Angela would sit quietly on a corner stool attempting to comprehend the words the old woman spoke with captivating style. But then a cousin or two would come looking for her, to play in the yard or down at the playground next door. Angela's most vivid memory of her *nonna* was in fifth grade. Her father had come to school to collect Angela and her brother and take them home. At first, she felt elated not to have to walk the long road home, until her father announced, "Your *Nonna Margherite* died last night."

That evening, dressed in their Sunday best, the family went to the mortuary. It had started to drizzle. Parking on the street, they hurried through a stone entrance with a carved overhanging sign that blew in the wind. Looking up, Angela stopped to read the words.

"What is Praisewater Funeral, Mama?"

"It's a name, Angela. Move on; you're getting wet, and we are late." Her mother waved her forward to a large wooden door where a tall basket of lilies stood beside the archway. She was the last to enter the darkened chapel with candles burning and more baskets of lilies filling the corners. Her mother had already moved into the last pew, followed by Angela's brother.

"Is this a church, Papa?" she whispered, genuflecting in the aisle.

"Sort of. Shhh, no talking."

Her father stopped her from entering the pew and grasped her hand firmly. She glanced at her mother, who was frowning and shaking her head. But her father was not looking, and he strode with her to the front of the room. As Angela's eyes acclimated to the dim light, she saw they were passing cousins sitting in the rear, and aunts and uncles in the forward pews. Most were following the priest's prayers, fingering their beads, and repeating the rosary out loud.

Angela felt special, excited to be the only child permitted in the front. The drizzle had turned to a hard rain, and the drops on the roof added a quiet symphony to the voices. Large white flickering candles spread shadows on the walls next to a large, strange-looking box at the end of the pews. Releasing his grip, her father knelt down in front of the box, eyes closed, head bent in prayer. Angela mimicked his movements. The temptation to peek irresistible, she opened her eyes and stretched her small frame to peer into the casket in front of her. Her *Nonna Margherite* lay there in her blue silk dress, her feet disappearing into the coverlet. The white satin-filled coffin gave her the appearance of floating on a cloud. The stillness mesmerized Angela, and then the understanding that something was very wrong. This woman, frozen, her cheeks unusually colored and her lips reddened, frightened Angela, until she recognized the dress with the small pink roses that her *nonna* wore every Christmas. The bony hands rested on the pink flowers clasped together; Angela knew those hands. She had seen them ladle soup, place cookies on her plate, press the dollar bill into her palm. They had touched her cheek at least once during every visit. A sense of loss that Angela didn't comprehend overwhelmed her. She started to cry and could not stop. Her father took her out of the room and comforted her, walking her quietly around the corridors surrounding the gardens in the dark. Finally, when she calmed down, they sat on a stone bench and listened to the rain.

"I'm sorry your mama is dead, Papa. We won't see her again?"

"No, we won't see her again. Not in this life."

"Will we see her in heaven?"

"Perhaps." Noticing Angela's frown, he added, "Yes, of course, we will all meet again in heaven."

Ten years later, Angela returned to San Francisco's Italian neighborhood in North Beach and steeped herself in the immigrant culture there; she could place words to her emotional longing. Here the immigrants retained their pride of the Old Country; some even wore it like a badge. She recognized that her sorrow had not been for her father but for herself. A piece of her had died before she could discover how valuable it was. Living in North Beach had been the final stimulus to travel back to the Old Country. But for her it was a new country.

Now, sitting in this stone kitchen, shape and color on the blank canvas of her *nonna's* early life were being added. Luisa spoke about her family's survival of the two great wars and how the lucky ones had migrated to North or South America. The rest, who stayed, were refugees in their own country, to put life back together again.

"It was not all easy in America, either," Angela interrupted. "My grandparents were very poor, and I'm not sure if they were the lucky ones. Our family has ended up scattered all over the United States, and no one wants to share where we came from. I think they are embarrassed of their early years, when being Italian was a dirty word. Luisa, your life here is a good one, no? Your farm, your house is beautiful, Formia is a pretty town, and the people are all family?"

"Yes, you're right, of course, and one does belong to the land, and the land belongs to the family. Maybe we were the lucky ones after all. I see you have come here wanting to know our ways and be a part of what your family left behind."

"Yes, none of my relatives will talk about it. I ask, and they would say, 'Angela, be grateful; we are in America now. Who cares about the past? Be happy your grandparents left the Old Country.'"

Luisa listened, shaking her head. "They are right! There were many hard years with little food and so much bloodshed and death. So much death ... Now things are good again; my children won't know of those times, just as you won't know of them either. I wondered why our simple life holds such an interest to you. The world you come from, America, is it not big and fancy?"

"Well, yes, it's wonderful and beautiful. But for me, it's like you said, I feel like I belong to this land."

"And so you do. What else would you like to know?"

"Well, there has been one curiosity in Formia that plagues me: Signora Fellini. Her shop is so wonderful, and she speaks English better than many Americans. Yet she is always alone, but it appears she has always been in Formia; so something doesn't seem to fit."

"Good observation. You're right; she doesn't fit. We grew up together, she and I, in Formia. But Sophia, that is her given name, always wanted to go to America. It was American soldiers that brought good news—the end of the war—with them. Her family did well with their store. She felt superior to the rest of us and that her life would be special, that she was not just some small-town girl. When Sophia was seventeen, she became involved with an American sailor stationed in Gaeta. Unchaperoned, she would leave with him to go to the American base—bars and dancing. Very scandalous! But Sophia was an only child, and her parents indulged her whims. How proud like a peacock she strutted around town showing him off to everyone! He didn't speak Italian, so we could not talk to him, but she introduced him as her fiancé. I remember how she beamed.

Ultimately, her papa demanded the young man do the proper thing and marry his daughter. I think he may have threatened to report the sailor to his American commanders about Sophia's underaged status. At any rate they were married after Sophia's eighteenth birthday in Chiesa Del San Luca. One of the biggest weddings ever, nothing was too good for her. Many of his company came, but not his family. Before they could move into the house her father bought for them, his ship put out to sea for Korea. She waited and waited for him to return. One year later, he sent passage for her to join him in America. Her dream came true. She left to live in America, in a place called Ginnia? Reginnia? Oh, I'm not sure."

"Virginia?"

"Yes, that was it; but in less than a year, she returned full-bellied, no bread under the arm, and no husband."

"No bread?"

"Ah, it's a saying that all *bambini* come with a loaf of bread under the arm; it means they are bringing abundance!"

"How wonderful. I'll remember that. So what happened to Sophia? Where was her husband?"

"I can only tell you what has been said behind closed doors. It seems she …" Luisa paused to stir the food, tasting it. "Ah, yes, the dinner is done. Gather the dishes, and set the table," Luisa directed as she removed the pan she had filled with the sausages, peppers, and gnocchi.

"Hmm, smells delicious. Now I'm very hungry. But, Luisa, please do not leave me hanging. What happened to Sophia?"

"Not now, cara, it's not polite to gossip at the table. After dinner, when we go upstairs to clean the willow, I'll tell you."

Luisa called out the window, "*Tutti a Tavola!* (Everyone to the table!) Stop your boasting, Sandro; call the children in to dinner and make sure their hands are clean."

The men, who were in a heated exchange about Italy's superiority over Argentina's soccer team, continued the call, *"Ragazzi a Tavola!"* Children to the table!

Seven animated faces stuffed into the rustic kitchen. The boys loudly exchanged silly insults, and Stella shared her excitement about a pending field trip to Roma. This family behaved not so different from one in America. Angela soaked in all the noises quietly, hoping they would retain their traditions and skills of making cheeses, sausages, and homemade remedies. After the meal, the younger children were put in charge of feeding the animals. Luisa and Angela went upstairs to prepare the willow bark medicine while the men stepped out to walk the fields and smoke their pungent cigarettes.

"Now, Luisa, tell me what happened!"

"Okay, but let's work while we talk. Start by pulling the leaves off the branches, and we will let them dry. I'll scrape and grind the bark. Now, let's see, where did I leave off?"

"Sophia returned pregnant, alone!"

"Yes, Sophia arrived in Formia and began helping her parents in the store. At first, we thought it was temporary, but when the time came to have the baby, and no husband appeared to celebrate the birth, more than clothes were flapping in the breeze. They said her young man didn't come from a good family and rumored that he beat her and drank too much. When he found her pregnant, he returned to military service, to avoid his responsibilities. Their marriage in Italy was not recognized in America, and he refused to marry her there. If she stayed, her child would be a *bastardo*. Impossible! At least here the child would be legal. So she returned, and soon after her son's birth, she put on the clothes of a widow, telling everyone that her husband was killed in Korea. Perhaps it was true; at least it would do. Well, Sophia, too proud, never accepted sympathy or help. Her son, a good boy, is smart like his mama, but very sweet. She insisted they speak only English to each other. She sent him to a school in Britain. I never know, is she heartbroken, or is it her pride? When he comes home on vacations, she is smiling the whole time, and he treats her like a queen. I think he might like to stay here, but she insists he will become someone important. The townspeople welcomed her home and tried to be friendly, but she would not let anyone in. After a while, we accepted her separateness; so life moves on. Her parents died a few years back, and, well, now she truly is all alone."

"Her son does not know his father or his American family?"

"Sophia did go back once, when the child was two years old, to visit the grandparents. We don't know what passed there, but after that, no, never! It will remain her mystery. The postman delivers every month a letter from America to the boy. And Signor Benito once told my Alessandro that there is an account in the bank for the son. So who knows what the truth is in this story, because Sophia closed the door and never reconnected with us, not really. She stayed here and took over the family store. Hers is the best in Formia, with much money. She could go anywhere, but no, she stays and never spends it. It's sad. All alone, no one to share, and always in black. She was quite a beauty in her day. Now, she is filled with resentment. You know what they say about resentment?"

"No, what do they say, Luisa?"

"It's like taking a poison pill and expecting the resented to die. Enough gossip now. Let's finish our work, and after, we make an espresso and find something to dunk."

The two women worked quietly, listening to the voices of the family outside. Angela sat eyeing her new friend moving tranquilly around her sanctuary.

"How strange life gives and takes, Luisa. Here I have found home and community so far from America, but Sophia, she cannot find peace, neither here nor there. I belong to both worlds, and she to none. It's sad, no?"

"*Si, Cara*, maybe it's sad. But it's also easy to figure out," Luisa said, and smiled.

Looking up confused, Angela asked, "Really, how so?"

Luisa stopped, walked over to the young woman, and touched her heart, "Here is where you choose to live and be at home." Then, shaking her head and tapping her own forehead, "Not here, where people like Sophia choose to live. Is this not so? You're open to life, and so life embraces you!" Grasping Angela's shoulders gently and giving them a tender squeeze, Luisa continued, "Now bring me the nice demitasse cups from my cabinet, and there is a bottle of anisette next to them. You deserve a little treat after your work today. You helped the sisters and now, me. We shall have to call you Saint Angela."

"Well, my mother might have something to say to that. The closest I ever came to saint for her was when she dressed me up as the sinner Saint Mary Magdalena for the All Saints Day parade."

"Not so bad; there are some who believe she was the first apostle."

"What? I have never heard that story."

"We will save that for another day, *cara*." Luisa took the cups and liqueur from Angela and placed them on the silver platter already brimming with the *cafetera* and biscotti. Handing the tray to Angela, and motioning her to follow, Luisa went to the large salon and pulled the curtain, unveiling french doors that opened onto a tiny veranda overlooking the Tyrrhenian, where a small table and two chairs waited.

"Luisa, how many more beautiful surprises do you have in your pockets?"

"This is one of my favorites; shhh, there is music, *cara*."

The two women sat and dunked their biscotti, listening to the summer crickets sing to the moon falling into the sea.

Into the Puddle

Her heart fell into the puddle. Barely a splash and a trifling ripple followed, with no more ceremony than tossing a spent match. The fullness of her wail pierced the open sky, sending the blackbirds in the trees scattering for shelter elsewhere, just like the autumn leaves that had trailed riotously behind her spinning tires, their melted sunshine specks dancing like whirling dervishes spewing out ten thousand prayers.

But the sky was not vast enough for the sorrow that draped over her. It was too small to take from her lean frame all the sorrow she could no longer contain. Nor had the road been wide enough to absorb it, or long enough for her to escape. No matter how fast she sped away, her sorrow caught her.

Sara stepped over the puddle, ignoring her still-beating heart and its call for her to retrieve it. She continued, walking deeper into those dark woods, so unfamiliar to her. Perhaps her heart would seep into the humus and feed the earth that had born it, like the decomposing red and gold leaves that crackled underfoot.

"Don't turn back!" was what everyone advised. "Just keep those feet moving forward. He's gone now. There's too much ahead of you, demanding your focus, critical to your survival. Later will be time enough to grieve." *But what if there was no later?* she thought. *How* could she not be afforded the time to mourn, being dumped two weeks before her wedding day?

The snaky trail wound around granite boulders, then fell sharply and unwrapped itself down a steep gully, eventually dumping her onto an asphalt road. She hoped she had gotten lost and therefore saved. As she walked along the unfamiliar pavement, praying for the unknown, imagining a new universe where all was right with the world, she came around a blind curve and saw the gold rental Ford Taurus waiting for her.

"Damn, I can't even get lost properly!"

Taking the keys from her coat pocket, she eyed the smiley face on the plastic heart-shaped tag and turned it over for the first time. The words "DON'T FORGET ME" glared back at her. *Unbelievable*, she thought. *What a cosmic joke. I bet this heart doesn't bleed. Perfect!* She removed the tag from the key ring and placed the small piece of plastic in her bra cup. *Now that's a fair trade*, she thought. *I guess there's no option but to go forward. I wonder if anyone will notice or care.*

—⁓—

She opened the door to the hotel room, and a blast of light shined too brightly at her. Her mother's voice called out from the bathroom. "Is that you, Sara? Did you have a nice drive? See anything special?"

Sara threw the key on the nightstand and plopped on the bed, pulling off her boots, which still had a few red splotchy leaves stuck to them. She peeled them away delicately, to preserve them. Why hadn't she picked up a few of the more unspoiled ones for her niece? Nicole would have been delighted to add one to her collection. There are no fall colors in Florida.

"No, nothing special," she replied. How could she explain that she had abandoned the most essential piece of her, deep in the woods? "It was pretty enough."

"Well, that's nice," said the elderly woman coming out of the bathroom, wrapped in a luxurious bathrobe, toweling her head as she walked, her stocky body covered by the sea of white chenille. "I was thinking that it would be nice to go into that quaint town we passed back on the road, the one that had the odd name. *Otis* or something, wasn't it? The main street had a number of charming cafes. I bet we could find a tasty country meal. Sound like a good idea?"

Sara fell over onto the bed. She removed her sunglasses, and then quickly pulled one of the plump feather pillows from under the lavish silk coverlet to cover her face and protect her eyes from the late-afternoon glare. "Sure, whatever you want," she said from under the pillow. "I don't have enough inspiration to plan anything more complicated than brushing my teeth. I'm just along for the ride, remember?"

"Oh, stop hiding, Sara. Come on over here and step onto the veranda and enjoy the flowers."

Sara peeked out from under her pillow. "Gosh, Mom, do you have to have all the shades up? This room is so bright it feels like being under the spotlights in an operating room."

"Oh, stop your whining, you party pooper," her mother chided. "The view over the garden is a celebration of the autumnal equinox, and it's so unusual for it to be this warm in Massachusetts this time of year. One must soak it in. Boston will have nothing but gray skies for who knows how long."

"Oh, excuse me for not dancing a jig. As you so aptly point out, I have nothing but gray in front of me for God knows how long. And that's only if I'm lucky to have sky at all!"

As soon as the words poured out her mouth she jumped up and went to where her mother stood toweling her head. The sting of Sara's words had already transformed her mother's tender smile. She watched her mother try to blink away the glossy tears that had immediately welled.

"Damn me and my too quick tongue. I should just put a sock in it, Mom. Can you forgive me? I'm grateful you brought us here. You're so right, and I don't deserve your cheery outlook." Sara reached her hand out to touch her mother's shoulder, and the towel dropped to the floor.

Sara stared at her sixty-two-year-old mother's slick white bald head.

"Shit, Mom, what have you done? How did you ... Why did you?" The words rushed into a dead end. Like an air mattress with a leak, Sara slumped down onto the plush carpet. Head bent over, her tears trickled and disappeared into the soft white wool, drop by precious drop like a leaking faucet, one at a time, running down her nose, and falling quietly.

"Oh, my darling Sara, I did it for you." Raquel bent down on her knees, put her arms around her daughter, and held on tight. She rocked her child. The nightstand clock ticked as loud as her heartbeat against her chest. She brushed the hair back from her daughter's face and wiped away the tears with the sleeve of the soft robe hem. "I had to do something. It's my small way of trying to take some of the burden from your heart. If only I could take the suffering. It's so unfair, every mother's worst nightmare. I thought that if I shaved my head first, when they shaved yours you wouldn't feel so different. You have three days to make fun of me. That way I can laugh, instead of cry, at all of this. Please get up. These knees can't bear to be bent like this anymore. Damn, I wish I could be stronger for you." She pushed on her daughter's shoulders to lift herself up. "Here I'm leaning on you, when all I wanted was for you to lean on me."

Sara looked up into her mother's eyes, probing the strength this short woman carried, and a fierce kindness mirrored back to her. Rising, they held on to each other; the daughter's lean frame towered over the sturdy lioness that was her mother.

"Oh, Mom, your strength is all I have left to carry me." Sara pushed back to get a good hard look at the smoothness that was her mother's crown. "I can't believe you shaved off your snowy mane. It's been your trademark your whole life. No one is going to believe it. Can I touch your head?"

"Well, of course you can touch it. I haven't been able to take my hands off of it. The girl in the salon downstairs laughed at me when I went in and asked for a buzz. I guess she thought I was joking, or misspoke. I think she was English, or she had an accent anyway. I asked her, 'What's so funny?'"

Molecules and Women

She replied, "I'm sorry, Mum. I thought you said you wanted me to shave your head."

"That's correct, no mistake; it's what I said, and what I want. And she refused. Can you imagine that?"

"Oh, my, she refused you? Is she still breathing? I wish I had seen that. So how did you get it shaved?"

"I told her that if she didn't, then I would just do it myself. I grabbed the electric shaver that lay plugged in on her workstation, inviting me, and flicked it on. Well, you can't believe the commotion that little girl caused. She started hollering 'Help,' as if I was threatening her, for land's sake. Next, the manager appeared, rushing from the back, but she slipped on a cord, knocked the cart over and broke her high heel. That brought all the rest of the staff scurrying, surrounding me like I was some sort of terrorist. The manager regained her balance and shouted, 'Put the electric razor down, Madam!' I felt like I was in a *Law and Order* episode. It was so ridiculous. Then she repeated, 'Put down the razor and step back.' I didn't know whether to cry or laugh. Everyone froze until a voice of reason finally spoke out loud over the din."

"It's okay, dear, let me take that and help you sit down," said the shampoo girl, of all people. In the pandemonium, I had begun to shake. She pressed everyone aside, took the razor from my trembling fingers, and helped me to a swivel chair. I tried to open my purse but was shaking too hard. She took charge, the little sweetheart. She opened my bag and retrieved my pills, quietly ordering the manager to get me a glass of water. She even rubbed my neck until the shakes stopped. Then she whispered in my ear, "You remind me of my grandmother. I do miss her. Now, what is it we can do for you?"

Raquel had begun to shiver in the telling of the story. Sara took her arm and led her to the wicker chaise on the veranda. "Come, let's sit and enjoy this beautiful garden." Sara went and opened the minifridge and took out a blue bottle. "Mom, you're not going to believe they have your favorite mineral water, Blu Italy!" Handing the small bottle to her mother, Sara noticed her mother's hands trembling. "Are you okay, Mom? Do you need another pill?"

"No, Sara, I'm all right, thank you. But it was rather exciting and silly too. I'm a little worked up remembering it. This water is all I need."

"I can't believe all this happened in the short time I left, so you could take your nap. How then did you get your head shaved?"

"After I explained to the manager what I needed and why, she sent everyone away. She ushered me to her private room and buzzed me, at no charge. Now, she didn't have to do that. Such a nice gesture. I made sure to leave the shampoo girl a nice tip."

Sara sat on the wicker ottoman in front of her mother, taking her small hands in her large ones. The two women silently caressed each other's fingers. Sara's attention was drawn to her mother's face. She released her hand and brushed her fingers lightly over Raquel's soft cheek, searching those gentle eyes for the comfort and safety that she knew dwelled there.

Raquel spoke first. "Since you were a little girl, you haven't let me gaze into your eyes like this. I remember holding you for hours, inventing stories. I cherished that time when you silently gazed up at me, barely breathing, trusting. It was me you would run to and share the caterpillars you found. How you loved those caterpillars. Do you remember the one you slipped in your mouth to keep me from taking it from you, and then accidentally crushed it in your teeth?"

"Only the story you've told me, Mom. They don't hold the same beauty for me now," Sara said, shuddering and smiling.

"Or when your goldfish dropped in the sink, and I was able to open the trap underneath and save the creature from a fate down the sewer? Then I held the magic wand that could patch up all trials. Now I can't fix anything. I couldn't stop Jason from running away. I keep thinking there must have been something I could have said to make him hang in there. Maybe he'll figure it out and show up."

"Mom, stop, please. I can't think of Jason right now. He showed his true colors; and as much as it hurts, better now than after we married. He'd better stay gone. Maybe you could make up one of those stories now. They always made everything better."

"You're right, of course. But I just feel so useless. Would you really like me to tell you a story?" Raquel brightened.

Molecules and Women

"I want to see Peewhittle the butterfly soar and Flotron the grasshopper bounce, escaping across the sea ... Oh, Mother, it's so hard being an adult. I planned my life so carefully, only to have chance steal it away. One tiny cell in my brain, so small, invisible even—until it decides to wake up and start multiplying, without considering that its progress could spell my doom. What did Dr. Grinch say, 'dumb chance'?"

"I hate when you call her that. I don't remember her saying that, Sara, but yes, there is no sense or reason for this, this ..."

"Tumor. Say it, Mother. It gets easier once you do."

"Okay, tumor. But remember what she did say. You're lucky it's not malignant, and after the surgery, it should be over. Just another one of life's ghastly mysteries."

"*Maybe* it will be over. This is why I never liked surprises or mystery novels. I look at your life: Father gone, and you, so young and widowed and alone. But you were never afraid. Somehow you made it look easy. Now I'm beginning to see how much I took for granted. Knowing you were there, we'd count on you, just like I thought I'd be able to count on Jason. Instead, life is confronting me. I thought I could do this all alone. And here you are with your shaved head, still letting me lean on you. This was not supposed to happen. I should be boarding a plane in two days with the man of my dreams, not lying down on an operating table like Frankenstein's bride."

"Sara, you must stop that, and stay positive. It will be good; you'll see. The surgery is what will save you, and in a short time will be behind you. Dr. Grendle is the best, and the location of the tumor is low-risk. And maybe you're right about Jason. He failed the first test of courage. This could turn out to be a blessing when it's all over."

"You know, I usually hate when you find a silver lining in everything disastrous. But you just might be right. Stroking her mother's smooth scalp, she smiled. "I don't know if I'll ever get used to seeing you without your mane, but I'm grateful you did this. And it will grow back, of course—maybe purple. Wouldn't that be a hoot? Somehow it feels almost possible now. How did you know?" Sara kissed her mother's small hand.

"We never know what to do. There's no plan to follow. Not afraid? I would wake in the middle of the night terrified. How was I to manage, with no job and two young children? But don't you ever think I did it alone. There were friends, neighbors, and most of all there was your brother and you. Your two smiling faces never let me feel lonely. We did have a pretty good time of it."

Raquel looked down and noticed she was still wrapped in the robe. "My goodness, look at me, outside on the veranda in nothing more than a robe. Help this old mother up, before I make another spectacle of myself. Once today is enough."

Taking her hand, Sara helped lift her mother. "Oh, pshaw, Mother, you never concerned yourself with what others thought. What was it you used to say? 'Keep the bastards guessing; keep the mystery alive'!"

"I never used that word! You always have to add the extra punch. But, yes, right fond of the unknown, I look for the mystery under rocks and other unlikely places. We just step into each day, mostly trying not to hold our breath too much, and let it wash over us. Sometimes we're sparkling clean, and we dance; other times, we get stuck in the mud and captured for a time. Then we clean up our mess and try all over again. Yes, my darling, the most important thing is we're never alone in this. We turn around and look up, and there is a hand holding ours. As yours is right now."

Sara bent down and kissed the bald crown of her mother. "We're going to have to get you a tattoo before the hair grows back, huh?"

"Funny. But I'll pass on that. You're the one that likes marking your body. Now, I don't know about you, but I'm starving. Let's go find an elegant dinner, if you're not too embarrassed to be seen with a bald-headed companion.

The Painting

The willowy young woman entered the portico with her arms full. She used her slight frame to push open the iron door.

"Don't slam the gate," her *Nonna* Isabella's voice would call down from the kitchen, every time she heard the squeaking hinges creak open.

She stood still, hoping to once again hear that voice, but as the gate clanked shut, only silence greeted her, silence and the sweet scent of *Nonno* Allesandro Datura trees. They arched over the walkway with long orange and white trumpet blooms dangling overhead, and she remembered herself as a little girl, climbing his garden ladder to pick armfuls to bring up to the kitchen. The immense blossoms would slump and wilt quickly, but their fragrance lingered, blending with the savory sauces that simmered on her grandmother's stove.

She inhaled deeply and reached for a golden trumpet, observing this portico that had seemed so large to her as a child. Many hours were spent here playing with chalk on the patio while *Nonno* read the *Roma Giorno* or pruned his plants. Gently she plucked the mature flowers from the branches. Careful not to drip the milk that flowed when the flowers were separated from the tree, she carried their heady scent up the stairs, hoping the kitchen would be filled with loud voices and steamy juices.

But as she pushed open the kitchen door, only the kettle's whistle greeted her, and Moriah found the shelves barren. No mixing bowls, no olive oil, no basket of garlic and peppers next to the stove. No fresh basil or rosemary tied and hanging in the window. She dropped her things onto the empty counter, laying the Datura blooms in a wooden bowl. She turned the stove off and peeked through the atrium to find the verbena in full bloom.

"Ah, thank you, *Nonno*, for your tender loving attention and green thumbs," she whispered to the herb garden. Remarkable bounty continued to ripen even five years after his death. She removed the gold-plated baby shears that hung from the window knob, tenderly clipped the leaves of the verbena plant and a few flowers from the chamomile as she had been taught, for *Nonna's* favorite tea. Lastly, she snipped a few sprigs of white jasmine to place in a tiny vase for the tray.

Moriah had the tray ready, the infusion already steeping in the teapot, when *Zia* Pasqualina entered the kitchen to check on the water and found her.

"Moriah, you're here! I didn't hear you come in."

"Afternoon *Zia*," Moriah greeted, bending over to kiss her aunt's cheeks. "It's all prepared. Why not go and rest awhile? I can sit with *Nonna* this afternoon."

"What blend did you make? Isabella cannot tolerate any caffeine, only gentle herbs *adesso!*" snapped *Zia* as she walked over to inspect the teapot.

"*Si, si, Zia*, I know. I made *Nonno's* special blend; it's gentle and the best for her."

Zia Pasqualina lifted the lid to inspect, sniffed and stirred the infusion, and finally nodded her head in reluctant approval.

"*Va bene*, it's OK. We must be very careful. Isabella's condition is very weak. And please don't get her excited with any of your fancy stuff, Moriah."

"I know, *Zia, faccio*. I'll do it. I am always careful. Now please go rest, and I'll sit with her quietly." Moriah gently placed her hands on her aunt's shoulders, then ushered her toward the hallway.

"Molto bene, Moriah, *Perdonomi, Io sono stanco."* You're correct. Moriah, I'm tired. "And she struggles so; every breath is work. Call me right away if anything happens." Her voice faded as she shuffled down the hall.

Moriah waited until the old woman had entered her bedroom, and she heard the door latch. Turning back into the kitchen, she picked up her backpack and, with tea tray in hand, quietly pressed on the blue door of her grandparent's room. So unusual to have the master bedroom off the kitchen these days; this house contained a medley of compositions. The family grew into it, each new section representing a slice of their lives: bedrooms for the twins, bathrooms to quell the morning trickery, larger dining salon to embrace Isabella's creations, wine and cheese cellar for Father's selections. Her grandparents' bedroom remained the only constant.

She lingered in the doorway for a moment while her eyes acclimated to the darkened room. The scent of her *nonna's* violet water permeated the air. Moriah's gaze fixed on the large oil painting of a voluptuous maiden carrying an earthen water jug on her bare shoulders, mysterious hazel eyes drawing the viewer into her panorama. The painting hung prominently above the four-poster bed, instead of the usual crucifix. She had graced this quiet room for five decades; all who entered the bedchamber were rewarded with a secret reflection of the love that had passed below it. No one ever spoke of the painting, but everyone had silently wondered who the peasant woman might be.

"Could it be Isabella or Mama or *Nonna?*" each had asked.

In a side alcove, red votives illuminated a small altar to Saint Francis of Assisi, his Tau cross hung above a simple wooden statue, the "Canticle of the Creatures" prayer embossed on a small card tacked onto the wall. Over the decades the prayer had yellowed and faded; its original gold leaf letters mostly flaked away. Moriah returned from Assisi two years ago, bringing a new copy for her grandmother to replace the wilted one, but it remained in its gold envelope behind the statue.

"Troppo bella, bambina, per questa vecchia" (Too beautiful for this old woman), Nonna had complained as she fingered the

beautiful linen paper, but she had kept it. Each morning thereafter Isabella secretly took the envelope and put it to her forehead, lips, and heart, whispering, "*Grazie mille San Francesco* for delivering my granddaughter home safe."

Beneath the small altar, a red velvet cushioned footrest survived where *Nonna* prayed twice a day every day of her life since arriving in the United States, her knee imprints still discernible even though it had been weeks since she had left her bed. As a child Moriah had snuck into the room to stare at the beautiful woman on the wall and kneel on the cushion herself, reading the words of the canticle in Italian aloud, imitating her *nonna's* voice.

Now as she crept in, an unfamiliar gloom enveloped her, replacing the soothing reassurance she usually encountered. She stepped quietly toward the bed, and whispered, "*Nonna*, it's Moriah. Are you awake?"

"Si, *Cara mia, finalmente,* someone has come to rescue me. Please open the drapes, and let the world in. I'm not dead yet. I cannot believe the silliness of my sister. She thinks because my body is failing that my mind is too!"

Crossing to the windows, Moriah flung back the heavy green and gold brocade curtains, filling the corners with warm sunshine.

"I have brought your favorite tea and a surprise, *Nonna*."

"*Perfetto, cara mia.* Come here and prop me up. The way Pasqualina covers me up, you would think she cannot wait for me to go. I still have life in my bones, breath in my heart."

"Don't be silly, *Nonna*, she just wants to protect and keep you safe. I'll ask her not to close it all up; it is a bit spooky. *Zia* means well; remember, you're the last of the sisters. What will she do when you're gone?"

Moriah spoke soothingly, surprised at the matter-of-factness in her voice. Certainly, she wasn't ready to let go of her grandmother; somehow, in this room, it didn't scare her.

"Okay, of course you're right. Just tell her not to try so hard, and to stop hovering. Now give me my tea. Did you bring my profiteroles?"

"As long as you eat them quickly so I don't get into trouble. We must be careful with your blood sugar. *Zia* will have my head if she finds me sneaking you these."

Placing the tray on her grandmother's lap, Moriah brought out three chocolate-filled Italian cream puffs from her bag and placed them next to the cup.

"Two for you, one for me."

"Ah, with your skinny body, you should eat all three. When are you going to put some meat on those bones, child? Such a shame, without me to fatten you, you will probably disappear. Come closer. Ahh, I like the gold streaks you put in your hair. It lightens your face and lets your green eyes shine. You have time, but I don't, so I just may eat all three."

Laughing, the old woman took a pastry and bit it in half, fluttered her eyes, and smiled. Like a child she placed the rest in her mouth, filling her cheeks. Her face flushed as she chewed and then slurped up the tea to wash down the evidence, already reaching for the second one.

"Careful, *Nonna*, that you don't choke."

"*Si, Si, bambina*, I tease you. The world has turned upside down. First I care and pamper you, and now you spoil me, filling me with *dolce, la vita pazza*."

"Well, I cannot argue that life isn't crazy, but beautiful too. I'm blessed to have this time with you, and I'm glad to leave the goody-child behind. I love being the naughty girl; even if it is only your chocolate sins I help you indulge. Now I have something else for you."

Opening her backpack, she pulled out a silver paper-wrapped box and held it out. Her grandmother took the box with her bony fingers, then put it to her puckered lips and nodded, handing the box back.

"What elegant paper; make sure to save it! Unwrap it for me, *cara*, while I eat *mi peccato* and drink my tea. Make it easy for me."

"Of course, it's what's inside that matters." Pulling off the paper, careful not to tear it, Moriah removed the lid and lifted out a leather-bound journal with the inscription "*Cara Nonna*" etched into the cover. Inside the first page lay a small golden pen. Moriah handed it to Isabella, bent over, and kissed her grandmother's golden-brown velvety cheek. Applying the special olive cream daily had defied the years, leaving this eighty-year-old protected from the usual ravages of the clock.

"This is for you, *Nonna*, to write anything and everything you want."

"*Cara*, what does an old woman like me have to write about?" Her *nonna* fingered the smooth embossed leather and turned the empty pages of the book.

"But you have so much. You could write the stories of *Nonno's* and your voyage to America or of your childhood in *Italia*, or secrets that no one knows. Or even who the woman in the painting is, just for starters. The remarkable life you have lived and all you have taught me, whatever you write will be my treasure. I remember some of the wonderful tales you told me, but the details are blurry. I need to convey your story to my children, when they arrive. They can only know you through your words; it will make losing you bearable. Please say yes!"

"But such a beautiful book, it's wasted on me and my stories, *Cara*." Nonna closed the book, offering it back to Moriah.

Moriah stood up, refusing to take the journal. Her face quickly flushed as she attempted to quell her rising anger. "*Basta Nonna*, it's not wasted! It would be your gift to me. Stop saying ridiculous things like that." Tears forming, her voice began to crack. "Why can you never accept the small gifts I bring? Is it so much that I ask? Give me your word you will write in it these next days—anything you feel like, even your recipes!"

Biting her lip, the quick flash of hurt dissolved, Moriah was thinking, *I am anything but ready.* She crawled onto the bed and rested her head next to the old woman's hands. Her grandmother caressed her cheeks, wiping away the tears, and dabbed their wetness to her mouth.

"*Adesso Cara, calmati'*. Don't fret so. I'll do what I can, *bambina*. We are prepared for what comes next. You and I more than anyone, we must be ready, *dobbiamo essere pronti*. Now calm yourself; I do love all that you bring. Watch me eat all our profiteroles, shhh, before my nosy sister comes and finds us."

⸺ ⸺

That proved to be their last visit alone together. Within weeks the old woman passed. After the funeral, *Zia* had taken Moriah into *Nonna's* bedroom and handed her the box, now wrapped with a red silk scarf, then pointed to the painting leaning against the window, covered in her *nonna's* shimmering gold shawl, a favorite treasure that *Nonno* had ordered from the finest millinery in Florence for their fiftieth wedding anniversary. Neither spoke. Looking up to the empty space behind the four-poster bed, Moriah began trembling; finally she allowed the river of sadness to flow.

"She's really gone, *Zia*. How will we live without her in our world? She was the glue that held us all together. I can't bear to see the painting off the wall; it feels like a sin."

"Hush, child, do not be foolish. Isabella wanted you to have it, before one of the daughters gets her eye on it. She made me promise to give it to you today."

Moriah bent down to hug the older woman and receive her aunt's kiss. When she tried to stand, *Zia* Pasqualina held her for a moment and spoke into her ear.

"Moriah, she loved you best of all, she told me many times that your smile lightened her heart. Now in her final hours she made me promise to say these words to you. *Ascolta!* So listen! You will never be alone. Open your heart, learn, then let go of the past, and love as she has loved. Remember this always."

⸺ ⸺

Weeks passed into months, and Moriah still could not find the courage to look at what she hoped her grandmother had put in the box. She was afraid that once this last secret unfolded, she would lose her grandmother forever. After the funeral, she had placed the painting under her bed, not sure where to hang it, not sure that she could bear to see it every day.

Abruptly, a chain of events moved Moriah forward into a new career. What started as an unexpected eviction manifested as an opportunity to rent a spacious home with a studio just for her, to create the embroidered pillows and shawls she loved making for gifts. To complete her good fortune, an expansive barren backyard laid waiting as an empty canvas to take her *nonno's* potted plants—she had been carting them around for years—and create a sanctuary in his honor.

Spring arrived, its warmth and promise emboldening Moriah, and one afternoon after cleaning, she reached under the bed and pulled out the painting. She freed it from the iridescent silk shawl and propped it against the window in her sun room. The light filtering in cast a glow on the maiden's face. What love must have moved the hands that painted this face? All those years it hung above the bed no one could get close enough to look carefully. Eyes more jade than hazel glowed back at her. *It must have been my nonna*, she thought. Moriah, overwhelmed by the beauty, quickly rewrapped the painting and placed it back under her bed. Having opened the bottom storage drawer where she had placed the silk-wrapped box, she slammed it closed again and cried out, "No, I'm just not ready!"

Moriah had thought herself prepared for her grandmother's passing, but peace of mind continued to elude her. Wretchedness occupied her chest. Those words of her *nonna* seeped into every nook and corner of her daily functions. No matter how much she pretended it didn't matter, she saw them, heard them, felt them: "Open your heart, learn, then let go of the past!"

How to let go of the past and its sorrows? Moriah had spent her childhood hiding from the shadows. At six, her mother's abandonment forced her to live with her father's parents. They embraced her with open arms, but in such a large household of grandparents, uncles, and aunts, she became lost. She relied heavily on her father's love. At first he lived there with her, but within a few months he began staying away for days, then weeks, at a time. She would ask, "*Dove sta Papa?*"

Nonna would pick her up and hold her in her arms. "*Non importa, bella.* You're safe with me."

When he finally did appear after weeks of absence, her father would argue with his father continuously. One night their voices raised so alarmingly that *Nonna* tried to intervene. "Calm down, both of you, this is no way ..."

"Be quiet, old woman; don't you start on me too!" her father yelled at his mother.

No one had ever yelled at Isabella. At each other, yes. At *Nonno*, yes, but never, never at *Mama*. The kitchen suddenly went silent.

Finally *Nonno Alessandro* spoke, his voice deep and quiet, "*Lasciala in pace, e non tornare mai piu qui, vai, vai.*" (Go, leave us in peace, and do not return here).

Moriah's father called to her to pack, and said they were leaving. He dragged her out of her room even though she was crying that she wanted to stay; her *nonna* pleaded for her son to leave the child.

"She is my child, not yours! I know what is best for her, and if I am not welcome, then neither is she."

"Yes, my son, but she needs a home. You must think of her safety. Go get your own home, and when you're settled, come take her with you, no?" His mother pleaded.

He stopped for a moment, then saw the tears in his mother's eyes and bowed his head. "No, Mama, this time it is my way, not yours," he whispered, in an attempt to control his anger.

He picked up Moriah, and with the child's arms clinging around his neck and a small bag clutched into her tiny fist hanging down her father's back, opened the door and left. Leaving the door ajar, he stomped down the stairs, with Moriah still crying, reaching for her grandmother.

The next weeks were spent in doorways and dark places among strange people who were sitting on dirty floors, talking funny, and smoking pipes. Her father, strangely tender and kind, spoke only softly to Moriah. When she complained that the floor was too hard to sleep on, he promised that he would find the best mattress—a pink one in fact, her favorite color. Then one day, in an alley not far away, there it stood waiting for them. Moriah believed he loved her now. He dragged it up the stairs, with Moriah pushing from behind.

He placed it in a corner, but before she could step on it, he ran out of the room, telling her, "Wait here darling; I almost forgot. Don't move." He called to her all the way down the stairwell, "Don't worry; I'll be right back." And he was. Within minutes, he returned holding something behind his back. "Close your eyes, and think, what would make this pink mattress perfect?"

Moriah closed her eyes tight, afraid to hope for what was impossible.

"You have it?"

She shook her head yes.

"Well, then, open your eyes and dance."

And just like she had dreamed, there on the mattress lay the softest pink blanket, exactly like the one in the Chinese store around the corner, but this one was even prettier. It had a purple unicorn in the middle.

"Oh, Papa, it's the best ever! May I lie on it now?"

"Of course, darling. This is our small castle, Moriah. When I go out, you stay here, and no harm will come to you. Can you remember that?"

Moriah had never noticed how kind her father's eyes could be. Scooping her up into his arms, he spun her around and around until they fell into the castle, laughing together.

"Are you happy, my darling?"

"Yes. I love our castle. But please, Papa, don't leave me here. I'll be good; let me come with you. I'm afraid when you leave me."

"As long as you stay in the castle you will be safe. I'm going out for a few minutes, to get some food."

Mostly he stayed there with her, but when he did leave, she pretended to be at her *nonna's* altar. Kneeling on the mattress, Moriah would bow her head and say the prayer to St. Francis to make her father come back. Sometimes he brought her cookies and milk, or an apple, but mostly he would just come back and go to sleep. At night he would play his guitar, and the room would fill with beautiful music until someone would yell for him to stop.

In the afternoons they'd walk around Washington Square in North Beach, and Moriah would be dropped off at the children's playground while her father would stand outside the fence and meet people. Usually, he would stay within sight, but one afternoon he left her, promising to come right back. He handed her a brown bag containing an orange and some potato chips. When it began to get dark, and all the children were gone, and still her father had not returned, she began to cry.

"Papa, Papa, where are you?" Wishing they had not left her pink castle, she ran to the fence and kept calling him.

Finally a tall man appeared at the children's gate and offered to take Moriah home. Her *nonna* had warned her to never go with strangers, but afraid to be alone, she took his hand.

"Can you help me find my papa?"

"Of course I can," he said, taking a hold of her hand. The man began walking very fast.

"Are you taking me to my home?" she asked.

The man pulled her hand tighter, hurting her. When she tried to pull it away, he sneered, "You're not going anywhere. You're mine now."

Terrified, but remembering *Nonna's* instructions, Moriah kicked the man with all her strength and pulled her hand from his. She began running as fast as she could, through the park, not looking back. A policeman standing on the corner noticed the child running, and began walking toward her. Moriah ran into his legs, crying, "Help, help," just as her *nonna* had taught her to do. Picking the child up, the officer recognized who she was. The night of the argument, her grandfather had alerted the neighborhood police that his son had taken his granddaughter, and left a picture of her with the watch commander. Knowing where she belonged, he brought Moriah directly to the Vannini home.

When Isabella opened the door, her prayers were answered. She scooped Moriah up and held her for the longest time, touching her hands, feet, arms, all her body parts, to make sure she had been returned intact. The rest of the family gathered, all talking to her at once. Where had she been? Where was Francesco? What had they been doing all these weeks? Isabella waved them away, saying, "Leave the child alone for now; she is frightened. Poor *bambina, tu sei con me, adesso.*" (You're safe.)

She carried her trembling granddaughter into the bathroom, removed her clothing, filled the claw-foot tub with bubbles and drops of her precious olive oil, and brushed all the snarls from her matted hair. *Nonna* sang Italian prayers in a soft tone while Moriah soaked, and then lifted her out, enveloping her in a satin camisole, so only the smoothest of fabric touched the child's skin—to erase any memories of harsher contact that she imagined Moriah might have endured. She carried the child into her own bed, calling out to Pasqualina, "Bring a tray with soup and a glass of water, and put a few drops of red wine in it."

She lay next to Moriah after she ate, and until the child's eyes closed, and her breath softened, she continuously whispered, "*Cara mia*, it's only a bad dream, and it's over. No worry; it's over."

The next morning the family treated her like a princess. *Nonna* made her favorite fried doughboys, with powdered sugar. Her aunts and uncles, who usually paid her no mind, arrived with hugs and gifts—a new doll and a pink stuffed unicorn.

When Moriah saw the animal, she leapt up for joy, thinking it was from her father. She pulled her cousin Sarah aside and told her about the castle and the unicorn that lived in it, but Sarah called Moriah a liar and ran and told their *nonna* that Moriah was making up stories. "But I'm not making it up! Ask *Papa*; he knows. When will he be here, *Nonna*?" she pleaded.

"Moriah, I don't know these things, but for now it's best we forget those days. They will only bring us sorrow. Your father will return, and all will be well again; you will see."

What Isabella didn't say was how.

Moriah couldn't forget her grandfather's harsh words the night they'd left. "Go out that door with that child and you are dead to me. Stop what you are doing, or surely you will die."

He forbade anyone to mention his son's name in front of him. At times, the others would whisper to Isabella, "Any words from Francesco?"

"Not yet," she would say, but her real response came in the form of keeping his bedroom clean and ready for his return.

Three months after Francesco's disappearance, a knock on the door interrupted dinner. "*Tutti seduti*!" *Nonna* said, rising to answer the door. Moriah had snuck out after her and hidden behind the curtain in the entryway. It was a policeman from the neighborhood. He took off his hat when he saw Isabella.

"I'm sorry to bother you, Mrs. Vannini. Francesco is your son?" Isabella nodded.

"Is there somewhere we can sit?"

"*Non e' necessario, dimmi.* (It's not necessary.) Say what you came to say."

"I'm sorry to have to tell you this, but we found him tonight. Well, we found his body. The paramedics did their best, but it was too late."

Isabella faltered. "*Alessandro! vieni qui.*" (Alessandro! Come here.) Their voices lowered, but Moriah heard the words.

"Overdose. It happens with these people."

Then Isabella fainted and was carried into the bedroom, where she would stay all night and all the next day. *Alessandro* left with the policeman to identify his youngest son. The house erupted in a tempest of people crying, arguing—a tumult of family members upended. The front door opened and closed. As the news spread, people came in, and the phone kept ringing and ringing. In all the chaos, no one looked for Moriah. She knelt there in the dark behind the curtain, her eyes closed, hands clasped over her ears, wishing she had not heard those words: "He is dead." She prayed to Saint Francis, "Please, please, let it be a lie. Bring my *papa* home."

The clamor subsided when her grandfather returned. He called for Moriah, and when she didn't answer, he searched the house and found her still hiding behind the curtain. She looked into his eyes when he picked her up and saw they were filled with tears. "Pasqualina, *veni qui*. Put Moriah to bed."

Pasqualina tried to take the child from his arms, but she refused to go. She slipped to the floor and ran to her grandmother's door and pounded on the door, begging to be let in. But the door remained closed.

Her grandfather picked her up again and walked her around until her sobbing ceased, and she fell asleep in his arms. He carried her to her bed and tucked her in. In the night she awoke and ran back to her grandparents' door, determined to wait until her *nonna* came out. In the morning, her grandfather discovered the child asleep outside their door. She refused to talk or move, and finally he relented, allowing the child to remain in the kitchen as long as she ate. Moriah dragged her pillows and dolls over, and camped next to the door. The family busied themselves around the child, leaving her alone. The noises of the kitchen soothed Moriah, helping her pretend that everything would return to normal.

On the second morning, when Isabella opened the door, she saw Moriah asleep against the wall.

"*O bambina dolce.* Come here sweet child. You're delivered to me from Madre Maria."

Moriah grabbed onto her leg. "*Nonna*, I'll never leave you!"

"*O mi Cara*, yes one day you will leave but not for a long, long time. But most important, I will never leave you."

"Promise me, *Nonna,* never ever?"

"Yes, child, never ever! Now we have work to do. Go wash your face, comb your hair, and put on your Sunday best. Don't forget your new black coat and patina shoes; we're going to Mass."

Moriah and her grandmother went to each of their neighbors' doors. Before they could knock, doors would open, and each friend handed Moriah a small saint card and *Nonna* an envelope. Then they left their homes and marched the ten blocks together in silence, to the oldest church in San Francisco, the Cathedral of Saint Francis of Assisi. The monsignor waited for them at the top of the stairs. When they entered, the church was full. The Vannini family was already sitting in the first pews. Moriah and Isabella went to the front, genuflected, and took their place in the first row next to her grandfather and all their children, their heads bowed.

A High Mass was performed. Afterward, the church choral chanted certain selections that Francesco Vannini loved. He grew up in the choir, which was perhaps the inspiration for his love of music. While they sang, *Nonna* took Moriah's hand in hers and tiptoed to the statue of St. Francis. There she put all the envelopes into the offering box and handed Moriah a long-stemmed match. Together they proceeded to light every single votive, over a hundred red candles. The child's face glowed in all the heat. Daughter and mother of Francesco knelt in front of the statue, soft voices repeating "The Simple Oration of Saint Francis." Moriah wanted to stay; there she felt safe. When they left that sanctuary, her father's death closed a door in her heart.

During adolescence, Moriah relied on a frequent routine of slight intoxication to keep the past in the past, always careful though not to go further than smoking marijuana, always cognizant of her father's addiction. Older now, her old methods conflicted with her spiritual practice; she was aware that to move forward, clean lungs and a clear mind were prerequisites. How to avoid opening the floodgates to her hidden self? She struggled between the knowing and the doing. Since her grandmother's death, the pounding in her chest begged to be released.

In an attempt to quell her dissonance, and determined to share her recent prosperity with beloved friends, Moriah decided to celebrate her thirty-third birthday. She organized a feast, inviting all the attendees to submit beforehand a favorite recipe, and suggesting each bring some herbs, flowers, or seeds to help plant the garden she'd designed for her new home. As each smiling friend arrived, delivering beautiful exotic plants or vegetables for the earth, the day unfolded as she hoped. Women bustled in the kitchen applying the final touches to enough food to feed five times the number of guests. In the oven, her *nonna's* pizza dough bubbled, scenting the kitchen. Every available countertop or table was cloaked in salads, pastas, and desserts. Moriah collected the recipes from all the entrees and would later publish a small cookbook, gifting a copy to all who'd had the good fortune to attend.

Antonia, the mother of one of Moriah's best friends, grabbed Moriah out of the fray and escorted her to the empty front porch.

The two of them sat on the stoop and Antonia handed Moriah a brown shopping bag.

"I spent hours wrapping it, as you can see," she laughed.

Moriah removed a baby blanket woven of many colors, crocheted into a spiral. "*Cara*, I began this blanket for a friend's unborn baby. As I worked on it, I had an inspiration to make it different than my usual. When I heard of your birthday celebration, I knew where the inspiration originated. In fact, I finished it on the way over in the car, so there may be a few loose strands. You will fix them, yes?"

She draped it on Moriah's shoulder, and it fit beautifully as a shawl. "Aha, now I see why! It fits you like magic. Happy birthday, darling," she whispered into Moriah's ear. "I love you."

Moriah ran to look in the mirror in the front room and came back, eyes flooded. "My *nonna* crocheted me a blanket once that I carried everywhere, and in one of my moves I lost it. I was heartbroken to think it could not be replaced. Now, another *nonna* brings me one just when I need it the most." She wrapped her arms around Antonia, repeating, "Thank you; thank you."

All of the memories, secrets, unspoken and unmentionable deeds, and the hours and days of losing her innocence, her father, and now her grandmother, came bubbling up to the surface, and she cried. More than in the soft wool, Moriah felt held in the embrace of her grandmother. Afraid that the spell might break, she didn't remove the shawl for the rest of the afternoon. While she shared the food and laughter with her guests, a rising desire began to awaken. She waited patiently for them to leave. Waving good-bye as the last car's wheels backed out over the crunching gravel, she entered her bedroom and removed the painting from under her bed. She opened the dresser and seized the sealed box and carried both items outside to her new garden. The sun's late afternoon glow warmed the stone bench she had placed in the middle of the herb patch. She unwrapped the painting and propped it in front of her, up on the chair next to the glass table.

"Okay, *Nonna*, I'm ready. Talk to me. Tell me of your deepest secrets."

Molecules and Women

Taking the box in her lap and holding her breath, she untied the string and removed the lid. Her heart sank when she removed the journal and found only empty pages as she thumbed through. The only words were a small paragraph on the inside page, below the note she had written to her *nonna*.

"These beautiful pages are for you now, to write to your children. Tell them of your loving heart and what you have waiting for them. And you can tell them about me if you wish. *Ti amo*, Isabella."

She closed the book and held it to her chest, holding back the disappointment, disillusioned by the brevity of her grandmother's final words.

Funny, she thought, she signed it *Isabella*. The box slipped off her lap and fell to the ground. White pages fell out from where they had been tucked tightly into the bottom of the box. Moriah fell to her knees to gather the paper, and the pages began to blow around the garden in the afternoon breeze. She chased after them, picking them up, and then recognized the paper and began laughing out loud.

Moriah remembered her grandmother showing her the butcher paper after one of their shopping expeditions. Isabella, always the thrifty saver, would take the outer wrapping that the imported Molinari salami came packaged in and cut it into small pieces and use the thick white paper to write her shopping lists or notes on. Isabella would save the big pieces from the two-foot salamis for Moriah to color and draw on. She would hang her grandchild's artwork on her sewing room wall and pointed out to all that entered the colorful drawings of unicorns and forests that Moriah loved to paint.

"Look, *Cara*, what wonderful paper; such a shame to throw it away. It's clean and lasts forever. No, no, I put everything to good use, not waste anything. You learn from me, you see. You will always have enough of everything, if you learn this!"

Moriah gathered up the pages, and noticed some had her nonna's special recipes written on them, including details about which meats were to be served with which pastas. Other pages had notes on how to care for her special herbs, and their medicinal usefulness. One sheet was devoted to when to serve *Anisette or Amaretto, Frangelico* or *Sambuca, Limoncelli* or *Grappa,* with espresso after a fine meal. Moriah had forgotten about the cabinet with homemade liqueurs that were Isabella's quiet indulgence. This woman with so many facets had become a devotee of the finest spirits, gathering and experimenting with recipes collected over the years. *"Misterioso, formula magica bella, vero!* she was fond of saying. The true elixir of the gods. Only persons of favored status were ever invited to share her potions.

The last page, written on both sides, started with her usual greeting, written in Italian. Moriah knew she would have to read it aloud in her best *Nonna* voice to understand the words:

Cara mia,
The one thing I have found in this life on earth to be true is energy. The nature of strength one receives with love is the best energy of all. Many persons imagine that money is the most important. Some believe it is power over others; some judge it is how smart you are in school or work. These energies can be important, but none of them are significant compared to love.

My long life has overflowed in blessings and the two great tragedies also brought my greatest joys. You asked about the painting. So I'll tell you of my first great sorrow and gift. Yes, it is me during the Big War in my village. I fell in love with a beautiful man, an artist from Portofino. I was only fifteen years old. In Campo Basso, there were few young men left, all gone to Greece. His father and brothers were soldiers, and as the youngest, he had been charged to take care of his mother. They had come to live with her brother to survive. Marcello helped out in his uncle's bar and was my first love. He first saw me carrying water from the well and painted the portrait. Very talented and so romantic. We were to be married, but on the road to Napoli he was killed by a bomb, like so many others. Terrible times.

Moriah paused, laying the pages on her lap, gazing at the painting. How young that girl at the well was. So much tragedy she endured. Yet, her *nonna* had always been joyful—the first one to laugh and the first one to dance. For the first time, Moriah grasped that Isabella's life didn't start as "wife" or "mama" or "nonna." Picking up the pages, she felt she could hear Isabella's voice.

After the war, I met your grandfather, Alessandro. A kinder man never have I known. He drove a delivery truck and came to Campo Basso to deliver building materials for the town carpenter. He stopped in the cafe for lunch and saw the painting hanging above the bar and fell in love with it. He begged the owner to sell it to him. The bar owner said that it belonged to the young woman portrayed in it. Alessandro went looking for me, no longer so young and joyful, just another lonely orphan living in the convent rectory, cooking for the nuns in exchange for food and a place to live. My sisters had fled to Roma to look for work like most of the single women. So many of our village had died, so many of my family. He found me and fell in love instantly, he said. There were no more formalities, no time for chaperones. Every week when he came though the village he would pick me up and take me to the local bar. No one dared question Alessandro. Did you know his name means the protector and keeper of mankind? He became my protector forever more. I didn't like wine or beer, so he would order me an Anisette. That is where I began my passion.

He understood matters of the heart and, with his patience, in time my love for him grew. Not a childish love, but a woman's love. After we were married, he insisted we hang the portrait wherever the road took us, as a tribute to all pure love. I remember the customs agent asking if Alessandro wanted to sell it. I would have sold it, for any money would have helped. One of the few times my husband grew angry with me.

"Woman, are you crazy? This painting brought us together. If I had not stopped and seen the portrait in the bar, I never would have found you. It's a reflection of love itself!"

He never exhibited jealousy and taught me to never fear or doubt his love. He would hold my hand at times, even in our last years, and tears would form in his eyes, "Non ci credo!" (I cannot believe my good fortune in finding you.) He would always say the words, so I could not take our love for granted. You see, my first great heartache brought me my great love.

The second great sorrow, you already know, was your father, my talented and crazy Francesco. I had lost him to drugs long before he died. So his death actually put an end to his suffering and part of mine. But he brought you to Nonno and me, and your shining heart healed my wound. But I know it was not enough for you. I had other sons; you had only one father. We did our best, and no one could have loved you more, mi Cara. We always tried to protect you from any more sorrow. I have prayed every day for you to be able to forgive me and your father and all his sins. We never spoke of all the pain he caused you, or all his deeds. Maybe, if I had been stronger, I would have helped you more, but I never wanted to know more than I could see. It almost broke your Nonno, the blame he carried until his death. Unbearable for him, to think that our son, my flesh, Alessandro's flesh, could cause an innocent angel like you such harm. But he did, and now I'm no longer there to protect you. It's time to forgive us all and let go of the past! So, mi cara, you must know that the only energy that matters is love: the love you have for your life, the love for your work, the love for your prayers, the love we will always have for you. Energy is not born, nor does it die; it's eternal. I have felt Alessandro's love every day since he left me. I know what I talk about. And our love for you continues, and you will need it. Reach out and take what is open to you, your inheritance from Nonno and me. Share it, and it will multiply.

Un Bacio e abbracci forte,
Nonna

Moriah pressed the letter to her heart and began to hum the chant "*Ave Maria*" that her *nonna* would sing after one of her bad dreams. The afternoon wind calmed as the twilight grew, and the last orange and red streaks faded from blue. Moriah had never thought of her grandmother as an orphan. To have lost so much as a child and still create such abundance in her life! To give so much, out of nothing? Moriah saw she had dwelled too long burying what she lost as a child instead of embracing the gifts that had replaced those losses. Her spiritual practice had prepared her for this moment, not to judge others so harshly, and to walk forward in this new awareness.

As she gazed into the darkening heaven, she saw Venus twinkle on the tip of the brightening crescent moon, and prayed, "Star light, star bright, the first star I see tonight, I wish I may, I wish I might, have the wish I wish tonight. Thank you Isabella. I am a woman no longer afraid of the dark. I accept my inheritance, and wish to find the love for me that you held. I promise to share it and watch it multiply."

Enora's Purse

At least the storm waited for the garden ceremony to end and all the guests to be seated at their tables before it hammered the tin roof with golf ball hail. The reverberation from nature's intrusive ice was drowned out by the sound of clinking glasses and loud voices rising with the pints of ale disappearing at the tables where the guests' throats and bellies were brimming. The lodge's customary adornments of dart boards, table skittles, and tally sheets of the long standing champions had been covered with yards of draped Scottish cloth, the colors of the groom's family.

Only the lodge's tartan apron above the stone hearth remained untouched, but just below it hung a collage of the bride and groom. The two billiard tables were lined up against the wall and covered to create a banquet counter holding the steaming dishes of haggis, hearty stews, vegetables, and fresh fish caught that morning. In one corner of the room sat an overstuffed plaid sofa whose dubious past was disguised as the innocent depository for the guests to place their gifts. What may have started out orderly had turned into a mosh pit of boxes, oddly shaped wrapped bottles, and even some unwrapped homemade cushions, quilts, and brooms.

A worn-comfortable, brown, wing-backed chair had been placed by the stone fireplace for Great-grandma Enora. She had settled in close, to be warmed by the fire. She could view the goings-on and still have her cup of tea at hand. After sixty years of living in the Highlands, she still maintained her English composure among "these heathens," as she so fondly referred to her adopted countrymen, even though her origins were nothing more than northern England factory stock.

Next to her a section had been set up where younger children could play on the floor. A few young mothers with sleeping babies in their arms were sitting in a circle, engaged in lively chat.

Their partners were, no doubt, by the bar trading toasts and cheers; someone had uncovered one of the TVs, and a soccer match was under way.

The band began to play, and with the eating done, guests were moving their chairs to get to the important business at hand, dancing! Enough whiskey had been poured, and the party was getting under way in earnest. The music mixed it up enough so that the younger crowd could dance to a modern beat, with an occasional waltz thrown in so the older ladies might coax their men away from drinking at the bar, whilst the younger ones refilled their glasses or pipes. Enora tapped her feet when the music settled in to a standard. A wry smile crossed her face as she gazed fondly across the room to her husband, who was standing with a group of men—whiskey shot in hand, conversation lit up, likely talking about football or the local MSP folly in Parliament.

Wending her way through the dance floor, a young mother walked hand in hand with her small daughter, who was clutching a daisy in her fist. She bent down and whispered to the child, pointing to Enora. The child let go of the safety of her mother's hand and charged through the crowd of dancers to greet the matriarch of the gathering.

"Oh, sweet Serafina, wherever did you get such a pretty flower? A daisy, no less, my favorite, to be sure," Enora exclaimed. Taking the flower in one hand and patting the chair with the other, Enora invited Serafina to crawl up onto the seat of the chair and receive the big hug that always followed a greeting with her Great-grandmum Enora, and a piece of something sweet she always carried in her purse. Enora continued, smiling up to her American granddaughter

Julia, "Dear, why not leave Serafina with me, and find that grandson of mine and have him twirl you 'round the floor some before he's too far past this side of sober to know how?"

"Normally I'd jump at the chance, Enora. But Fina and I didn't sleep much last night, with the time change and all; takes us a few days to catch up, crossing a continent and an ocean. I'm so tired. Besides, I think Joey needs more to rouse with his mates tonight; he does miss them so. I've a bit of a headache, too. I think I'd rather just sit here with you and enjoy the goings-on from the sidelines. You do have the best seat in the lodge."

"Go fetch yourself some water then, and bring a chair over. I have a compound here, made up from the chemist at the local pharmacy, guaranteed to take away any headache."

"Enora, you always have a solution." The weary mother left for a glass of water and returned with a chair. Serafina, who had sunk into the large lap of the elder woman, her lids growing heavy, would soon be napping. One of the young teens ran over to Enora and whispered into the elder's ear, who then reached into her purse and took out a small packet, which she pushed into the girl's hands. Julia's eyes widened, noticing that the packet was for feminine needs, and mouthed, "Really?"

Enora shook her head yes, and after the young lass ran off to the loo, announced, "Always come prepared for me girls."

Not five minutes later a young boy, tears wetting his cheeks, came over to show Enora a scrape he'd received jumping onto the stone entryway. Again her hand reached into her purse and, like magic, a Band-Aid appeared. A deft application of the bandage was followed by a kiss, and the youngster ran off right as new.

"Wow, Enora," Julia asked, "is there anything you don't carry in that bag?"

"Oh, Darlin', it seems that way sometimes. But the fact of the matter is you can tell a lot about a woman by what she carries in her purse. Now it seems mine has become the local medicine cabinet for my family." Opening it for a minute, she said, "Yes, here are the magnesium tablets for Tavish over there, who will be asking for them before we set off home, after the whiskey has done him in. I even keep my own special elixir, if you catch me meaning. But it wasn't always the case." She brought out a small silver flask and took a nip, then offered it to Julia.

"No, thanks, my head is just easing with your magic compound. Wouldn't want to risk it with whiskey."

"Oh, for gracious sake, I wouldn't think to put that Scottish poison in me gullet. No this here is the finest of Portuguese port. Since the 1600s and King Billy of Scotland, we English have savored the best port in the world. The best inheritance the Scots ever bestowed on the kingdom, I'd say."

Julia looked up, confused. "King Billy?"

"Oh, William the Third to you, I'm sure. Anyway, don't want to waste it on anyone who couldn't appreciate it, that's for sure."

"I'll gladly take a sip now that I know how special it is. After all, it's medicine, right?"

"Here's to us," Enora said, passing the silver flask to Julia.

"Hmm, it's so delicious. You have once again taught me a new delight. It warms my throat, gently. Thank you," she said, passing the container back.

Taking the flask and placing it carefully into a concealed side pocket, Enora laughed, "Our little secret, yes, girl?"

"I adore the chance to share in your secrets, Enora. Now what did you mean by 'it wasn't always the case'?"

"Why, I can remember me first purse. I was all of seventeen, in Newcastle. Did you know that's where I am from?" Julia nodded yes. "Of course you do, I seem to recall it a lot of late, no matter. I was off to work in the factories, during the war, and me mum taught me a proper lady always carried a purse. She gave me her favorite black bag. I tried to refuse, but she was having none of it. 'No, Enora, you do have to go to work to keep us in food rations for the family. You earned it.' She even put a one-pence coin in the bottom for good luck. 'Now, me young lady, remember your purse is your private possession. You don't let anyone hold it or borrow.' Proud I was to have a proper leather bag with a gold clasp. We had few belongings to speak of, modest we were to begin with, but with me pop and older brother gone off to fight, poor is what we became. Mind you, most in our town were no better off. Company we had. Me ma always gave me a few pence from my pay, and insisted I buy something, for me. Even now, I can tell you what that first purse had in it."

"Really? That's amazing, Enora. I couldn't tell you what mine had; I'm not even sure I know what's in my purse today."

"You must remember, back in those times, the war and all, it was the only private effect. Except for clothes, that is, but they were mostly hand-me-downs; and besides, clothes don't count. I can tell you, mine had a compartment for a small hand mirror and comb, a leather coin pocket that mostly was empty, a small lipstick case that came with a thin mirror on the inside to apply the ruby red, and, lastly, a sleeve for my food ration card. At the bottom is where I hid my three treasures."

"What were they?" Julia asked. She leaned in close to hear, as Enora's voice had dropped, and the room's noise had increased to a low din.

"Silk stockings, my diary, and my letters!" Enora said, and laughed. "Funny, isn't it?" Her laughter startled Serafina, who had been lulled to sleep in the women's lap. "Shhh-shhh, little one, go back to sleep," Enora whispered to the child, and like magic the child's eyes closed, she repositioned herself, and fell back to sleep.

"Oh, Enora, I wish I could take you home with me. You do have a way with her. Silk stockings—they don't seem like such a treasure. Why did you keep them in your purse?"

"It was an unusual time for young women. We were afforded a freedom that before the war we never knew. Our men mostly gone to battle, and us working in the factories, we could come and go more as we pleased. Some nights after work, we set off to the public house to listen to the singers and poets that might be gathering there. We only put them on for dancing. One good thing we could do for free. They were so special, it made one feel glamorous. So you had to keep them with you, just in case an opportunity arose. You didn't want to ruin them. I remember before I bought mine, I'd draw a line down the back of my legs, so it would look like I was wearing some."

"That's so odd; now no one wears stockings unless we have to. It certainly was a different time," Julia said, then added, "Is that where you met Grandpa Tavish? Were the letters from him?"

"You must remember child, they were silk, and not that horrible nylon you get today; awful scratchy they are. And, yes, as a matter of fact, Tavish was on leave in Newcastle with some of his mates, a lean specimen in those days. The kilt was a badge that won me over. Hard to resist; quite the charmer, he was."

Glancing over to the bar, Enora caught Tavish's eye, and he raised his glass to her with a wink.

"Still is, the ol' coot," she said, nodding his way. "And as soon as the war was over, he whooshed me up here to the Highlands, and my silk stocking days were over. But, no, the letters were not from him, but another boy."

"Oh, Enora, another boy. How romantic. Who was he?"

"Ah, well, romantic they might have been, but so long ago now, who can remember? The lad was one of your kind from somewhere across the pond."

"Enora, you mean to tell me you can remember the details of all the things you carried in a purse some sixty years ago, but who some letters were from, that you carried in the very same purse, you cannot? I don't believe you."

"Believe me you better, lassie; true I am telling it. He was an airman from the States, but once Tavish arrived, my eyes were only on him. It was the fun of having the letters, more than the substance, you see. Then off to the Highlands and soon Susan was born, and the contents of my black purse quickly changed to carrying nappies, bottles, and bum lotions. I needed a bigger one by the time Mickey was born. I turned in my stylish one for a larger brown leather bag that could carry the small purchases from the store, crayons, biscuits, and anything I wanted to keep secret. I did always maintain me mum's rule; no one was allowed in the purse. No one, not even Tavish."

"What happened to that black one?" Julia asked.

"Not sure. Probably crushed into a corner of my wardrobe. I save everything, you know. I thought to give it to Susan, when she turned sixteen, but she scoffed. 'Wouldn't be caught dead with that old thing, Mum,' she cried. Why look at her over there, standing out separate from all the rest. She always had her own sense of taste."

The two women's attention was momentarily drawn to the mother of the bride, wearing an elegant corral gown with a matching shoulder purse that glittered, in sharp contrast to all the plaid filling the dance floor. A striking woman, it was clear where the bride had received her beauty.

"She worked hard, she did, and I know she had hopes for a bigger deal than this here for her Blair."

"But it's a wonderful wedding, and take a good look at her, Enora. She is smiling so grand there, dancing with the groom's brother. You have to admit, amongst all the plaid, she does bring an elegant touch to the scene, and so does her beaded purse. Wonder what she has in it?"

"Oh, that tiny bag, it isn't big enough to carry more than a gum drop. It's for show. But true, it is a beauty; no wonder she never stood for no hand-me-downs. Lucky she learned to sew early. And now I carry another black bag, loaded with a medicine chest of sorts, like a doctor's bag, you might say." Enora pointed to the soft leather pink handbag by Julia's feet. "So tell me, lass, what have you got in your purse?"

"Probably nothing too surprising," Julia said, laughing. Picking it up, she opened it and called out the items. "Two disposable diapers; a Sippy cup; a packet of colored pencils with a pad of paper; a small storybook; my keys, certainly don't need them here; cell phone; a small brush; and a wallet filled with plastic but no cash. I see what you mean; if someone were to open my purse they would know immediately that I was the mother of a small child. When I was younger, besides my wallet, I'd have had a makeup bag, a jewelry pouch for my earrings or a necklace, an MP3 player with headphones, and a sweatband or a heart monitor. I loved cross-training before Serafina was born and, oh yes, maybe even a book to read when I took the Muni to work. Don't have time for any of that anymore."

Enora gently caressed Serafina's head. "No, I don't imagine you have much time, chasing 'round this angel most the day. But your time will come again. You'll see. I remember, when Susan and Mickey first left home for the university, I bought myself a new purse, the first in twenty years—a large black bag with a shoulder strap—and I vowed I'd never carry someone else's bits and pieces again. I took to filling it with my new passion. I loved to sketch small pictures of our village."

Julia interrupted. "Enora, I didn't know you sketched. You're an artist, too? Your talents run deep."

"Oh no, I was never very good at-tal'. I just loved doing it. But I'd keep a few pads, pencils or charcoal with me at all times. I got pretty good and used the small pictures I drew for cards to send people on their birthdays. I even bought a ticket to London once. I was going to visit all the galleries and study the important artists. I dreamed maybe I could go to ECA. Silly dreamer I was, but I was still a young woman and all. It could have happened."

"ECA, what is that, Enora?"

"Edinburgh College of Art, been around forever, more than a hundred years. Famous it is. I never told anyone, 'cept Tavish, of course. Didn't want the family to feel bad and have to lie and tell me how much they liked my drawings or anything."

"Are those small framed pictures that Susan has in the guest room yours? Why, they are lovely sketches. And Susan doesn't know you drew them? I must tell her. It's not fair she doesn't know. What made you stop?"

"Now stop your blather and promise you'll not say a word. No need to bring up the past; best to let it lie. After Blair and Joey were born, their pop was killed in a car accident. Poor Susan, two small children with no money to speak of, so of course I offered to watch the wee ones so she could return to school and get her degree, to make a good living for her children. And she did fine by them. Why look at Blair up there dancing, so happy. She is one of me favorites, you know. "

"Yes, I think she's everyone's favorite," Julia agreed.

"I like to think I had a hand in it. I never could get close to Susan like I did with Blair. Two different peas in a pod, you might say. So serious, Susan was. I think she sees me as a wee bit provincial," and looking over at her daughter, added, "Maybe more than a wee bit." Enora laughed.

"Blair was more 'bout the outdoors and getting dirty. When she was eight, I bought her first camera. She loved to capture everything in photos. I tried to get her to draw, but she had no use for it. She wanted to see the real thing come to life. We'd walk the meadows behind the church some afternoons, and as she took pictures, I picked up rocks and small wildflowers. And if we went to the shore, I'd come home with shells gathered along the beaches. That's how I came to have all those vases filled with stones and shells. At least once a week, I would have to shake out my bag to clean out all the earth and sand that might have fallen to the bottom. That one sure was the worse for wear. Can you imagine what someone would have thought to look in that bag then? Thank goodness for me mum's rule."

"And what happened to that one?"

"Oh, Blair always admired the soft leather of that bag, so when she started at the university, I gifted it to her to hold her different lenses and film canisters—one pocket for exposed and the other for the fresh. She still uses it today. She told me once it brought her good luck, she did. Maybe so, famous photographer she is. That child never throws anything away either. I'd have to say, it was one of my favorite times in life, and my favorite purse, but no more silk stockings. I still keep my secrets in my purse."

Stroking Serafina's hair, Enora looked up to Julia and said, "My, how you let an ol' woman go wafflin' on. Now this child won't be in the dream much longer; go give your Joey a kiss and take a whirl 'round the floor before the night be over."

Julia stood up and gave Enora a kiss on the cheek. "I do love you so, Grandmum, better than my own blood one, you must know. You better keep that a secret!"

"Cha sgeul-ruin e's fios truer air," Enora said, and laughed at Julia's expression. "It's no secret if three know it. A little bit of Gaelic I picked up over the years."

"I don't know if I could say it, but I love the way it sounds. I always feel better after a chat with you. I'll take you up on the offer. And I'll make your rule my own; my purse from this day forward will be off limits to everyone. But I will never look at another woman's purse quite the same. I'll always want to take a peek."

Watching the young woman walk away, Enora opened her purse and dug her hands deep to the bottom and, finding what she sought, drew it out for just a moment. Fingering the red envelope that held a withered London ticket and folded letters, she smiled. *I might give it all to Blair, one day, as a memento of a foolish ol' lady.* Then realizing there would be too much explaining to do, she placed the envelope back in the bottom of the purse.

Cape House

Herding Eli and Jacob out the door, she heard the phone. *To know or not to know, which is better?* It had been two months since Felicity returned from the cape; still, every time the phone rang, she thought, *Granddad*. It is still better to know.

"Jacob, help Eli get in the car. Mommy has to answer the phone."

"No, Mom, we'll be late for school."

"Don't worry; we have plenty of time."

"But, Mom!" Jacob complained.

"Hush now, and hurry up, boys. I promise Mommy will be right back."

Running back into the house, she picked up the receiver just as the machine answered, *Happy summer to you. John, Jacob, Eli, and Felicity can't get to the phone. Know that we cared you took the time to call; please take the time …*

"Hallo, I'm here," she spoke into the mouthpiece, her breathing labored from the dash to reach the phone.

"Hi, girl, glad I caught you."

"Well, actually, we were just leaving for school. The boys are already in the car, Mom. Can I call you back?"

"Your granddad's gone."

She held the phone against her eyes, exhaling, aware of her mother's breath, as the tears began to drip from her eyes; she knew that her mother's were dripping too.

"Death doesn't come quickly, does it, Mother?"

"No—not if we're lucky. And it isn't ever easy. We'll talk later." Her mother whispered, "I love you," and hung up. Felicity stood holding the earpiece, listening to the droning dial tone.

For two months it had been a waiting game, every phone call back to Massachusetts for an update, a held breath. At first, the weekly check-in consoled Felicity, allowing her the luxury that perhaps they would continue indefinitely. By September, the weekly hour-long calls became short chats every few days. As his breath became labored, and he was relegated to bed rest, most calls consisted of his "Hello," and then Felicity recapping the latest adventure of Jacob or Eli, attempting to keep up both sides of the conversation, and ending with their mutual "I love you." Two nights ago he surprised her and ended with, "Too much time. Foolish waste of time, staying here. Girl, you know I'm ready, so there's nothing to fret about. See you on the other side."

Too much time here, she thought. "And now, no more time left," Felicity spoke to the empty room. She had not called him back.

She walked to the car, no longer in a hurry. Her two little men were plopped in their seats, struggling to get their seat belts snapped.

"Change of plans, guys. We're going to take the day off. Woo-hoo, today is a very special day. And before you go worrying, Jacob, I'll talk to your teacher, and we'll do your homework together. But first, let's go to The Bagelry. We can each pick out our favorite bagel and spread. Then, let's go down to Twin Lakes and eat our snack on the benches."

Felicity reached in and unhooked Eli's latch; lifting him from the car, she squeezed him and gently placed him on the walkway. "Eli, run back in the house and grab the old bread from the back porch for the ducks. They will want to join our party." In the front seat Jacob was fumbling with his backpack. "Here, pass it over to me. I'll put it into the trunk, where your books will be safe."

"Mom, what are we celebrating?"

"It will be a surprise, Jacob."

When the rusted Volvo pulled out of the driveway and sputtered down the street, Felicity's thoughts returned to the cape house, to the last day spent with her granddad.

She had awoken to the August morning's brilliant salutation, aglow through the arched window. She pulled the pillow away from her face, eyes closed, and warmth spread over her skin; the heat exhaling from her nostrils cheered her heart. Pushing her feet against the yellow threadbare sheet until it fell to the floor, her body savored the wave that bathed down her neck, painting a glossy sheen over her bare skin. Slowly, as if releasing from a lover's embrace, she turned over; her sore back muscles softened beneath the sun's touch. She crawled back under the downy pillow, prepared to stay in this blissful state a while longer, adrift on the sea breeze that floated in through the window.

Felicity remembered her yoga teacher's soft instructions in the studio darkness: "Quiet the conscious breath, and the mind will follow with grace." *I should do some yoga this morning*, she thought.

Noises from below broke through her rumination. Granddad's tender voice wended its way up the back stairs, followed by the twitter of morning birds cantering outside his kitchen window. Even with eyes still closed, she could see him laying out the birdseed on the open sill, a silent invitation to indulge to their beaks' delight.

She imagined his tanned arms reaching up to the top shelf to retrieve the red Folgers coffee can, and then carefully measuring eight spoons, not spilling a single ground on the counter. She could hear the tap water slosh into the coffee pot and the burst of the flame as the old gas stove lit. The only thing missing was the soft murmuring of her grandmother Daisy's voice, as the couple discussed their chores or the shopping that might be their day's task, all the while stirring the daily oatmeal in her cast-iron pot, throwing in raisins, apples, or any other summer fruit available. Her worn blue slippers brushed the tile floor as she moved around the kitchen.

In this quaint cottage where she had spent her childhood summers, Felicity always felt protected, alongside Daisy's skirts or holding Granddad's strong hands. This sanctuary on a Cape Cod beach, with its sweeping porches and rickety stairs falling into the sand, had been where Felicity felt free. Away from parents' expectations or demands, she would roam the dunes, searching for buried treasures. Or, on rainy days, rummaging through Daisy's old trunks in the attic; dressing up and imagining another life, she would write plays for the three of them to perform in the evening.

Soaked in these familiar sounds and memories, Felicity waited until the percolator began its "plop plop" as the coffee bubbled into the glass top. She kept her eyes closed until the coffee's aroma wafted up the stairs. Unable to resist further, she sprang from her nest and wrapped her grandmother's blue chenille robe, the one with the paint stains, around her. A few years back, they had decided to repaint the porch rockers. That night, Daisy and Felicity came out to watch the Perseid meteor shower cross the night sky, forgetting about the wet paint. Daisy rocked in the chair, while Felicity lay on the ground at her feet, soaking up the celestial event. The oil-based paint permeated the robe. "No fuss," her grandmother said. "It will remind me of this wonderful night forever."

Felicity had rescued it from the giveaway box; a hint of rosewater still lingered. At the top of the stairs, her senses betrayed her intellect. She would never think to drink such unrefined coffee at home. What with all her imported beans and special tea blends, no contest, and yet, here in this house, Granddad's coffee was perfect. Bounding down the stairs two at a time, she slipped and missed the last corner, crash-landing on the sturdy wringer washer tub.

"Whoa there, girl; such a hell racket you're making. What chased you out of the attic, bats or demons?"

"No, Granddad, just your amazing brew percolating on the stove and memories of you and Grandma. Remember when I could fly down those stairs, and Daisy would wait at the bottom to catch me? But I guess my body doesn't quite have the ability to fly no more."

"Well, Felicity, I guess none of our bodies can do what they once could. Ready for a cup?"

"Fill her up with your magic potion," Felicity teased, wrapping her arms around this gentle lean sentry.

"Magic? Why, child, nothing special about this coffee—been making it the same for over fifty years. I'm just grateful that I saved this big old red can last year. Everything's always changing. Why, the new ones are plastic. Just doesn't seem right, coffee in a plastic tub. New and improved, my foot; the red can worked fine all these years. No need to improve it!"

"But that's what makes it so special, Granddad." Felicity reached for a fat mug off the wooden stand. They had made the rack her second summer at the cape. Granddad had showed her how to sand the driftwood into a base, then insert and glue dowels into it. Daisy had brought out her paints, and cheered Felicity on to decorate it with anything she gathered while beachcombing.

"I sure do miss Grandma. Do you ever get used to her not being here?" Felicity asked, blinking a tear.

"Oh, she's still here, Sweetie Pie. She's in the wood, the tile, and the glass, even the earth outside. And, yes, I do miss her, especially between the sheets."

Felicity covered her ears playfully. "More information than I want to think about, you dirty old man."

"Well, better than a grumpy old man, don't you think?" he chided. Granddad patted the top of her head and scooted her out of his kitchen. Felicity took her cup out to the sun porch, eager to revel a bit in Daisy's old rocker.

She was disappointed to see her mother occupying her favorite spot. Faith's lean muscular legs were propped up on the slide ottoman. She casually sipped the silver straw from her gourd of mate´, an electric kettle and a plate with a croissant on the side table.

Felicity, a shorter reproduction of her mother, sometimes felt diminished in her company. Being the runt in a family of long-legged beauties could have hobbled Felicity, but inheriting her grandmother's fiery resilience had secured her a superior allure.

Trying to suppress her irritation, Felicity smiled and asked, "Morning, Mother. Glad to see you're up early this morning. Hope you are ready to attack the boxes of paperwork."

"Oh, Felicity, how can you drink that dreg? Wouldn't you like to sip mate´? I brought a fresh sack of yerba with me from Argentina—your favorite, Fleur de Lis."

"No, this is just perfect." Felicity sat down next to Faith on the hanging wicker bench and curled her legs under her. The sway of the swing soothed the irritation she had been developing toward her mother all week. "We can begin on the boxes as soon as you finish your breakfast, okay, Mother? We should get an early start back to the airport."

"Don't stress, darling. We have plenty of time," Faith countered. "Our flight doesn't take off until this evening. There's this great little shop over in Pilgrim's Heights I want to check out. Sue updated me the other day; the Grey Whale opened their studio for local artists to exhibit. Sound interesting?"

Felicity pushed the warm mug to the side of her head, struggling to lock out a week's worth of frustration rising in her throat. "Mother, what are you thinking? We only have this morning left to sort through Daisy's paperwork. Every day you have found something else to while away your time. You promised to sort through the boxes filled with letters and cards. I don't know what you might want to keep or save. We can't leave it for Granddad. After all, that's what we came out here to do, isn't it?"

"Oh, honey, don't frown so. It hardens your face. I'm aware what I promised, sweetheart, and we'll get to it as soon as we get back. I mean it. Who knows when we'll be out this way again, what with our separate lives and your boys growing so fast?"

Faith placed the gourd on the table, leaned over, and reached out to rub Felicity's neck. "Let's put that beautiful smile back on your face. The one you came out here with. We can stop at the bakery for some of those buns you love so much. We'll finish our drinks and get dressed. No sense wasting a single moment of this brilliant morning. Not a cloud or fog bank in sight."

Felicity stood up, not wanting to give Faith the opportunity to avoid the topic. "Come on, Mother, you're doing it again. We need to start now, not later."

"Yes, we'll do it. Now let me give you a five-minute rub, while you relax a moment. All work and only work, never fills the heart at the end of the day, for anyone. Remember, Daisy always taught us that."

Felicity exhaled and surrendered. No use arguing. Faith was the only person more headstrong then herself. The woman had survived years of isolation and clinical depression due to relentless chronic pain. The illness that had incapacitated her eventually became Faith's portal to the outside world. In her desperation to cope, she had begun a daily routine of breathing exercises, and a journal of her suffering and the thoughts that accompanied it.

Encouraged by her doctor to publish her work, to help others, she discovered financial success that set her in motion to travel to China, where doctors utilized acupuncture to treat the condition successfully. The one downside to her recovery was that Faith, a previous borderline doormat, transformed into an immovable force when she had an inspiration. Felicity, although grateful for her mother's restored health, at times longed for a devoted overbearing mother, the type her friends complained about—a doting mother who might sacrifice for her daughter's wishes.

This week had stretched Felicity's compassion. The opportunity she had fantasized—a week away from her boys, a week of leisure and unfettered meanderings—never materialized. Felicity had been left to sort through fifty years of her grandparents' lives; packing old dishes, household items, and clothes, and hauling them over to a local shelter, had occupied her days.

Granddad had surprised her, though, with his enthusiasm and willingness to let things go. "I can't believe she kept all these theater billings. She was a pistol. Pretty enough to play the leading lady, but she preferred the offbeat roles. She could have been a big star, but she had no longing for the limelight."

Fingering the programs from Daisy's life as an actress with the Berkshire Theatre Troupe, he generously shared intimate stories of the different items. Then, just as easily, he boxed up the books, clothes, and everything else not attached to the floors. Even a beautiful Tiffany lamp had not been safe from the purging that took place.

"But, Granddad, you said yourself it was a wedding gift and probably very valuable. Don't you want to save it, or sell it?"

"Nope, Felicity. Haven't used that old lamp since we had the track lighting installed. It still works though; might as well let someone else get some use out of it. How can I sell what brought years of pleasure? No, let it be a gift for a lucky person."

They had reduced the rooms to their bare minimum, erasing fifty years of summer living. It had been hard work, and each night after dinner Felicity had plopped onto the mattress, grateful for its comfort. The hours to explore the expansive shoreline, gathering shells or treasure-hunting the dunes, never materialized.

In contrast, Faith had managed to find excuses to keep her occupied elsewhere. Monday, an old friend called with an urgent request that could not be ignored. Tuesday, a group from the library, hearing of her arrival on the island, asked if she wouldn't have an impromptu reading; they had featured her latest publication as a summer "must read." Then, Thursday, she got it in her head to bring out Grandma Daisy's old recipe book and bake up a batch of her mother's gourmet cookies. She baked more than three people could eat in a month, necessitating that the delicious abundance be delivered to the local senior centers, just as Daisy might have done.

Coming down the stairs, Felicity found Faith already waiting in the car. Her mother casually hummed a melody and tapped a beat with her fingers on the window. While driving out to the highway, moving farther away from the boxes that waited for them, a groan escaped Felicity.

"I hope you know what we're doing, Mother, because I certainly don't."

Faith looked over at her daughter and smiled but did not shift the gentle tune she purred. When they came to the junction at Pilgrims Heights, she motioned for her daughter to go straight to Meadow Heads Road instead of into town.

"I have a better idea. Trust me."

Her mother's quiet demeanor had calmed Felicity, so she dutifully turned east to the end of the cape, off the main road and onto a dune trail. They rolled over the black broken asphalt. The previous night's brief summer storm had blown sand across the road in shallow piles that made a watery mirage as they drove, granules splashing off the tires. The early-morning sun, bouncing yellow off the powdery grass, further softened Felicity's mood.

As the car came to a stop at the end of the road, Faith quickly jumped out before her daughter turned the ignition off. She crossed around to the driver's side, opened the door, and pulled Felicity out of the car.

"Remember when you were little, when I would come to pick you up, what the last thing we would do before we would go home to Boston?"

Not waiting for an answer, she kicked off her shoes and grabbed her daughter's hand, pulling her over the top of the dunes. "Ready, aim, and roll," she yelled. Faith lay down on the edge, her lean body taut and her arms stretched out behind her. "Last one down's a rotten egg," she said with a laugh, as she let herself go rolling down the steep dune.

"Oh, no, you don't," cried Felicity. "No fair, head starts," she yelled out as she threw herself down and began to roll after her mother. Limbs flailed and childish voices screamed as the two tumbled down the embankment. Felicity landed on top of her mother as they crashed to the bottom.

"I win; I win!" she celebrated, lifting herself off her mother.

Felicity stood and wiped the sand from her face and eyes, shaking her head to and fro, like a dog wagging off water.

Faith, unable to stop laughing, continued until the laughter turned to tears.

"Mother, are you all right?" Felicity stooped down to offer her a hand.

"Yes, I'm okay. I laughed so hard that I almost wet my pants!" Trying to lift up on her daughter's reach, Faith pulled Felicity down on top of her again, and their giggles returned.

"Oh, stop, please stop, or I'll pee Granddad's coffee all over me."

"Serve you right for drinking such dreg," teased Faith.

"You are such a food snob."

"It takes one to know one," Faith retorted, standing up. "Now, let's change these shorts, dump the pound of sand we just collected, and get a move on."

After climbing back up the dune to the car, the two women stripped down to their birthday suits and brushed the fine white granules off each other as best they could. Faith leaned into the backseat and pulled out the raffia bag she always carried. They wrapped themselves in red hibiscus sarongs topped off with the straw hats that she had adopted for summer wear. The two women walked along the shoreline hand in hand. About a mile down the beach, they came across two weathered wicker chairs partially buried below some battered, crumbling stairs.

"I wonder who they belong to. There doesn't appear to be any house up above," Felicity said.

"Buried treasure," mocked Faith. "Perhaps they once belonged to a summer bungalow owned by a lonely writer now lost and forgotten, and were long since taken away by nor'easter storms."

Felicity shook her head and smiled. "Well, maybe not quite treasure, but definitely not a bad find."

They dug them out and dragged them down to the water's edge. The sun reached its zenith in the cerulean sky, reflecting a hot whiteness that absorbed the sand and left the beach shimmering. To keep cool, they placed the rickety chairs on the wet sand in the gentle lapping of the surf. Neither woman spoke for fear that words might break the spell that had spun between them.

A flock of sleek seafaring gannets appeared skimming the surface of the ocean, one with the water. Their snowy white wings glistened in the bright sun; breaking formation, they soared high in the bright sky and began to plunge, diving to the sea.

"They are so dazzling. I love watching the pelicans in Santa Cruz, but these birds are regal. Oftentimes I feel my life is skimming the surface, each day passing. Is it all for those moments that we soar and plunge recklessly into the deep, knowing, or not, what lies below? You were right, Mother; this was a great idea," Felicity whispered as she took her mother's hand in hers.

"Well, glad you approve of something I've done, my dear," Faith nodded, her gaze fixated on the slow rollers that were beginning to come in. With each new wave, the water lapped a little higher on their chairs. "I'm sorry I let you down this week, girl. I guess I just didn't realize how hard it would be for me. I can't trim my mother down to her effects. So many days I still reach for the phone to call her, and when I hold the receiver and realize there's no number to dial, I ache. When I was most ill, not a day went by that she did not call me. She never allowed me to give up on myself. There were days that her voice was all I heard outside of my own thoughts. It grounded me so to this earth, held me until I could hold myself again."

"I'm sorry, Mother. I tried to be there too. When I went away to college, it became easy to distance myself. Maybe too easy? You never mentioned this before, even in your writings."

"Honey, no blame, please. It was enough that you had to deal with me during high school; I know it wasn't easy. I was not your job. You had your life, and you took it. It saved me from adding culpability to my plate. Daisy always said, 'Guilt is a most useless state of mind, a lose/lose situation, highly overrated.' When I wrote my acknowledgments in my book, I realized that there were not words to describe the essence of my mother's touch, her birthing me twice. In my heart, I cannot box that. I'm not ready to reduce her to memories just yet. Sometimes I talk to her, and I can hear her answer me, you know. I guess I'm afraid I'll lose that sense of her, jeopardize what I still have. Granddad will be leaving us soon, too. I know it in my bones."

Felicity looked over incredulously. "Oh, no, he's not sick again, is he? I thought he looked pretty good, especially after all he's been through this year. I did notice his coughing yesterday in the attic, but he told me not to worry, it was just the dust."

"Well, he hasn't told me directly, but that's not my father's way. 'Stubborn and stoic, a deadly combination,' my mother would say. When he made her mad, she would declare, 'Dash it all. The SS Stuart must have sailed in last night.'"

"I remember her mumbling that sometimes, but I never understood what she meant by it. It didn't seem like a good thing to ask about, and Granddad would offer to take me for a walk. I just thought it was their code or something. Hmm, I guess it was."

"He called us out here, asked us to pack away the summer home; that's his way. It never really was about the furnishings. He's not sure whether to sell the property or leave it to me and you. We did speak briefly, after the funeral, about it. I, for one, do not want the headache. That's why I didn't have you bring the boys. I don't think he has the strength for their energies, and it would only bring it all out in the open."

"But then I would have wanted them to come out too, at least one more time. I'm not ready for him to leave. It's only been nine months since Daisy's been gone."

"Not necessary, sweetheart." Wiping a tear from her daughter's cheeks and taking Felicity's hands in hers, Faith continued, "Honey, you were always his Sweetie Pie. He needed you here now. Besides, they spent Easter together. Granddad had those two monkeys climbing all over him for days. We couldn't separate them, remember? All the fishing, sailing, and fires on the beach. He doesn't have that strength now, and it would have only served to sadden him. 'Good-byes are highly overrated.' Another favorite on my mother's list appears to be my father's favorite too. He has not been robust for a while, and, well, Daisy embodied his strength. Fifty-seven years together is a long run. They planned for him to go first, you know. After all, he was ten years her senior. This time together is his way of giving us the opportunity to take whatever we want. I don't need anything, but you might."

"Mom, why didn't he tell me, or you, for that matter? I might have looked at their belongings differently if I had known."

"Really, Felicity? Would you have traded this time, this week with him? Can any object give you more than this? I don't think so." The next wave swept up, licking their knees. "Guess it's time to go, darling. Help me up, please. Those rolls down the dune may be a bit much for an old girl like me. Maybe I should have done some yoga stretches before attempting it," Faith said, and laughed.

Molecules and Women

Felicity rose, extended her hand, and helped lift Faith up, hugging her as she stood out of the chair.

"Mom, why tell me now instead of later, when we're home?"

"That's easy, girl. I didn't want you brooding and angry at me all the way back to California. Besides, I don't agree with all of my father's methods. I will be returning here in a few weeks to stay with him and close the house. He's not going back to Boston, and has decided to go live in a senior facility. He brought the brochures with him to show me. Even though it's hard to imagine him not in his home, without Daisy, it's more difficult than comfortable. I know, with your complicated life, you won't get the opportunity to come back. I need you to relax with me while you finish off those boxes, or not. Use the time wisely. In the end, isn't it the most precious gift we have?"

The two women gathered themselves up and, hand in hand, walked up the beach in silence. A wave sloshed up their legs and soaked their sarongs. The cool water was a welcome relief to their steaming bodies. When they reached the car and began changing into dry wear, Felicity asked, "Mom, do you have any room in your suitcase? I only brought a small carry-on."

"Sure, I can make some for you. What do you need to put in?"

"Just some clothes I need you to take back. I want to make room in mine for a big red can and a mug stand."

"You silly sentimental darling, I have watched you all week with Granddad. And I have learned a few things about my father and daughter. His grace and your diligence will guide me through the next months. You know what they say; the fruit doesn't fall far from the tree. I think that you fell off the Daisy tree, lucky you. A fine tree to have fallen from."

They arrived at Twin Lakes, and Felicity turned off the car. She turned to her boys, and seeing Jacob's big brown eyes staring up at her reminded her of her granddad. She'd never noticed how much alike they looked. Tousling Jacob's mop much like Granddad had always tousled hers, Felicity let out a whoop. "Why, we're celebrating your great-granddad's big adventure. He has gone to join your great-grandmother, Daisy. He left this morning on a shooting star. Eli, grab the bread, Jacob you bring the juice and the water. I'll grab the bagels, and I'm thinking we can sit around the lake, and I'll tell you stories about how it was growing up, and spending my summers with them at the cape house. We could sing the silly songs he taught me. What do you say? Think that's a good idea?"

Return Home

A silver-haired woman sat in the car, eyes softly opened, hands folded in her lap, breathing in the silence. The rattle of the cooling car engine finally subsided, allowing the quiet of the land to seep in. The windshield framed the pastoral scene before her, a painting she felt compelled to step into.

She pushed open the car door, and a warm summer breeze greeted her. The leaves in the woods beyond the field filled the hush with their voices. Lured by the promise of answers, Elena walked from the road toward the farmhouse, her pace quickening, half expecting Aunt Amelia to open the porch screen door to greet her. She recalled how she had loved her aunt's blue tennis shoes, the ones Amelia had cut the sides out of, so she could wiggle her toes and keep her bunions from rubbing.

Why, of all the things to remember, she thought, *would I think of that?*

She stopped next to the creaking windmill that sputtered due to its bent and missing blades. The loose barn door slammed in the wind, releasing a long moan from its graying timbers. Built by her Finnish ancestors in the 1840s after leaving the Midwest to venture to California, the whole western side appeared to be kneeling down to the setting sun. The massive landmark barn had been collapsing forty years earlier, when Elena had run through chasing her kittens. She was comforted that it still stood.

She envisioned Uncle Charlie carrying full milk buckets, his black field boots covered in sticky hay as he marched from the barn to the back porch. He would pause to wipe them on the iron shoe grate before he entered Amelia's sanctuary. As the memories flooded in, Elena reached for the railing on the garden fence to steady herself.

The stone bench her father Virgil had placed next to the birdbath came into view. She went through the gate and sat down. Now empty, the basin, had green stains from where mildew streaked its bottom. Elena lingered and yielded to the moment.

After her father's disappearance, she searched for him every day in hopes that he would come out of hiding. Elena remembered circling the whole yard yearning to see his blue and green striped shirt emerge from behind the grain tower or woodpile, or appear from the fields, hopeful that if her father returned, then her mother, Beth, would come home too.

She remembered the day he got lost. She had been playing near the barn with her pets. He'd come out of the house through the back garden with his shotgun over his shoulder.

"Papa, can I come with you into the woods?"

He didn't turn or answer, just kept walking away into the field. She stood to run after him but remembered the kittens that were her responsibility. Later, as she ran around the garden teasing them with a red skein of yarn to chase in the grass, she heard the familiar shotgun blast. Aunt Amelia, who busily hung sheets on the line close by, said, "Sounds like Virgil caught us something for dinner."

But dinner never came. Sometime later, Uncle Charlie appeared out of the field in a hard run, hollering to Aunt Amelia. The two began conversing loudly in the old language, the grunts and sharp sounds that Elena couldn't understand. With all the commotion, Aunt Sarah scurried out of the house. As she stood listening to her siblings, she began to wail, startling Elena. Amelia grabbed Sarah and spoke harshly, pointing to the child, and mentioned Beth's name, and then Charlie and Amelia ran off. Aunt Sarah rushed over and lifted Elena up from the grass and held her too tightly as she carried her into the living room. Elena remembered that Aunt Sarah's cheeks were wet, and her own shirtsleeve was damp when she put her on the couch.

"I'll go gather your kittens and lock them into the barn where they'll be safe. When I come back I'll fix you something to eat. You stay put and read your book until I return."

Elena heard the back screen door slam, and she waited in the quiet room. Shortly after, she heard Sarah's footsteps up the stairs, and the porch door open. The clatter of pans in the kitchen reverberated, mixing with funny groans. Sarah appeared with a tray of cabbage and carrot soup and a chunk of brown bread covered in honey. Unexpectedly, she placed the tray on the coffee table, where no one ever ate.

"It's okay, Elena; it will be our secret. Just be careful to not spill a drop on Amelia's rug."

The usual bubbly aunt sat silently, looked at magazines and listened to the Zenith radio that stood in the center of the living room while the child ate. When she finished, Sarah carried the tray into the kitchen. The rattle of scrubbing the plates muffled the woman's weeping. Aunt Sarah reappeared with cookies and milk in one hand while wiping her eyes with the other.

"What's wrong with your eyes, Auntie? Where has everyone gone? Can't I go outside and play with my kittens again?"

"No child, better we stay in. How about we cut out pictures of the pretty clothes in the magazines? I could make new clothes for your paper dolls."

When night fell, she combed out Elena's ponytail, slowly brushing her long blonde tresses, then tying them in a fancy pink ribbon.

"Aren't Mama and Papa going to tuck me in, Auntie?" Elena looked up into Sarah's red eyes.

Blinking back the tears, Sarah hugged her niece. "No, sweetie, not tonight."

"But where have they gone? And Uncle Charlie and Aunt Amelia, too?"

Just then, Amelia's steps could be heard on the stairs, and Sarah ran out of the bedroom to greet her on the landing. Elena listened to the two women speaking, again, in the old language. Then Amelia swooped in and picked up Elena and gently rocked her. "It will be okay, child. Your mother will be home tomorrow. I am here now and will always be here for you. We will say our prayers together tonight, you and I. And afterwards, I'll sit with you until you fall asleep. If you like, I'll sing you a lullaby that your grandmother sang to all us girls."

And she did. She held the little girl for the longest time before tucking her in. Elena felt confused, unaccustomed to Aunt Amelia at bedtime. This had been her special time with her parents. Mama Beth would read stories of faraway places, and Papa Virgil would draw pictures of the house that he would build for them one day. They would map out where they each wanted their rooms. Sometimes, Elena would stay up late with them, hatching big plans. She insisted she could not fall asleep unless they both tucked her in together. Her mother called them the Three Musketeers—one for all, all for one.

Elena roused in the middle of the night and found Aunt Amelia slumbering in the chair next to her bed, her hand still resting on the child's shoulder. She fell back to sleep and was awakened in the morning by Amelia's shake. It would be the first time she gave Elena the velvety pink towel, the first time Amelia dressed her. And it was the first time Elena looked into those blue eyes, though that day they were red and puffy. She began to feel afraid. The house was silent and cold; the familiar sounds of the men's boots tromping around down below were missing. Only the kettle whistled.

"Where are Mama and Papa?"

"Don't fret child, your mama will be here soon. After you go outside and do your business, you can help me put together a new recipe for berry pancakes. You can even stir in the fruit," Aunt Amelia consoled.

But her mama never really did come home again, only another woman who looked like her. That afternoon, when Beth walked through the door, Elena ran and threw her arms around her mother's legs.

"Mama, I'm so glad you are back. It was so scary when I woke, and you were not here. Where is Papa? Isn't he with you?"

"No. He will not be coming home, ever. Now run along; go play with your kittens," she blurted, then hurried from the kitchen.

Amelia knelt down next to Elena, taking her hand and patting it. "It's okay child; your mama has a lot to take care of now, and needs to rest a while. Sarah, take Elena and go collect the fallen walnuts before they rot on the ground. They will spice up my strudel tonight."

As they walked out into the porch Elena overheard someone say, "Virgil was lost, poor man."

Elena did not understand. Why didn't someone go find him? That is what you're supposed to do when someone gets lost. She had a lost kitten once and searched everywhere until she found it in the pantry behind the flour sacks. It had been locked there for hours. Another time all the men went out looking for a new calf that had wandered off from the field. They found it after dark in the woods crying for its mama. But who was searching to find Virgil?

After her husband vanished, Beth asked the family to call her by her given name, Inga, instead of the nickname Virgil preferred, confusing the child even more. Every night before bed, mother and daughter knelt to pray. But Beth never named Virgil in the long list of family names for the angels to watch over. After her mother would leave, the child would creep from the covers, kneel down again, and whisper her own prayer to the angels.

"Please bring Papa home, and Mama Beth too. I promise to be the best little girl—do my chores and never make anyone angry."

The memories jarred Elena. She was surprised she could remember every single word spoken and the feelings from so long ago. *Stop*, she told herself. *Stop! You did not come all this way to rehash this pain! What's the point?*

Leaving the garden, careful to close the gate behind her, Elena looked up into the walnut tree by the back porch and saw the last strands of the hemp rope that had held her swing twisting in the afternoon breeze. How many children might have swung in it long after she had left the farm? She walked up the steps but found the door nailed shut, and so sat down on the stoop. The mooing of cows in a neighboring pasture brought back its own flood of images.

She remembered jumping off the swing to follow Uncle Charlie into the house after the evening milking while Aunt Sarah parked herself at the sewing machine, busily attaching white lace to a set of curtains for the living room. The bone buttons of Sarah's blouse danced on her belly from her frequent giggles and laughter. The only child in this tall Finnish family, Elena had been afraid to look up at their large faces.

"Come here, Elena. What are you waiting for? Step up on the stool and scrub your hands before dinner," Inga called, holding out a bar for her.

Climbing up, she took the giant bar of lye soap that she needed both hands to hold. Slippery and wet, it required all her strength not to drop it, and she was afraid it would be impossible to reach to the bottom of the basin if she did. Uncle Charlie's sturdy reach arrived just in time. One quick pump on the handle and water flowed over the soap, suds dripping from his hands above Elena's like falling snow. She caught the bubbles into her hands and then squished them and then squirted them back up to his. Another longer thrust on the lever, and water poured out, splashing her all the way up her arms.

"Charlie, don't drown the child, for pity's sake," Aunt Amelia scolded her brother.

"Ah, Amelia, we're just having fun. Look, Elena has found a smile in her pocket."

He laughed as he took his enormous fingers and shook them into her smiling face. Grabbing a towel, he wiped his hands in the middle and Elena dried hers on the bottom of the towel. Uncle Charlie's red-checkered shirt rubbed against her cheeks as he stood over her. The fragrant scent of fresh cow's milk still lingered there. Every day her uncle would grasp the cows by their ears to lead them to the milking pens, and kiss each one on the top of the head before he tied the cow to the post.

"Elena, enough already," her mama's sharp voice intruded, ending the cheerfulness. "Help your Aunt Sarah set the table, child."

Uncle Charlie's warm hands lifted Elena up, swung her next to the table, gently stood her on the stone floor, and kissed the top of her head as he had the cows. She watched his black shiny belt walk away and disappear into the porch as he went to gather wood for the stove. Aunt Sarah's chubby pink hands passed Elena a dish from the sideboard to place on the wooden table that stood in the middle of the kitchen. Her aunt offered the heavy plates one at a time, instead of six all at once like her mother did.

"Fewer trips to the hutch, child; you will learn to save time and save energy!" she'd state.

Inga's middle name should have been Efficiency. The crisp white shirt, long black skirt, and gray woolen sweater she wore every day perplexed Elena. She recalled being rocked in her mama's lap, caressed by a velvety blue skirt, her head nuzzled on a silk blouse as her mother sang her lullabies. Elena could not be sure if this was an imagined memory or true. Her mama's soft, downy skin stretched around plump lips; her sapphire eyes were speckled with flecks of gold. Elena had felt the smiling song caress her cheeks.

Where had that soft woman gone? "Beth," that's what they had called that mother. Inga stood straight, ready with her black-stockinged legs sunk into taut laces and hard wooden heels, resolute and organized, keeping Elena out of harm's way.

"Don't move too quickly or jump down stairs. Elena, walk, don't run, and you won't skin your knees," she'd warn. "Careful child! Place the glasses down quietly. Don't clink the silverware."

Inga would force a tuck in Elena's shirt, lick her finger to push back an errant hair from the ponytail, brush lint off her daughter's skirt; but nevermore the caress, or long hug and hold. Except for the kiss goodnight on the forehead after their nightly prayers, Elena never got to feel those plum lips anymore.

During the week, Inga left the farm before daylight, to walk the three miles to San Miguel, where she taught at the one-room schoolhouse. She didn't return till evening. It hadn't always been that way. Beth used to come home at noon to care for her daughter and husband. Mother and daughter would work together, laundering the clothes or readying box lunches for afternoon picnics and berry-picking.

On Fridays, they always rode to town on her papa's chestnut mare to do the household shopping, finishing at the candy bins for a bag of penny candy. Her parents had promised her a pony of her own, when they had their own home. Now, instead of coming home at noon, Inga boarded the bus to Paso Robles to attend classes at the community college, studying to complete her teaching degree. That goal had been set aside when she married.

With Inga gone early in the mornings, Elena awoke to Aunt Amelia pulling back the covers on the bed and gently patting her behind, with those red, rough hands scooting the child to the white basin. "Rise and shine, you sleepy monkey; daylight's wasting." Amelia, ready with the small pink towel, would kneel on the floor and wait for Elena to finish sponging up; then, she would help her into clothes, socks, and shoes. Elena cherished Amelia's caring twinkling blue eyes and her graying red locks that escaped from the yellow plaid scarf she wore every day except Sundays.

Doted on by Amelia and Sarah, Elena thrived in the mornings. She savored the fire's crackle in the woodstove and the smell of bubbling dough filled with cranberries or blueberries baking in the oven. Aunt Amelia covered the hot scones with fresh butter from the larder and sometimes even spooned honey into Elena's warm milk.

"Come here, child; let me brush your hair." Aunt Sarah's belly bounced against Elena's bony shoulders, never pulling too hard as her mother might, singing Finnish children's songs or some silly commercial she remembered from the previous night's radio shows. When they finished eating, Sarah read aloud the stories from *Tots and Toys*, the same primer Inga used to teach her first-graders. It was to be a surprise: to read to her mother once she knew all the words. Sitting there, practicing writing words that were new to her, Elena studied the blue tennis shoes as Aunt Amelia worked around the kitchen, imagining words written in yellow crayon on the white sides of the soles, dancing above the floor. The two sisters would talk and talk around her. Sometimes they lowered their voices, or spoke in the old tongue about the minister's wife or the time the sheriff's son ran off and joined the army. Elena learned to stay quiet, and she listened to many things that perhaps she shouldn't have heard.

She loved when she was freed to do her chores. She clicked her tongue like the Pied Piper, as Amelia had taught her, so the chickens would follow her out of the coop. She scattered the corn to woo them, instead of playing them a song. She collected the eggs from the hutches in her wicker basket, always careful to inspect each nest; the chickens would hide the eggs and try to sit on them.

She remembered a time, or at least she thought she remembered a time, when her papa had held her by the waist and raised her high up so she could look into the top hutch. Then she had climbed the short wooden ladder he had built for her at the metal tank. She scooped water into her small bucket to fill the birdbaths Virgil had sculpted, each one unique, and placed around the garden. Elena recalled that his hands were smooth, not rough like Uncle Charlie's; and the brown hair on his arms was much darker than his brother's, too. Virgil's clothes smelled of paint thinner, not hay, milk, or wood, and his hands speckled in white plaster, okra, and crimson dye. They would play hide-and-go-seek in the barn. And no matter how many times Elena would take cover beneath the hay piles, he never remembered to look there. She would listen to his breath as he would pass over her and hear his teasing.

"Where have you gone, my pumpkin? Fee, Fie, Foe, Fum, I smell the sweetness of my little one!" He would look in the stalls and behind the tools, and would walk right by and not hear her gasp until she pushed her red tennis shoe up from the hay or coughed out loud. Once he did find her, he would scoop her up in his long arms and tickle her until she pleaded for him to stop.

After Virgil became lost, the boisterous family grew quiet. The tall ones patted Elena's head and sighed. They stopped conversing, so Elena did too.

It fell to Amelia to begin the healing. She planned Sunday excursions to the coast and created new chores for everyone, leaving little time to dwell about what could not be fixed. Her resilience and peaceful courage glued the adults together. Slowly the days turned into months, and the family, one by one, came back to themselves, all except Beth, who had now become Inga. Her sapphire eyes never shone gold again; her sweet songs were never sung again. All was replaced by the hard-working provider concerned about bills and planning a new life. This mother was distant, far removed from the Three Musketeers. Elena's aunts took good care of her, but no one ever mentioned Virgil again. When Elena would ask about her father, tears would form in their eyes. They would shake their heads and hush her.

"He's gone child, and that's that."

After a while Elena stopped mentioning him. She became quiet, astute in listening to their voices, eager to hear a clue, a detail that could answer her prayers. Their kindness in other matters kept her safe, but it could not displace the ache the child carried, the longing that turned into blame. Maybe it had been her fault that her father left them; maybe she had done something wrong. She should have followed him to go hunting. He would not have gotten lost with her there. Maybe that's why her mother didn't love her anymore.

Dinnertime became the most trying part of Elena's day; all the family's activities would be discussed around the table. Her mother listened politely. Amelia attempted to engage her.

"Inga, is it exciting to return to your studies, at the new college in Paso Robles?"

"It is nice." Inga kept her head down and continued to eat her food.

"Are there many young men, what with the war effort and all?" Sarah asked.

Amelia shot Sarah a sharp glance and answered for her, "Oh, Sarah, of course there are. We still need teachers, war or no war. But tell me, Inga, is it true, they are expanding the high school next year to four years?"

"Well, that is the talk."

"Then you will have fewer grade levels crammed into your schoolhouse. That will be nice for you, won't it?"

Inga looked up briefly at Amelia, nodding her head, then back down at her plate. "Hmm, yes, that would make it more structured for teaching."

After dinner, Inga would bury herself in books and papers on the kitchen table, while the rest of the family retired to the sewing room to listen to the radio. *Oxydol's Own Ma Perkins* was their favorite show. Inga never joined in the evening reprieve or had time to play with Elena or finish decorating the dollhouse they had started in the spring. Sarah replaced Inga, helping the child make the miniature furniture, but Elena missed her mama's touch.

The next fall mother and daughter left the farm and moved to San Jose, closer to her own family, where Inga was raised, away from all that existed of Virgil. She earned her teaching degree and devoted her life to her career. Her days were filled with instructing eager young faces, answering their questions—only to come home and not answer her own child's most pressing one. Inga found it easier to lose herself this way. Plus, a fatherless child in a city during wartime was more understandable, and there were fewer questions. It was easier to allow assumptions to shape the truth.

Elena ceased probing for answers about her father and started school. Her life on the farm drifted seamlessly apart from this reality. The turmoil of the times required sacrifices, and a small child's prayers were defensibly abandoned to the era. Elena grew straight and tall like her father's family, a constant reminder of the difference between Inga and her. She looked forward to their visits to the farm. Unafraid anymore to look into those large adult eyes, she regained her voice. Once again, she laughed at their jokes and appreciated their doting. On Elena's tenth birthday, Amelia brought out Virgil's easel and paints, setting them up in his garden.

"Elena, why not paint the birds."

Inga frowned. "Oh, Amelia, now what did you bring those old things out for? Elena doesn't paint. Such a silly waste of time."

"Maybe it's time she learned. No harm can come from her painting; it was the best part of him."

They still could not even say his name.

"Well, all right then, but she will have to leave them here. We certainly don't have room in our apartment."

Elena loved Aunt Amelia the best. She always prepared Elena's favorite dinner, walnut pancakes. After she married and had her own children, she used Aunt Amelia's example as a model for how to be with her children, serving them pancakes for dinner when they needed a little extra love.

The whispers and silent nods finally came together. One day in her early teens, without ever being told, Elena knew what had happened to her father. The knowing added more questions that could not be asked, and her deep yearning to be told the details went unfulfilled. The unmentionable remained unsaid. Underneath, the pain sank deeper, unnoticed by others, and in the family tradition, unspoken.

Her mother never regained the softness or emotional presence that once carried her beauty. In an effort to compensate, Inga strove to afford her daughter the opportunity to pursue higher education and feed her intellect. After years of living meagerly, Inga saw her dream realized when her only child enrolled at the University of California at Berkeley. Vindicated, she thought her daughter would not fall prey to the shiny luster of love and betrayal. But it was only another beginning.

Elena found this new freedom intoxicating, and, out from under mother's stern scrutiny, she began a social life of her own making. Dating for a six-foot young woman had many complications. Most young men were intimated by her height, and mistook her shyness as superiority. In her sophomore year, she attended a dance of upperclassman with a group of daring young women she had met in a poetry class. They had coached her, explaining that her height could be a source of attraction.

"Hold yourself tall and look directly into a man's face. You're so striking; they will not be able to resist," they teased.

As she strode into the hall smiling and laughing with her companions, her attention was drawn across the room by the vision of what she thought to be her destined match. Swept away by an elegantly tall and mysterious man, she was filled with expectations of belonging to something outside herself. She confided to no one, but in her mind she spoke. *He is the one for me!*

By the end of her second school year, Elena, as her mother before, left the safety of her community, hoping to recover in this man the love she lost. She had married what she knew best, a silent person unable to unveil his interior. Agreeing to abandon her studies and follow him in his career as a chemist working for the government in the desert of Southern California, the cycle repeated. Her marriage soon turned to disappointment, and, once again, she failed to break the code of a silent soul meant to nurture her. Abandoned, empty-hearted, and bonded to another emotional cripple was the truth that eventually replaced the whirlwind courtship and marriage. The events played out with the woman mirroring the child, seeking dialog, captured in a monologue of her own voice that resounded against her husband's silence.

Unacceptable as a divorce was in her times, she was not a candidate for suffering, realizing that she had a choice now. She took her small children and returned to northern California. A single mother, Elena dedicated herself to being emotional available to her children, unlike Inga had been for her. Following her mother in other ways, she returned to college and completed her degree.

Studying philosophy and deep self-exploration, she cultivated her own powerful voice, ultimately leaving her family's silence behind. She found unusual jobs that afforded her freedom to be home in the afternoons. Working in a cannery with farm workers during the Cold War, she was invited to visit Russia with some of the union organizers. When she returned, her boss threatened to terminate her position unless she quit her union associations, and she stayed silent. Silence had never been her friend, so she refused, and the company recanted its threats.

Later, when her children were grown, she accepted a post as a temporary Unitarian minister, and new doors opened to her own spirituality. When called upon to deliver occasional sermons before the congregation, she found the community welcomed her voice. Her ideas gave comfort and confidence, and people began to seek her out for counseling, asking her advice and comfort with their sorrows and family wounds. Their sufferings Elena knew all too well, and in this role she came to understand and accept the unyielding force that was Inga's silence, making peace with her own wounded heart.

Decades later, advanced throat cancer had left Inga physically unable to speak. As she neared her final days, she gave Elena written instructions detailing her wishes for her burial. Ignoring the fact that her brothers and parents were buried in a family tomb in Santa Clara, where she had lived the past forty years, Inga had bought a plot in the cemetery outside San Miguel, near where her husband's family had lived. Stunned, Elena knew that asking her mother would bear no answers, and once again she was left alone to ponder the enigma.

Why would she break with her own family to go to San Miguel? Elena, unable to make sense of her mother's wish, had no choice but to honor it. The day after Inga's death, she drove out to San Miguel. She had called the mortuary to inquire about the details over the phone. The mortician informed her that everything had been taken care of, and there would be no need to come before the service, but Elena insisted.

"No, I need to come and see where it is my mother wants to rest."

Even in death this woman couldn't break her code. When Elena arrived, the undertaker politely gave her the file with all the instructions from Inga. He was correct. In her most efficient manner, nothing was left undone. He gave Elena a small hand-drawn map so she could go and visit the plot her mother had purchased. In an old part of the cemetery, farthest away from the chapel, he explained, she would find it, already cordoned off. They were to prepare it the next day. As Elena walked through the cemetery, she recognized each name: Amelia, Charlie, Sarah, and Grandma Kitchen. All were buried here. It had been over twenty-years since the last of them had died. When she reached the cordoned ground, a portal of understanding opened about her mama's life. Next to Inga's intended plot, Virgil's simple tombstone stood; it revealed only his name and that he was survived by his loving wife "Beth" and blessed Angel "Elena."

Years of wanting to find her father, to understand his reasons for depression and final desertion, would end in this simple marker? Somehow Uncle Charlie must have gained approval to bury his brother here, quietly, without a service. Suicides were usually not allowed in consecrated ground, but here he rested, the word indelibly written only in her mind, the unspoken word Elena had learned to use only in therapy. She had come to call it an "unfortunate accident" to her children and to any others that would question her.

How cruel, Mother. Why could you not share your sorrow with me and my sorrow too? At least you knew where to find him. What about me? She stood there, her feet beginning to sink in the San Miguel barrow, an immovable force meeting up with time. An opening in her ear, an inner voice answered. *To wish to be buried here, how you must have loved him still, after all these years.*

This place, where Beth had been her best, her true self; of course this is where she belonged, to rest here finally, with her long-lost love. Looking down at mud-soaked shoes, the same mud that as a child she had loved to run around in with bare feet, squeezing the wet, light-brown mush between her toes, this same earth that now prepared to take her mother's worldly self. Elena recalled words from a favorite Rumi poem that she had quoted often at the memorial of others.

"The tomb looks like a prison but it is really a release into union."

Yes, Mama, it will be your release into union with Papa Virgil.

She left the cemetery. A compelling force pushing her to complete the puzzle unveiled the direction for her to take next. She drove out of town through the golden California hills, now covered in vineyards. She found the Rancherito iron bridge that crossed over the dry creek bed that cut through the farm. It had been her favorite place to play, among the river willows and the rattlers.

"You mind your step, young lady, while you play down there. They won't bother you as long as you keep a good distance," Aunt Amelia would warn when she saw Elena light out, a burlap sack over her shoulder with her kittens following. "Better put those babies in the barn; they're not smart enough to know to stay clear. And don't you try catching anything but frogs. You leave the rattlers to Uncle Charlie. He's so mean they would probably die from biting him."

Elena returned home after decades of life that separated that child from this woman; now she would bury the woman whose very breath had given her life. Elena came to recover the piece of her that was forsaken that afternoon, forty years before. She found the property neglected, and the old farmhouse boarded up. But returning to this land had opened a window to the ultimate mystery that fueled her heart's longing.

She rose from the stoop, walking past the garden and around to the front of the house. Finally coming to rest by the corral, she could smell what remained there. The billowing trees that bordered the oak woods sang a melancholy tune in the afternoon breeze. Elena walked along the white picket fence that bordered the lush emerald pasture, and listened. The others' voices returned, rupturing the silence.

Elena imagined Beth's blue skirt billowing on the clothesline, kittens running in the tall golden grass, and heard her mama's voice singing a lullaby. Her aunts' laughter echoed in the kitchen. Uncle Charlie in his red shirt ambled in the distant pasture calling the cows to the barn, a family blended together to be their best. Good people. All gone but Elena.

Leaning on a fence post, she noticed there were horses frolicking in the neighboring meadow. A young colt galloped after a chestnut mare to keep up. The mother allowed the colt to reach her and nuzzle, rubbing his short body under hers. She stepped aside and playfully nipped at the colt and suddenly trotted off to another patch of grass to nibble. The colt whinnied loudly, seeming to beg the mother to return.

Elena remembered her promise to God she made all those years ago: *to be her best and never make anyone angry*, an impossible pledge that had colored so much of her relationships.

A lone dark stallion suddenly approached her at the railing. He stopped short and stared down at her. Elena looked up into those cobalt eyes, held onto the post for support, and stretched out her hand over the fence. The horse put his nuzzle into her open palm, snorted, and licked her cheek, the salt of her tears pleasing to him. He took the last pace forward and tapped the top of her head with his chin, pushed against her shoulder, and whinnied. Then he galloped off. The mare and colt waited for him in the pasture.

It was these animals in front of her—real, not imagined or remembered—that released her heart from its prison. An inner awareness rose up, fracturing the dam, her love overflowing its boundaries; a wellspring called forgiveness poured out, for her family, who had not the courage to speak the unspeakable. Those gentle souls had done what they could to care for and love the lonely child. Compassion flowed for Inga, Beth, her mother, who had lost so much that afternoon, understanding that she had no answers either. No one had. Virgil had fallen into a darkness no one could have recognized; the mystery would remain his forever. Acceptance for the suffering Inga chose to bear alone, never opening herself to love again, too vulnerable to chance it.

"Thank you, Mother, for bringing me here now, to give me in your passing what you could not in your living." Elena spoke out loud so her words could be heard, in this land where her earliest memories were of love. "Better late than never. Good-bye, Mother. Good-bye, Father. If only you both could have found the peace in this life, while you breathed this air, walked this sacred earth, instead of waiting for the next to love again. But those were your choices, and I have mine. I'll love and cherish our Three Musketeers."

Elena turned to leave, grateful that the sacred had waited for her to return, all these years later, to finally let her take a whole heart home.

The Promise

High concrete barriers lined the construction next to the fast lane of the 101 Freeway. Maneuvering through them at seventy-five miles an hour, the blue Jaguar defied comparisons, handling that speed as smoothly as a gentle Sunday drive in a park.

"Faster, go faster, please," Zoë begged. "Can't we go faster?"

"Sure we can, but who's going to pay for the ticket if we get stopped? Not to mention, getting pulled over means we lose our window of open road; it could close at any time. Do you want to be stuck all the way home bumper to bumper?"

"We won't get stopped, and so what? I'll pull off my wig and play the terminal case. A cop wouldn't dare give you a ticket."

Looking over at the child with the crescent moon smile beaming back at me, I shook my head, laughing. "How'd you get so sneaky? Oh that's right, I remember; you're a teenager."

As I pushed the accelerator pedal down, Zoë let out a whoop.

"Faster, faster! It feels like the Matterhorn at Disneyland. All we need now is a big splash to land in."

"At ninety-five miles per hour I don't think that would be a good idea, playing roller coaster with my pretty blue Jag."

"Oh, Laura, you won't crash. You're the best driver ever."

"Why, Zoë, besides radiation, what else did they zap your head with this morning, horse paddy rays? Not that I don't agree with you, but I'm not risking that perfectly round head of yours, after all your work to keep it ticking. Dr. Giovanni would be furious if I damaged a single new hair, not to mention your mom, Cielo, Santo, Dorian, Marcello, Michael ..."

"Yes, I get it already."

Sensing a shift, I eased off the pedal until the speed reached 65 mph; silence filled the void as the exhilaration waned.

"You get to pick the music, no complaints. Do you have your cassettes in the front seat?"

"I'm mad," Zoë whispered.

Not sure of what I heard, "I'm sorry, what did you say?"

"I said, I'm mad, angry."

"Well, that's no surprise. I can think of a lot of reasons, but let's hear yours, and we'll see if I'm close."

"I'm angry at my dad."

"Okay, that wasn't my top pick; I'm wrong again. But, honey, he has been gone for two years, so why now?"

"I'm mad at him for dying. He is supposed to be here now to help me. He copped out. Why didn't he quit smoking and drinking like the doctors told him? It's not fair. If he really loved me he should have, he would have, and could have been here now to help mom and me!"

In all these months she had never spoken Alex's name. Zoë, up until then, had been the most optimistic of us all. Contrary to what the shrinks had warned, the diagnosed depression we prepared for never materialized. No way around it; she hit the mark. Alex had failed his daughter.

"Wow, you always know how to get my attention. I haven't heard you mention him since his death. You never wanted to talk about it, at least to me. Now is good though; look at me Zoë. I'm here for you, you know that?" I searched her face for tears, but there were none. Her frail white hands clenched on her lap, silently pounding on her legs.

"That's just it; I don't want to talk about his dying. I want to talk about his living. Why did he waste his life? I'm doing everything to fight for mine, and he abandoned his. He gave me away. Why couldn't he fight to be here for me? Aren't fathers supposed to do that? I'm so afraid, and tired of all this."

"Yes, parents are meant to protect us, guide us, and love us. And we are people too. We fail or fall short. I can't tell you why your father lost his way, but I do know that he loved you, Zoë. The smile appeared the minute you bounded into a room, and his eyes shone at the sight of you. He resides in your heart, even now; that is where your hurt comes from. You could ask for his help from the other side."

My words felt empty, and they were. I knew it, and so did she. Shaking my head back and forth to let her know I hadn't fooled even me, I let out a growl.

"Damn it all, Zoë, I can't answer for him. I can speak for me as your godmother. I'll fight for you, no matter what. Your mother and I won't let it be any other way. You will win this battle, promise. Now you got me mad too. I wish I could just slap him, and that's a good thing."

Her eyes grew even rounder as she interrupted me. "Now what is that supposed to mean, Laura? Everyone else is always trying to calm me down, so I can do my visualizing of Pac-Man eating the cancer, making it go away. They tell me if I do it right, it will work."

"There you have it. They want you to see the cancer as little bubbles floating up and pop them. Calming you is one technique. I'm saying you can use your anger to vanquish demons as another approach. Feelings toward your father are part of those demons, the part of him that didn't stay here for you. Turn your anger loose on the cancer and the hurt from your father, to move it out of you. Then you can take back the other part of him that loved you. This is hard work." I looked over at her and saw confusion.

A light bulb popped on in my mind. "Zoë, you're not afraid that if it doesn't work, you've done it wrong, are you?"

"Well, that Doctor-Who-Smiles-All-The-Time keeps telling me that this is my school now, and that my job is important and to keep it up at least three times a day. Some days I just don't feel like it, and then I get scared; what if I *die* because I didn't do my homework?"

It was the first time I had ever heard her say *the word*. I struggled to get over to the right lane and pulled off the freeway to park below the overpass. The reverberation above our heads reminded us that the rest of the world continued on in fast-forward.

"Oh, Zoë, I'm so sorry you have had that burden placed on you. No, you're not going to die because you didn't practice some meditation. These white-coats want to leave no stone unturned, and each doctor believes in his or her method. But remember, Sweetie, that's their job. But this disease is not your fault. Your body replicates those cancer cells; no one knows why. It's one of many mysteries that fill our lives."

"Well, this mystery sucks!"

"Yes, it sucks the big one. Listen, your dad became ill because of his use of alcohol and smoking. These are behaviors he directed into his body. The addictions overwhelmed his life force. He could not control them, even to save his own life. We cannot judge how another person deals with disease and illness. But most importantly, we know we are not responsible for their choices."

"He still sucks."

"Yes, I do agree, but it's different for you. We can change what you eat and drink and breathe, but there is much more we cannot control. Remember the three-year-old girl we saw in rehab? They were teaching her to build blocks. She certainly couldn't do the Pac-Man visualizations, but does that mean she can't get better? None of us knows what's in store. We are guessing every day at what will work and what won't."

I watched her, waiting for a sign. None came, so I continued, "Right now your real job is to listen to your music, feel all the love that surrounds you, and let it soak into your bones. Find the place in you that makes you smile and at other times lets you cry. And when your anger rises, as it should, express it, use it. We will help you in whatever way you need."

I unbuckled myself and reached over to hug her and whispered, "I can't imagine how scary this must be for you. I would give anything to trade places so you could be free of this, but I can't. And that sucks. I'm left loving you deeply."

Molecules and Women

I could feel her tears wet my shirt, and the soft quivers as she pressed into my chest. I waited until calm returned, then pushed back to look into her newly composed face with streaked tears drying. She was staring ahead, past the window, into where? I waited until she looked at me and nodded. I resettled into my seat. "Let's buckle up and drive like the monorail. Swoosh!" I tried a laugh.

"Will you drive fast again, please?" she asked as she pulled a cassette out of her bag and plopped it into the player and turned it up loud, smiling at me.

"*Don't worry, be happy, everything is going to be all right now …,*" Bob Marley blasted out of the speakers.

Why not? I thought. Happiness is not a destination but a vehicle in which to travel. Why settle for a Ford if you can drive a Jaguar. "You got it, sweetheart!"

I maneuvered the car back onto the freeway. The song continued, and I snuck a peek at Zoë, her eyes closed and her hands resting unclenched on her lap. Grateful for the reprieve, I looked out as we passed the Capitol Record building, a Hollywood landmark, a building built to resemble a stack of records atop a record player. I noticed for the first time the flag on top designed to appear as a needle on a record. The architect thought it would be relevant for eons, and here in only three decades, with records going the way of the dinosaur, it was outmoded and lost in an ever-expanding concrete city that dwarfed their vision.

And here I was, the architect of my own vision, in a constant challenge to remain relevant in the face of tragedy and insurmountable concrete mountains erected by our fragile lives. Accepting the role of godmother was an honored tender position, but the reality of the responsibility in these times was daunting.

With the death of Alex, a few years earlier, I assumed a quiet position. Hoping to create a joyful, stable presence in the face of his daughter's loss, and to be available to help Tammy, Zoë's mother, digest the loss of her husband, I never imagined what future adversity awaited mother and daughter.

It had taken us months to get up to snuff on all the medical terms and lies. We didn't know it yet, but there was hope in ignorance. The not-knowing was a lot better than the knowing. We had begun with Doctor-Shining-Star-From-Another-Planet surgeon, whose magic sword excised 95 percent of the tumor in *only* ten hours. A good thing?

That took us then to chemotherapy, or radiation? Tammy and I sat on baby chairs in a children's playroom in the oncology department, my attention drawn to little hand-painted hearts on all the backs of the chairs. I wondered who painted these symbols of love in this room where loss prevailed. Doctor-Gray-Hair-Sage-Who-Speaks-Only-the-TTammy sat across from us, his large body overflowing the small wooden seat, somehow comfortably, perhaps after years of practice.

He met our eyes directly and elucidated that they are nothing more than witch doctors with experimental voodoo in this kind of disease. In his view, quality of life was the real question. So, heeding what we guessed was his silent message, we opted for Doctor-Sure-of-Herself-Steady-Aim radiologist, whose success rate was higher, the risks lower.

Tammy, tenderly present during all the endless decisions, never flinched in front of Zoë; a calm abiding coated her voice in all the translations from medical jargon to child speak. The courage was mirrored from mother to daughter and back to mother. Her fragile state, disguised in front of Zoë, was ever-present in the hallway, waiting room, and corridor. A sentry outside operating rooms and treatment settings, she was the only constant timbre in Zoë's world, providing reassurance every day.

After four weeks of critical care, sleeping in the hotel across from the hospital or at the Ronald McDonald House when rooms were available, I needed to return to my life, my family, and my work. Observing the magnitude of the sacrifice that my children were asked to bear, I cringed at my demands on them. But when I put it into perspective, the loss that Tammy faced made my concerns pale. My ex-husband, magnanimous in this one act of support, aided me in my absence. Others in my family were much less encouraging. There were not words to explain, so I didn't try.

Soon, Zoë and Tammy came to live with my children and me until Zoë completed her arduous months of treatments and rehab. We formed a triangle of shelter as a buffer between the brokenness of the exterior and the wholeness of the interior—a shell for the soul. A silent conversation of love among the three of us carried on beneath the routine trips to radiation and vomiting into buckets. At times, the words would escape our lips and float around the room like dust. We wouldn't try to capture them, but just let them settle where they wanted. Occasions like my drive with Zoë were never repeated to Tammy; they were entrusted to me as a piece of our inner bond, and were meant to be held quietly. We each had another to turn to. On rare moments, Tammy broke down in the empty passageways, or outside in open concrete cubicles that led to the fresh air of downtown Los Angeles, or on the small decks between floors that had been tucked away from the general public—secret sanctuaries where she could openly weep at the horror of the possibilities that lay in her future. I would say, "Breathe, Tammy; remember to breathe." And I in my Jaguar, traveling at high speeds, wept alone openly, sometimes catching the widened eyes of other drivers reflecting back sympathy.

The medical community held the hope-carrot out in front of us, and, of course, we snatched it up. We grabbed it during the six weeks of physical rehab to regain strength from the devastating brain surgery. We grabbed it when the eight weeks of radiation destroyed her immune system along with the cancer. We grabbed it during the slow advance toward healing, and we held onto it at the Make-a-Wish Foundation's gift to send her to Hawaii. She returned with real signs of recovery. We won the brass ring when her CAT scan showed no new growth. We fiercely guarded remission, a return to ordinary. Joy and celebration spread through the hospital staff. Our miracle Zoë returned home with Tammy after nine months of battling windmills. Their lives, a fragile peace, demanded a new attention. It required that they abandon their rustic hillside property and move into town so Zoë could be close to everything. We managed weekly phone updates, to affirm a return to normal. Holding the pretense for each other encouraged the promise of a future. High school dreams were being hatched, along with a sixteenth birthday in just a few months, and the treasured driver's license.

Relying on just a cane now, Zoë began to ride her horse around the corral. At first strapped into the saddle, after only a month she had the strength to hold herself up, giving way to excited expectations of upcoming equestrian events. Hope drove her and her trainer Dorian to practice daily. The goal appeared within reach until one Saturday morning she slid off the saddle in slow motion.

She'd suffered a new attack. All progress halted. One day later, behind a door marked Do Not Enter, Staff Only, in a darkened radiology analysis room, her mother and I stood holding hands, leaning into each other, heads touching one another's as her scans lit up on the screen to reveal new dark spots on the brain stem. A translucent finger pointed and then traced an outline to what no one wanted to see.

The start gun went off, the final heat set in motion. We surrendered to the once-rejected poisons they offered, leaving her after only one course gasping for air as her lungs failed. We yielded to blood transfusions as her liver shut down. We stared as they inserted a feeding tube to replace her damaged digestive tract, and we nodded when they delivered the hi-tech joystick-driven motorized wheelchair to replace the legs that would no longer carry her wafer frame.

The last stop was the private office of the leading pediatric cancer researcher on the West Coast, who demanded that we leave our swords in the waiting room. "You have no time to wait. She must undergo another course. I give her less than two weeks with the spread of the tumors left unchecked. What has she to lose?"

"Maybe two weeks," I blurted out, followed by, "considering your first course just about killed her less than forty-eight hours ago."

Up until that moment it was my duty to remain cool and collected in those meetings, ensuring me a purpose, a foundation for my strength. I took the notes and asked the questions. Vanquished and disoriented, I walked out, choosing to wait in the open air, adrift in the realization that only nonsolutions were left. Tammy appeared a few moments later, leaving Uncle John alone to listen to the rest of the specialist's lies. We walked across the pavilion to the main hospital and waited until we found an empty waiting room to talk. I had my head bent, resting on a wall, unable to meet her eyes.

"It can't be this … All the work, wasted? All the fight to just walk away defeated? How can you think that way? You can't mean it. Laura, look at me," Tammy glared.

"Because I can't bear to watch her undergo one more poison, one more zap, one more cut. She has given so much to be here in this life. Hasn't she given enough? Why call it defeated! She has lived and laughed fourteen months more than that first insane diagnosis from Doctor-Who-Had-No-Heart in Ventura. Tammy, he gave her less than a week. As hard as it has been, it's been beautiful too, all the smiles, laughter, tears, and hours together. You two have lived more in the last year than most parents and children get to in a lifetime. This is not defeat!"

I looked back and saw what I had not wanted to see. The glint of her dark eyes gone, Tammy's trademark corner smile that never failed to sooth my brow was nowhere to be found.

"Well, *I* can't make this decision!"

"Nor I," I whispered.

"It has to be *her's* now."

"Yes, you're right."

Upstairs, on the sixth floor terminal ward, I watched out the window as the cars entered and left the parking lot; the brown haze loosely called LA air hovered over the skyscrapers. I listened and wished for some pool of water or green forest to escape into as Tammy sat on Zoë's bed, carefully explaining how Doctor-World-Famous-Authority-with-Super-Credentials wanted to proceed, laying out the risks and the alternative—do nothing. She held back that he gave her daughter a maximum of two weeks to live in her current condition.

"What do you think I should do, Mom?"

"Honey, it's your decision now. I can't make any more."

"What do you think, though? What would *you* do?"

"I'm not sure. Maybe it's worth a try? This could be the miracle drug they are always talking about."

Zoe turned her attention to me. "Laura, what do you think?'

I turned and saw the child warrior's IVs delivering precious fluids into her bony arms, her pug nose resting on an oxygen tube helping her lungs complete the job, the exhausted body propped up on pillows, and her fiery eyes alert, alive, demanding.

"Zoë, your mom is right; this has to be your choice, and it's time your voice be heard. I know you will know what to do."

"No, not good enough," she demanded. "Tell me what you think. You promised you always would."

There it manifested: "The Promise." After Alex's death, Zoë came to stay with us for a week before returning to school. Thinking it safer to be lost in the chaos generated by my five children than the silence of a mourning home, I had attempted to console her during one rare moment alone. I caught her from behind and held her in my arms and whispered in her ear. "Do you have any questions, anything at all you want to talk about? I promise you, Zoë. I'll never lie, or keep any secrets from you, no matter what."

She nodded, waited a minute, then breaking free from my embrace, smiled and returned to the TV room to play *Mario Brothers* and disappear among the children.

Then again, that first night all those months ago, while we waited for dawn and Doctor-Shining-Star to sharpen his sword, Tammy asleep in the chair next to her, I had reminded her that she could talk to me about anything. "Are you afraid about tomorrow? Do you have any questions? I'm here for you if you want to talk."

She shook her head no, and said, "I know, I know," and waved me off.

I walked over to her bed. "You sure know how to pick your moment, darling." Taking her hand, I kissed it, and then looked at Tammy. Her eyes struggling to stay dry and her heart quietly breaking, her small nod gave me permission.

"Well, let's see now. I'm alone in my opinion. Your mom, all the specialists, and even Uncle John think that you going for another course of chemo as soon as your white cell count moves up *is* a no-brainer. Shit, Zoë, I'm sorry, I didn't mean …"

"Laura, stop; it's okay. It's funny, you know, 'no brainer,'" Zoë interrupted me. "But, what do you think?"

"Me? I think you should blow this taco stand, take your sweet life and get out. Pack that pretty head of yours up with your mother and travel to Wilmington to see Marcello and the family. Escape as far away from here as possible and live! You know how I feel about most of *these* doctors. You know more about your body than they do; my money's on you, girl. Now, having said that, you have to understand that this isn't considered the wise choice, and it's easy for me to say and much harder for you to do. *I get that.*"

Looking over to Tammy, I was greeted with the tiniest of smiles to let me know it was as okay as it could be. I so needed that. Squeezing Zoë ever so gently, so as not to crack a tender rib, I made my escape.

"I have to go to a parent/teacher conference tonight for Angela, but I'll be back in the morning, first thing. Call me if you need me to bring up anything tomorrow. You know, a steak, fries, or smoothie?"

They both smiled at my feeble attempt. I quickly kissed them and practically ran out the door. I contained my desperate urge to scream obscenities at the universe through the long green hallways, past the doors of dying children, into the white padded utility elevator with staff members who knew not to look too hard into the face of a nonuniformed adult.

I even managed to get to my car and drive the blur of sixty miles home without smashing into anything, weaving through the tall gray structures of downtown and onto the infinite ribbon of concrete and steel that is the LA Freeway configuration. Traveling in that encasement, I was temporarily immune to the ravages of blood, tissue, and diseased organisms that refuse to be controlled or conquered, grateful for the reprieve to focus on nothing more than heavy metal and noxious fumes, speeding with the millions of others not concerned with the significance of an astrocytoma-glioblastoma bomb that can tick in one's own cerebellum, or worse yet, in a child's. Of all the nefarious decisions of the last year, this had to be, was by far, no doubt, the ugliest. There would be no turning back from this one.

As I eased my blue Jaguar off the concrete freeway and onto black asphalt, I exhaled deeply, another mission carried out. The emptiness of the long mountain road winding through the granite canyon to my home in Malibu Lake was salve to the eyes, a portal between that culpable world and my own. Five beautiful, healthy children with not even a toothache to disturb their peace, and Tammy's one angel called to arms. A sense of guilt for my blessings stirred in my heart. A true measure of acceptance demanded attention to what is, and what cannot be.

I noticed my daughter Cielo's car gone and knew she was picking up her siblings. How much I had relied on my oldest, only seventeen years old, during this last year; how much I had leaned on all of my children, to fend alone or for each other.

I heard the quiet criticism from my mother, "Aren't you spending too much time away from your children? Tammy has a sister and a brother. Couldn't they help more?"

"She is my godchild, Mother. You, of anyone, should remember what that means."

But never reproach from my children. We had grown closer, kinder to each other in the witnessing of such loss. They had given me permission, not always pleased when I forgot one of their events, but grateful in a way, for their health, and grateful it wasn't one of them.

"Mom, is it wrong to be glad it's not me that has cancer?" Cielo had confided in me recently. "It's so sad to see Zoë. I was happy when she went home to Ojai."

"No, it's not wrong to feel joy that you're blessed; of course you were glad. We all were glad to return to our lives."

I parked my car in the driveway, too tired to lift the garage door. *Got to get that garage door opener fixed before the rains*, I thought. As I approached the garden fence I was surprised not to see our giant black Labrador bounding from the backyard, as I always braced to be pounced on. It was eerily quiet. Opening the front door, I called out, "Anyone home?"

Greeted only by Dozer, who, slip-sliding out of the kitchen, brushed by me in a dash, and out the front door, not waiting for my scolding, "Who let you in?" Looking around to the silent house, I wished I could gather one of my babies in my arms. I noticed my hands were shaking.

"I need a shower." I was talking to the emptiness, simultaneously lonely and grateful for a momentary reprieve. Kicking off my shoes at the bottom of the stairs, I heard the phone ring.

Let it ring, I thought. *Five minutes to myself.* Then thinking, *what if it's my daughter?* I ran up the stairs to my bedroom and picked up the receiver, out of breath. Taken aback to hear Tammy's gentle voice coming through the plastic, "Laura, is that you? Zoë has something to tell you."

I sat down on the edge of my bed as I heard the phone being passed.

"I made my decision, Laura, and I wanted to tell you right away."

"Okay, sweetheart, I'm here. What is it?"

"I'm done. I want to go home now. No more treatments."

Yielding to the space between the words, an abyss I didn't want to look into, opened my heart. She continued, "Aren't you proud of me? Did you hear me?"

I couldn't believe she asked me that. *Such courage!*

"Yes, darling, I heard you. I cannot tell you how proud I am, and how grateful for all you teach me. Do you hear me? I love you."

"I love you too. See you in the morning?"

"I'll be there first thing, and we'll plan your escape."

I placed the phone back in its cradle and walked to the sliding doors off the deck, staring up at the mountain. "Yes, we will plan your freedom," I spoke to the blue sky above, "and it will be good."

Zoë chose to live her days, not suffer them. She made it to the Outer Banks in North Carolina. She mastered driving her high-tech wheelchair with a joystick, having never regained sufficient strength to walk on her own. Cousin Marcello and Zoë terrorized the Village of Bald Head, taking turns popping wheelies on the boardwalks around the island. The family in North Carolina visited

Duke University with Zoë's records, in the hopes of leaving no stone unturned, but those doctors' protocols were no better.

As the family spokesperson and medical advocate, I received the phone call from Doctor-Whose-Research-Was-The-Newest-Cutting-Edge to ask my support for the opportunity to administer their voodoo, but wisdom won the day. He explained for ten minutes how he was researching a different avenue, and it was showing great promise. I listened attentively, and when he was finished, he inquired whether I had any questions.

"Only one," I replied. "Do you have any survivors?"

There was a long pause, and he began to repeat his whole protocol. I interrupted, "Excuse me, Doctor; I don't wish to appear rude, but I asked a question and am waiting for that answer."

Again, another long silence. "Well, at this time no, but ..."

"No, Doctor, there is nothing more. Zoë won't be your guinea pig. We do appreciate your work, and we wish you success."

I was reminded of Doctor-Gray-Hair-Sage-Who-Speaks-Only-the-TTammy. "At the end of the day, quality of life is what matters."

When a star goes nova, its brightness increases many thousands of times, and so it was during Zoë's trip to North Carolina. The light burned bright on her trip east. The photos they sent me were of a vibrant teen, laughing, mouth full of braces. After Thanksgiving, Tammy and Zoë returned home, and her condition deteriorated rapidly. She celebrated Christmas and her sixteenth birthday days apart. Her dream to sit at the wheel of a Beamer, driver's license in hand, would not be realized. Tammy elected to stay in Ojai to allow for what would be to be. The doctors advised us to admit her to Children's Hospital. "The care she requires, too intense for a mother to bear."

They no longer had a vote. This child had outlived their entire medical prognosis and their best estimates. Seventeen months since Doctor-Who-Had-No-Heart blurted out in a green drab hallway, "Maybe a week or two to live." Three months had passed since we drove out of the hospital, vowing to never see any of them again.

Zoë lived her days and nights under her control, not others'. Hospice staff came daily to relieve Tammy and oversee the meds; I came on weekends. A motorized hospital bed occupied the center of Zoë's room like a throne. Tammy's small cot was pushed up against the wall. All of her daughter's blue and red ribbons and trophies lined the shelf erected across from her bed. From six years old as a champion show rider, photos of her astride her horse, straight and tall in the saddle, hung throughout the room. Confined to her bed, a smile usually greeted whoever came into her sanctuary. Sometimes, though, the strain creased her brow, and Tammy was quick to react and insist that it was time to rest.

Fortunately, that January the weather was exceptionally warm, and the sun shone into the room, reflecting the shiny trophies, medals, and ribbons. The open window swept the room of the smells that accompany all things medical.

Tammy's bedroom had become a minipharmacy with equipment, needles, tubes, and monitors. Harnesses and slings that mostly went unused, and her wheelchair, were all shoved into the corner and covered with plastic pads and bedding. She required IV feedings for nourishment, and meds to ward off infection and help her organs function, but no respirator.

We were instructed on all the possible ways the end might come. None were comforting, and all were full of various degrees of suffering. Our miracle was having it her way, not the doctors'. She didn't want to use the morphine because it made her sleepy. Her music played continuously, masking the sounds of the equipment.

The Sunday after New Year's, 1992, as I bent to kiss Zoë goodbye, she whispered for me to wait. "Mom, can I please have a smoothie?" When Tammy left the room, she made me promise that I would take care of her mother.

"Oh, sweetie, don't you worry about such things."

"Not good enough! Give me your word you will take care of my mom. Say it. Say it out loud."

"All right, I vow to always be there for Tammy, and take care of her when she needs it."

A light opened into my heart. This child had willed her body to stay alive so her mother wouldn't be left alone. She would not abandon her, as her father had done. Her mother should not suffer, but now Zoë was too weak to prevent anything. "I'm so tired. I can't work anymore."

"Darling, your job here is done. Rest now; everything will be taken care of."

The next Friday, I dropped my children off at their father's for the weekend. We had picked up a birthday cake for him, and I had intended to come in and join in singing "Happy Birthday." I entered his house, and he was on the phone; when he saw me he handed me the receiver. No one had ever called me there.

"Where are you?" Tammy's shrill voice demanded. I had begun keeping a packed bag in the car like when you're about to deliver a baby, always prepared.

"I'm on my way." I kissed my children and left.

Once again the 101 Freeway became the bridge from the ordinary mundane to the Sacred Portal. Night had fallen when I arrived in Ojai, but the house lights were off. All was dark when I opened the door, except for the light coming from Zoë's room. I met Tammy in the hall on her way to the bedroom pharmacy. She nodded, not stopping to hug, our usual greeting. She entered the room, flicked the light switch, and whispered, "Help me."

"I'll be right in; let me say hello to Zoë."

I peeked into Zoë's room to see her sleeping, her breathing shallow. Quietly I moved to her side and held her hand in mine and realized she was barely there. She was leaving us. I bent to kiss her forehead, and a tear fell on her cheek. Dabbing her tender skin with my sleeve, grateful she didn't stir, I crept away. I found Tammy pulling on the welder's magnifying mask so that she could see to make sure no bubbles entered the IV infusion feeding tube. A nurse had made that mistake once, causing Zoë to suffer needlessly. Holding back the rain filling my heart, I whispered, "We don't have to do it tonight."

Pulling up her mask so I could see her eyes, she snapped back at me, "Yes, we do!"

Such effort, for three small words; her eyes were beyond bloodshot. *When had she last slept?* I didn't know. I gently reached over and took the tubing.

"I'll do it. Please let me. I swear to be careful, not one bubble. Go lie down, and close your eyes. Zoë is sleeping."

I donned the mask and gloves and beseeched the tender mercies to guide my hands. Tammy stood for a moment watching me, and then silently left. When I had the medications and bottles ready, I pushed the IV stand into Zoë's room. Tammy was standing by the bed, staring. I hung the fresh bottles on the bedside pole and pushed her out into the living room to lie on the couch. In the dark, I covered her with a blanket, promising to come for her as soon as I finished the feeding.

The ritual of preparing the Hickman, flushing the apparatus, removing the empty bottles, replacing them with full ones, monitoring their flow, and redressing the area took an hour. Mother and daughter slept through the whole process. The quiet humming of the equipment was all the company I had, all the company I needed; the emotionless tone soothed.

After the feeding, I went to wake Tammy for the bathing, but she waved me away. Without opening her eyes, she mumbled, "I need to sleep; let me stay in the living room. You know what to do, how to do …" Her voice drifted off, replaced by a light snore.

Stunned, I stood there in the dark, not sure what to do. For seventeen months, Tammy had slept in plastic chairs in waiting rooms, army cots when available, foldout bed-chairs in some wards—every night as close to her child as possible, and now she slept away. Her breathing deepened.

I returned to Zoë and began the vigil. I played all the steps over in my head and duplicated them as best I could. I had witnessed Tammy, led by a fierce determination, complete the nightly ritual of bathing and moisturizing this withered child whose heart had opened to so many and now could no longer be contained in this receptacle.

Zoë opened her eyes. A similar exhaustion to Tammy's smiled up at me; silently she allowed this invasion without protest. She spoke once to remind me of her teeth and sat up so I could brush her braces. A final act of hope, she had refused to have them removed, even when the nurse suggested it would make her more comfortable. She asked for Pachabel, one of her favorite composers, and then drifted back to sleep. The birth had begun, and I was the last to catch on.

The final step was her hands. When I took those once elegant fingers in my palm, I saw they had begun to swell. Her rings were constricting the blood flow. I would have to remove them, but they were already stuck. She'd refused to remove her rings, all ten of them, her signature. I lathered her hands in cream, whispering through my tears how sorry I was to have to hurt her and to please forgive me. When finally I pulled them off, I suggested, "How about I massage your feet to make up for it?"

Her eyes fluttered open, looked into mine. She slightly nodded her head and mouthed yes.

It was after midnight when I finished. I dimmed the light and listened to her breathing intermingled with Bach and Pachabel. The night hours passed gently. I would check on Tammy every few hours; her breath just as deep and labored as Zoë's, she never changed position.

As the morning light began to fill the room I awoke with a startle. I hadn't meant to sleep. I was holding Zoë's hand in mine. I bent down to kiss it and her eyes opened.

"Can I get you something, darling?"

She just looked at me and then closed her eyes. I watched and noticed that she hadn't inhaled. I waited and finally after a long interval she breathed in.

"Tammy!"

She popped her head in the door on the way to the bathroom.

"Tammy, I think it's time."

She continued into the bathroom.

"Tammy, did you hear me?"

I heard the shower turn on and the glass door close shut. I began to panic.

Standing over my goddaughter, I began counting the seconds between the breaths. Fifteen seconds, then thirty; I called her to me.

"Breathe, Zoë. You've got to remember to breathe."

When she didn't respond, I panicked. I hit her on her chest and put my ear to her breast.

"Please, please breathe, please!"

The sound of water running was the only response. The room was filling with sunlight. I stopped and realized I was doing it all wrong. I climbed on the bed and lay my head next to hers. Caressing her hands and face, I began whispering prayers of peace into her ears. I gathered her up into my arms.

"It's okay, Zoë, you can go now. Look for the angels and the dolphins, and look for your father; they're all waiting for you. Your time to be free of this body has arrived. Soar, my darling Zoë. Your mother will be safe. You're my angel now; please watch over me."

Radiance enveloped the room, warming it, and then a shadow cast over her body, slowly darkening her. The brilliance concentrated on the area behind her head, then began to travel up the wall and out though the ceiling. For a moment the whole room darkened as in twilight. My eyes closed in tears. I reopened them to sunlight filtering through the lace curtains, warming the sanctuary a second time. I heard Tammy's footsteps leave the bathroom and come through the door. I looked up to her; head bent, she was toweling her hair. My tears were everywhere, and I was holding her baby in my arms.

"She's gone," I mumbled.

Tammy dropped the towel and ran to the bed. She called to her daughter, "Zoë, can you hear me? Mama's here, baby."

She struggled to take her child from my embrace. "We need to do CPR. She's still here. I can feel her. I can hear her. Don't you see?'

"No, Tammy, that's the motorized bed. She is gone. I watched her leave."

I moved over as she rocked her child in her arms. She began to weep uncontrollably. We wept together for the first time on this journey of fierce compassion, arriving home.

Louisa's Cardboard Box of Life

Most everyone she knew did not know that she was named Luisa Eleanor Mangini at birth. They knew her as Louise Giorgio. And those that had known were long since gone. During what would be our last visit, we sat at her favorite table at the Four and Twenty Pie Shop on Laurel Canyon Boulevard. She liked coming here. Though the food was only adequate, the staff always recognized her and called her by name, and she loved their pie. I always ordered her a piece to take home.

Pretending gluttony, she chided me, "You'd better order yourself one too. I will not share this one."

I had arrived secretly the night before, not telling Mother I was attending an impromptu meeting with my two siblings, David and Vanessa. We were sailing on different ships, sidestepping around the real issue, not agreeing on how best to care for our mother. Her condition greatly diminished and me trapped by my middle position between them, the three of us were on separate courses, me clearly not wanting to side with either. Equally clear was that a change was imminent, with our cooperation or without it. Sitting with my mother now, my earlier angst dissolved, my heart softened, and I ceded to my sister's position: do nothing and let my visit be nothing more than a visit.

I watched my mother's eyes, still bright and blue; but behind them, I saw the fragile flower she'd become. I held her arm gently as we walked to the car, her gait unsteady, and the proud six-inch stiletto strut which once had been her signature now a distant memory.

A beautiful rose that had long since blossomed, even now in its final days still held profound beauty, grace, and fragrance. After our errands were completed, we returned to her home, and Mom wanted to sort through certain belongings. I knew not to question this process of shedding her skins as preparation for her final journey.

A life of images in a cardboard box awaited us on her favorite red chair. At least fifty years old, with the words "Rhode Island Red Hens, The Very Best" written on the side, it was filled to the top. Someone, perhaps the nurse, had been cajoled into taking it down from the closet, its home for decades. A slipshod container of total chaos was so unlike anything else in my mother's life. Everything in its place, tidy, neat, and clean had been her battle cry my whole life. Yet, here, photos and cards, some loose, others placed in manila accounting folders from her working days, and some still in their original thin, worn, green paper sleeves, easily torn by careless handling. Green molecules held together by air, falling prey to the wear of time, like her purplish skin that had grown paper-thin also.

As we traveled through the decades in her old box, I observed her face, lighting up at some photos and turning inward at others. I was reminded then, she was not always my elderly mother ... Not, always, even my mother.

Brown and beige snaps of three lean girls, maybe eighteen, riding bicycles, dressed in skirts, gloves, and hats. Other glossies taken at the seashore in East Greenwich, Rhode Island: pulled-down blue sailor hats, and Louisa, hamming for the camera, making silly faces, a side I didn't remember seeing, growing up with the serious bookkeeper that was our provider and mother. One tiny dark photo of them on a small rowboat in Goddard Park fell to the floor, a smiling trio waving, always the same two best childhood friends,

Mary and Dora. Friendships that would span seventy-five years, Louise now the last one left.

"You sure were dressed up riding bikes!"

"We were probably off to a dance at the Italian Hall. You must remember that was our main method of transportation." Taking the picture from me, she laughed, "No, I remember this one; we were going to catch a bus to Cranston for a night on the town with the Giorgio sisters. Matter of fact, I think I met your father that night." Peering at the snap, she continued, "Yes, we went to dance the jitterbug at a dance hall, and your father stood on the sideline, pretending not to watch me all night. The last song for the evening was a foxtrot, and he ambled over and tapped the young man that had been dancing with me most of the evening, cut in, and took my arm. Before I could say anything he danced me away around the floor until finishing up by my friends just as the music ended. He bowed and left. Just like that, off he went. I should have known then," she said, and grimaced.

"Sounds awfully romantic," I said. "Did you know who he was?"

"Oh, Margie had told me her youngest brother had eyes for me, but didn't like crowds."

"So?"

"So what?" my mother frowned. "You can't expect me to remember every detail." She brushed her hand in the air, as if brushing the memory away.

I dug into the heap and uncovered two more sepia snaps of the three friends at the red wooden bridge in the Japanese Tea Garden at Golden Gate Park, wearing gray and white striped shirts, their signature uniform. Attached on the back of one was a Polaroid shot from the '80s, of three older women. Posed identically, more rounded, hair cut short, Dora and Louise were stylishly blonde, but Mary could not be outshined, still glorious with her red flaming Irish crown.

Handing the picture over to her, I asked, "Mom, when were the three of you in San Francisco?"

"After you were born they took a trip out to meet the first Californian. Forty-five years later we met again in San Francisco, on the other side of our lives. It was the year before Mary died."

She glanced up to me, with her smile and a tear. "I do miss them both," she said.

I nodded and pulled out another large file folder marked "1985," and more sepia-tone images slipped out and stared back at me: baby Luisa on a pinto pony in a white dress with brown leather shoes held by her mother, my *nonnie*; Catherine, Mike, and Anne on a bench behind her, waiting their turn to sit and pose; the four siblings lined up like little soldiers in front of the family porch on Queen Street; and shots of me and my brother David on the same porch thirty years later. And then I found the almost ghostly image of my mother at eight years old, dressed in her first communion lace dress, with veil and bouquet, standing somber and still. When I passed it to her, she shrieked, "What a terrible haircut my mother always gave me." Frowning, she said, "I look like a boy."

"Well, Mom, you made up for it, with the next eighty years of glamour."

"Yes, I did," she said with a laugh. "And still do."

Her face grew younger as she laughed, and I wondered, *How does she do it? Keep up the endless beauty? Smooth forehead, only baby crow's feet at the edge of her smile. Is there a portrait somewhere aging?* Then I noticed her hands shaking as she held a glass of water to her lips. I took it from her.

"Don't worry. I won't drop it. That's why I only fill things halfway, so I don't spill."

"Do you need to take a break and rest?"

"No, don't be silly. The shaking is not from being tired, just from being too damn old. Getting old sucks, you know. Let's keep going. This is fun."

Next we came across the young bride swimming in a sea of white silk, a dress that needed two sets of hands to hold the train, a dress she had sewn, copying it out of a magazine. There had been an elegant wedding album that was stored in a special box. I remembered, when I was a child, home alone after school on rainy days, I would open

Molecules and Women

the box and thumb through the pages. Staring at the images of my older relatives, who had been young once, some even children, I wondered, *How was it they were so old now?* Looking at the image, remembering that the book had been destroyed in our house fire, I thought, *Was this all that was left of her wedding photos?*

Taking the large photo from my hands, her voice softened, and wistfully she said, "I strung a hundred baby orchids and white rosebuds on silk threads."

"They are so unique, definitely one of a kind—like you and Dad, so elegant. I remember the album being burned up in the fire, no?" I asked.

"Yes, it suffered terrible smoke damage. When Catherine died, Arlene sent me her photos of my wedding. She thought I would want these. I never really looked at them again though, just threw them in the box. Didn't really need them, but it was a nice thought."

"I'm glad she did; I would like to have this one."

"Take it; it's yours. We did make a handsome couple."

She pulled out her honeymoon picture of boarding a train for New York, cashmere hat and coat with a fur collar, gloves and purse, smiling gently at a camera. "Held by whom?" I asked. She could not remember.

"He promised me Niagara Falls, but a blizzard canceled our plans," she sighed.

"December 27th in New York. Isn't snowfall assured back East that time of year?"

She nodded. "I guess you're right."

I returned the sepia shots to the folder and placed them next to me on the coffee table.

"I would love to take that folder with me and prepare a photo collage for you. My friend Christy could help me, and I could bring it to you on my next visit." Picking up the other pictures of the three friends, I stealthily slipped them in the same folder.

"I saw that. I am not sure it is what I want, you taking them. Let me think about it."

Dipping back into the box, I pulled out a small Kodak preaffixed red booklet, held together with grey plastic tabs. The back of the cover with the scalloped edge was stamped 1951. There was a faded gray snapshot of my young mother, a baby in her arms, and my brother David at her feet on a sidewalk in San Francisco. She was joined by her mother. We all stood in front of a '40s Buick.

"I didn't know *Nonnie* came to live with us in San Francisco," I said. "I remember she came for Vanessa, so you could go back to work."

"She came each time one of you was born," she said, and sighed. "I always had to go back to work."

I took the picture and looked closer at my *nonnie's* stern face, remembering her kindness not portrayed here in her reflection, and her sardonic humor. Suddenly recognizing that my mother's humor must have started with her mother's, their similarity having never occurred to me, I questioned. *Does one inherit a sense of humor? The two of them, so different on the exterior, not unlike me and my mother, incompatible on so many levels. What more similarities might there have been, might there be?*

"Let me see what has caught your attention so raptly." Her shaking fingers took the booklet from mine. "Oh, how sad these are mostly blurry; cameras were not always very reliable back then," she said, handing them back to me.

"Yes, they are mostly blurry, but these close-ups of our family at Ocean Beach are wonderful. Look at Dad holding you in his lap, the two of you smiling. I can't believe you sat in the sand. You always hated sand on your body. You both look pretty happy then."

"We had our moments. He could charm a snake out of its skin."

"To do that, he must have given you something too?" I asked.

She ignored my question and dropped the booklet back into the box. She grabbed a small handful and passed them to me.

Seeing she was tired, I moved closer to her and sorted the photos neatly so we could thumb through them together as she leaned against me. "Oh, Mom, here you are with the Giorgio sisters, Auntie Pat and Aunt Margie. Look at you three women all dressed up showing off your sexy legs, laughing at the camera. How old were you there?"

"Yes, we sure thought we were something. Thirty years? I guess. Gosh, those styles were awful. Look at my bubble hairdo."

"I'm guessing it was the most up-to-date style then, no doubt."

She crunched her face in her signature fake scowl, and then laughed, bringing the picture closer into view. "Thirty-four years old, I was. That would make Margie thirty-six and Pasqualina thirty-nine."

"Even by today's standards, you three look great. Why were you all wearing black?"

"I remember. We had all come back from Mass on Good Friday, and the men were cooking the fish in the kitchen."

"Ugh, I do remember that holiday. I hated when it was at our house. Our kitchen smelled like fish for a week. I remember Dad tricking me and taking the frogs' legs and making them jump. The worst was skinning the eel, creepy eyes."

"That was the one holiday when I refused to enter the kitchen," she laughed.

Next were black and white shots of my brother David and me, smiling shirtless and standing proudly on a mound of dirt in front of our new home on Vintage in Granada Hills, so happy. "Our first home … So many promises, so many hopes," she spoke to herself more than to me.

"Ahh," we sighed together at the first colored photos, muted pastels of my baby sister Vanessa.

"Here come the '60s," I said. I caught the reflection of an eleven-year-old me, bobbed and gleaming, holding a baby up to the camera in a baptismal gown. "Hey, look at the boy-cut you had me wear. You can't blame *Nonnie* for what you did to me."

"Well, you wouldn't sit still, and didn't care that I cropped it short."

"Not true! I hated going to the beauty parlor with you. You would stand behind me and say, 'Short, very short.' Why do you think I have kept it long most of my adult life?"

"No, you were a tomboy! I remember clearly, you hated having your hair combed. Climbing the tree above the arbor, your face buried in a book. What was the name of that series you were constantly reading?"

"Nancy Drew detective stories. She always got her villain. And no boy could beat her. She wasn't afraid of anything. I so wanted to be like her, but I was so afraid of the dark."

"I don't remember that. Why were you so afraid?" She took off her glasses and took my hand.

"Because of the Saturday matinees David always took me to. You had to work, and he wanted to see every horror movie that came out: *The House on the Haunted Hill, The Tingler, Invasion of the Body Snatchers,* and then the ultimate capper, *Psycho*!" I almost yelled at her. "I can still remember trying to find my seat, slowly creeping down the darkened aisle in the theater, terrified. I had run out earlier, after the infamous shower scene, now forever imbedded into my DNA. Waiting for the theater to grow quiet, I had mistakenly reentered just as the second appearance of the ghoulish mother streaked across a hallway. The soda that David had bribed me with got thrown up in the air as my scream joined the rest of the theater." When I finished the telling of it, my heart was racing.

"Oh, Paula, how did I never know? You always acted like you wanted to go."

"Of course I wanted to go to the movies, and if I complained, David would make me pay. I began taking my Nancy Drew books with me, and when it got too scary I went to the lobby and read until the screaming was over. It's okay, Mom. You were working so hard. I didn't want to make you worry. Didn't you ever wonder why I never would take a shower? Besides, most of the times it was wonderful. I loved theaters and didn't want to miss out on popcorn. It was like watching my books come to life. But I still loved reading best. My favorite book was called *Shangri-La*; no, wait, the story was about Shangri-La. The book was called *Lost Horizon*, I think. I read it a hundred times. I can't believe I just remembered all that." I glanced down and for the first time noticed the pain in her face.

"I am so sorry, dear. I never knew." Her face was stricken with remorse.

Wow, I thought, *another thing she never knew, that I never told.* Noticing my breath was still shallow. I realized there was still an unresolved issue here for me. Looking at my mother, I knew it was mine, not hers anymore.

"No, I'm sorry to get so excited. I guess these pictures can uncover memories and emotions we don't realize still pack a punch. That was fifty years ago, and, believe me, I'm not afraid of the dark now. There is nothing to be sorry for. You always took good care of us. It wasn't always easy, with Dad gone so much. I only wish you would let us return the favor now."

"Now, let's not go there again."

"No, we do have to talk about it. You can't keep falling down. I see the black and blue on your side. The next time you fall could be your last. You could die, or worse yet, end up in a nursing home. Assisted living or with Vanessa would be much better than that."

"I am not moving anywhere, and that's final. If I die, I die in my home, not burdening someone else."

Seeing the immovable force that was my double bull mother, a Taurus in conventional astrology and a Water Buffalo in Chinese, I accepted defeat. I stood up stretching, seeing that night had fallen, and it was after nine. "Amazing, we have been on the couch since six. Let's call it a night. We can start again after breakfast, if you want. Do you need help getting into bed?"

"That would be nice. You could sleep in my bed, instead of on the couch. Much more comfortable, and I promise not to snore."

"Mom, it's not the snoring. It's the oxygen machine that would keep me awake."

"I could sleep without it," she offered.

"Oh, yes, that would be a great idea; just what the doctor ordered. No, I'm fine on the couch for one night."

The next day, after our coffee, I arranged the pictures in groups. The first era was the years of instant pictures. "You sure made that camera last. There must be ten years at least of Polaroids here!"

She brought over a box of plastic sandwich bags. "It wasn't one camera, silly. I replaced it every few years when they came out with a newer model. I still have my last one, I'm sure. Maybe you can look for it later and take it with you?"

I nodded. In these moments, I was grateful for her failing memory. Not wanting to open a can of worms, I remembered that camera, archaic and broken, disposed of two years ago. She would forget about it again, I hoped. I still could see her snapping out the pictures and carefully blowing on them, her impeccable red polished nails placing them on a table to dry, never a smudge. Only when it was her turn to get in the picture was anyone allowed to touch the priceless Polaroid. I always deferred to my brother or sister, in those moments when we listened to her strict instructions. I did not want to get caught with a thumbprint on the wet film.

She pulled out a baggy and suggested we organize them by years or events. This was the mother I knew. "That's a great idea." I peered at all the photos stacked on one side of the box. After we'd examined them the day before, I'd placed them in neat piles, but not organized by any scheme.

"Wish we had done that yesterday. Do you want me to go back and start again?"

"No, let's move forward. The rest are color photos, more fun."

In the first one I picked up, I saw my mother on her balcony surrounded by luscious flowering spider plants, her first grandchild, a two-year-old Cielo, newly arrived from South America, in her arms. They stood next to my teenage sister, Vanessa. The year 1975 was stamped on the back.

"Wow, Mom, you looked great at fifty. I never thought of you as fifty, only young. I love your hair." She took the photo from me, her delicate fingers running over the faded faces staring back from the glossy paper.

"No, it was too bouffant. And I was younger there, thirty-six years ago. But I look good, and Cielo is letting me hold her. Remember how much she cried when you first came? You couldn't leave the room, or she would break down caterwauling."

"I know, Mother, and you never seemed to appreciate the shock to her of moving here. I took her from a farm in Argentina, where she reined queen among the animals and Roberto's family, boarded her on a plane, in the dead of winter, pouring rain, and landed in sunny Los Angeles, where concrete ruled, and no one spoke her language."

"Well, maybe so, but it was foolish of you not to teach her English in the first place," she muttered.

"She was only two years old! You learned English and Italian together when you were raised, but you needed English first to get along in America, no? Well I was making sure she understood everyone in Argentina first," I exclaimed in a raised voice.

"It was different when I was growing up. Besides, we were Italian. You're not Spanish."

"You are such a bilingual snob. A second language is only good if it's Italian."

"I don't know what you're talking about."

"Really, if we go anywhere where they speak Chinese or Korean or Spanish, you frown and exclaim, 'Why can't they talk English? They're in America now.' You wonder if they are saying mean things about you. But we go into Montella's Market, and you love when Allesandro speaks to you in Italian. *No e' vero?*" I snapped at her.

"Okay, but that's different. I have been going there for fifty years." She wasn't backing down.

I caught myself, hearing the anger in my voice, and apologized. "You're right, Mom, and it is different." *When was I going to let go of my prejudices regarding her prejudices? Why do I insist on carrying the unimportant issues that no longer matter? More meditation and practice needed here*, I noted. Looking at the frail image before me fading before my eyes, not the brown sepia-toned photos, but this flesh and blood, I felt the guilt rise in my throat. My old hurt, not feeling heard by her, still had the power to sting.

The last pile was her with her grandchildren when they were babies: Santo and Angela in her lap, the three of them smiling at the camera; Julia tiny, minutes old, my mother flushed and beaming after witnessing her third granddaughter's birth; another with her holding the newborn Alexander. She had stayed alone with him for two days, by herself protecting him, only hours old, as I was rushed hemorrhaging back to the hospital, with her standing in for me as mother.

There were the times when she knew just the right thing to say or do. She could cut through the distractions that I'd bought into, and zone in to my core.

A cardboard box: of photos telling her story of eighty-six years of living, loving, laughing, and, yes, tears too; of days that were sad, and the loss of so many that had passed before her; and of Mass cards calling out the names of the dearly departed. The best discovery was found last. Crammed on the bottom of the box was her high school yearbook, *The Crimson*.

I opened to see her name, Louisa Mangini, reclaiming her heritage as a pen name, followed by *Editor-in-Chief*. Before I had time to review it, I noticed the clock. It was late. Afraid she might refuse me, I stuffed this precious item next to the sepia folder and hid everything in my already packed suitcase next to the door while she was in the bathroom.

We spent that last morning laughing and crying, until my time was cut short by my ride back to the airport. Regretting I had not made my visit longer, I now knew time was all we had left to give each other. I promised her that next month we would sort, date, and place the photos in envelopes or albums. When I bent down to kiss her good-bye, she held me close for an extra long hug and whispered, "I wish there were two of you."

"Two of me? *Two* of me? Why? Mom, one of me is usually enough to drive you bonkers. One is more than you can handle already," I quipped.

"Because then one of you could stay here with me, and the other could return to her life. Thank you for all you do."

"But I don't do anything, Mom. I wish I could do more." Tears filled our eyes as I turned to leave.

— —

Hours later, sitting in the airport, angry that my flight had been delayed, thinking about how I could have stayed longer with her, I was angrier with myself for arriving not-so-happy only three days earlier, dreading the possibility of having to demand she allow us to place her in another living situation. Now I was hoping it had not rubbed off on her. Time was disappearing, and the clock had wound down. *How many visits do I even have left?* I wondered.

Remembering my larceny, I pulled her yearbook out of my carry-on. Finding her picture, I was stunned by the caption: *Deadlines, rewrites, dummies, all problems met by conscientious editor-in-chief of Crimson, jitterbug and mystery novel fan and writer, efficient in all undertakings."* Another entry, on the class prophecy page, read, *Luisa Mangini, columnist for a newspaper,* and the byline, *My Busy Day.*

Exhaling, seeing my teardrop hit her face on the page, I closed the book. *A writer? She never spoke of this to me, all of my childhood poems and stories ... She never encouraged me, never acknowledged my passion.* I thought to call her right then and ask her why. *She wanted to be a writer; perhaps my talent started with her. Were we more alike than I ever knew? When I get home, I will call her.*

Then I thought better of it. *That Luisa Mangini is long gone, and some mysteries must remain just that.* As I walked down the boarding ramp, still holding the book pressed against my chest, with more questions than answers, it occurred to me. All of the women my mother Luisa Mangene, Mangini, and Louise Giorgio had been: daughter, sister, best friend to many; lover, healer and teacher to others; mother and mentor to many lucky souls; grandmother and great-grandmother—and still a mystery to me.

When I crawled into bed that night I saw the small hand-painted card she had made on a long-ago birthday, which lived on my windowsill. I reached over and blew the dust off as I opened it.

Dearest Daughter,

I realized soon after you arrived that you were born a "Free Soul." The purple in your aura that surrounds you is also in your eyes every time I look at you, representing the cooperation with yourself that you have been mastering all these forty-nine years to gain your "Freedom." The Blue Sky represents the endless travel of your Soul—no limits—no boundaries, as the birds in flight, you have and are still following your Spiritual Light. Happy Birthday. I love you very much, my beautiful daughter, Mom

Holding the card to my lips, I answered my own question. She saw me, she knew me, and she *knew* the best in me. Maybe not how I wanted her to, but in the only way she could—her way. *I love you too, Mom.*

Acknowledgments

Most importantly, I offer my gratitude to the following women, whose generosity knew no bounds: Beatrix, Cielo, Lei Ling, Carol, Jung, Leona, Willow, Cathy, Moriah, Angela, Sophia, Susan, Brenda, Coco, Felicity, Elena, Raquel, Nicole, Helen, Amelia, Inga, Tamara, Zoë, Julia, Ann Marie, Vanessa, Sweetie Pie, and Louisa Mangini.

Also to all my readers, whose unwavering support pushed me to continue when I was unsure of where I was going: Aaron, Xander, John, Jim, Santo, Christy, Jewel, Catherine, Anne, Jeanine, Kimberly, Dawn, and more.

To Mari's beautiful painting that has hung above my desk, a constant reminder from the depths of the waters that nourish my heart.

To my editors—to Deb Mckew, whose early enthusiasm permitted me to believe in the project; to Kate Hitt's red pen and laughter; Elaine's good timely suggestions; to Clive Matson's poet heart and pen, to recognize and confirm the real direction I was headed; and to Sister Mary Clare's appearance at the end of the journey, to spend the marathon weekends in laughter, tears, and glasses of spirits, bifurcating the pathways, rummaging through the punctuation, italics, periods, ellipses, dots, apostrophes, quotes, points, colons (semi or not), and ultimately, the maze of possible commas that can make or break a sentence.

COVER ART—
ARTIST'S STATEMENT:

THE REGENERATING POWER OF INTUITIVE HEALING COMMUNICATION, WHICH IS THE POWER OF LOVE, IS CELEBRATED IN "OCEAN'S EDGE."
MAY THIS IMAGE INSPIRE OTHERS TO SHARE AUTHENTICITY AND SUSTAINABLE JOY!
MY LOVE OF THE LANDSCAPES AROUND SAN FRANCISCO BAY AREA AND APPRECIATION OF THE HUMAN FIGURE INFORMED THIS WORK.

MARI AARONSOUTH
http://www.mari-aaronsouth.com

CPSIA information can be obtained at www.ICGtesting.com
Printed in the USA
BVOW011337201112

306041BV00001B/50/P

9 781475 949940